My
FIRST
COLOURING
BOOK

To Skvar the boy,
Edwin the man

My
FIRST COLOURING BOOK

Lloyd Jones

seren

Seren is the book imprint of
Poetry Wales Press Ltd
57 Nolton Street, Bridgend, CF31 3AE, Wales
www.seren-books.com

ISBN 978-1-85411-478-5

A CIP record for this title is available from
the British Library.

The publisher works with the financial assistance
of the Welsh Books Council.

Printed in Plantin by Bell and Bain Ltd, Glasgow

contents

brown

LATELY I've had time to sit and watch the world slow down. There's still life out there, but it's moving away from me gradually. Clouds drift across the sky; lawn mowers burble and drone like party bores on unseen lawns; a leisurely tabby cat stalks in Mrs Morley's garden, her tail doing the Indian rope trick.

Ours is a family business, gone very quiet in the last few years. New Tesco's down the road, same old story. Corner shop and sub post office – a thing of the past. Makes me feel ancient and antiquated just sitting here inside the place. What's that old saying about money? The first generation makes it, the second keeps it, the third spends it. I'm the third generation behind this counter, and the only thing I can spend freely is time. Waiting and watching, ticking like an old clock in the corner, marking time. My family has petrified slowly over millions of hours waiting for customers... makes me think of the old oak beams, crooked and iron-hard, in the church porch. I don't even bother dusting under the counter now. We'll close sooner or later, it's only a matter of time. The accountant gets quieter every time I visit. His place is gathering dust too, I've noticed. Both of us well past our sell-by dates. So I spend far too much of my day looking through the window, ticking off the day's anticipated events, come rain or shine: the bread van first, a fat green beetle scuttling down the hill frantically with the hedgerows whirling behind it, doing a dervish dance; then Postman Pat, shovelling the mail into a box outside our shop, kicking it in – this one's so young and spotty he doesn't even bother looking at me through the window.

Then there's a trickle of professionals going to good jobs an hour or more away; they only come here when they've forgotten something at Tesco's. Birthday balloons and firelighters, that sort of thing. They're all so well groomed. Nice teeth, nice hair, clean fingernails, lovely bedside manner. Look into their eyes and you see a Microsoft logo where the pupils used to be. We call them the Llandroids.

I open at eight, ready for the school kids. Little shits. You need eyes in the back of your head. Good homes, too, most of them. Afterwards it's down to a trickle – the old regulars come here for bread and hope, to know they're still alive; to mumble a litany of surgery bulletins and rolling village news, cheerless gossip nurtured hydroponically behind net curtains. They count their small change out of cracked plastic purses, penny by penny – as if they were grey-haired children playing a final, silent game of shop with the old money.

Death is the centrepoint: Latitude nought degrees, Longitude nought degrees, Year Zero, the Capital City; it hovers quietly above the town, a titanic mother ship waiting for the shuttles, each coffin a pod returning to the cargo hold, ready for the final journey to deep space. Home. When they stand outside my window pointing to the sky I know they're not picking out a buzzard or an owl – they're celebrating another departure, silently streaking the sky. Time they measure in rainfall and funerals. But there's another construct out there on the streets and it weaves a captivating pattern – it's the criss-crossing of individuals as they go about their daily grind. It's as delicate as a sampler – a cross-stitch of pathways and pavements, tracks and alleyways weaving through the town, all with junctions and interstices where people meet each other almost every day on the way to somewhere, or as they move away from someone, literally and metaphorically. Some of these meetings are haphazard but fairly regular, while others are as habitual as clockwork. Here's an example of the irregular: young Carrie Little is having a red hot scene with Iwan Roberts the trainee gamekeeper, newly separated, and she leaves his rumpled bed between five-thirty and six every morning, still all a-tingle and flushed, presumably, otherwise it's a waste of time Carrie dear; more often than not she meets the milkman on the corner by the postbox. They nod and smile but never say a word. Sometimes she looks back, after she's passed him, and smirks. Me too. We're all conspirators at heart, and I treasure this beautifully-crafted piece of knowledge – yes, I hold it up to the light and polish it gently whenever Iwan's mother, she of the tartan skirt and a history of depression, harks on about her precious heartbroken son while she's getting her weekly ration of shortbread biscuits.

There are plenty of other meetings every day, as regular as clockwork, excepting holidays and illness. I could cite any number, but for convenience I'll use my own daily encounter with Mr Barker. He's an old codger, knocking on ninety, and I meet him every afternoon between four-thirty and five in a particularly dreary part of town, a T-junction near the hospital. I wish I could flatter the place, but it's a stunningly boring part of Planet Earth: bland, empty-looking houses (with dirty windows) rising straight out of the dog-spattered pavements, on an abused stretch of highway scarred by countless handpicks and drills, as if it were a practice ground for apprentice road workers. There's one redeeming feature – a tiny public garden on the corner, with a few bullied trees and a dilapidated bench. It's the remains of an old park which has disappeared under an urban jungle – the corner of a stamp torn off accidentally and left attached to the serrations in a stamp book. I pass this place every day on my way to the botanical gardens, where I stroll for an hour or so before returning to the shop to relieve my husband. And it's at the T-junction, every day, that I meet Mr Barker. Or perhaps I should be more precise and say it's where I used to meet Mr Barker until recently.

For months we nodded to each other as we passed. Then an element of humour crept in, and for a while we smiled and greeted each other in an exaggerated way. There followed a period when we observed normal social custom, saying a breezy *Good afternoon!* or *Dreadful weather!* or *Isn't it lovely!*

Finally, we stopped. One day, I can't remember when, we came to a halt as we passed, and eyed each other. Why that particular moment, I don't know. Sometimes I think we all have meters inside us, counting everything consumed or experienced, just as we have electric and gas meters in our homes. A mileometer/smileometer which clocks and logs everything we do and everybody we meet. Sooner or later the dial stops spinning and we come to rest, looking at somewhere or someone in a different way. It's when a landscape becomes a landmark, or when yet another face becomes a familiar person. So I introduced myself, and Mr Barker did the same. During the following year one or other of us would sit on the bench in the park and wait. But there was no development of the relationship – no cosy chats or cups of tea in the nearest café, and certainly no secret yearnings because Mr Barker is old enough to be my father, and if you must know, I have a taste for toy boys. People often mistake my husband for my son. When pleasure is thin on the ground one must grab what's available with both hands, so to speak.

I must describe this man, Mr Barker. His head is too big for his body, and he has huge jugs, so he reminds me of Wallace in *Wallace and Gromit* with a pork pie hat (too small) jammed on top. He has short arms and legs, so if you imagine a walking Potato Man you're close to the mark. The only hair evident is a bushy moustache, droopy and nicotine yellow (though I've never seen him smoke); and the incongruity of his continued existence on this earth is heightened by his upright, almost regal bearing – as if he were a cartoon character come to life for the day, with one eye staring backwards into the past and the other staring forwards into the future. He's a knot between two colours in a knitted pullover – a singular day between two epochs. Dolefully, his chestnut eyes – once beautiful no doubt – regard everyone with the spaniel's dread of the size twelve boot. But Mr Barker is still alive, yes he's still very much alive: he's a living example of the lottery of existence. Somehow his blood struggles round every hour, somehow his brain tallies each day in its ancient ledger.

He fought in the war and carries his medals with him always, hidden away in an inside pocket. I got to know about his mates in the army, and the big events: injuries and near-misses, a month in the glasshouse for decking a sergeant.

So I grew fond of him. These things happen. We'd sit for a few minutes on the bench, dusting a few selected topics, one of which was the allotment he went to every day of the year, and therefore the cause of our daily meeting. We'd discuss onions and beans, carrot fly and blight; the warm friability of soil in spring. He talked tenderly of humus and haulm: his gnarled, earthy fingers became a puppeteer's as he re-enacted the drama of the soil. Seedlings were his chorus and slugs were the forces of evil in his version of Lear on the blasted heath, myself starring as Cordelia. And then other things became apparent, slowly. Subtly and poignantly.

One afternoon, in a light warm shower, he transferred a dirt-streaked carrier bag to my right hand suddenly, with no opportunity for me to refuse: inside it a clutch of new potatoes and a baby lettuce, still necklaced with a cobweb of rootlets and soil particles. Into my hand he thrust a posy of sweet peas, freshly picked and still sparkling with water droplets. They were a gift from this ancient man to a woman he hardly knew. Eventually I learnt to parley with gifts of my own – out-of-date mints, a packet of seeds come apart at the seam. I felt something gracious and true in the air, a minor exposition of the latent nobility of civilised society. Every day he came in the same clothes: the pork pie hat, shiny and denuded at the front, where his fingers grasped it; a thornproof tweed jacket which looked indestructible, over a clean white shirt and brown tie, carefully knotted; grey slacks tucked into his socks, and once-white trainers, which looked as absurd as a tutu on a navvy. I felt he might have discovered them in his grandson's bin and couldn't bear the waste.

Every hospital has a patient who should have died but didn't, sparking a TV documentary; Mr Barker was a man who defied death not because he wanted to, but because death had paid him a visit and felt so much at home it stayed, putting off the inevitable until the last possible moment, just as a young man who's just enjoyed his first heady holiday romance refuses to go home and stalks around moodily.

But there's another point to this story, and it involves the theatre, or an element of drama at least. Because Mr Barker was a solo dramatist of exceptional skill, I realised gradually. I learnt to sit back, relax, and enjoy the production.

He got up at five o'clock every morning, without any need for an alarm clock – his body was finely tuned, to the exact minute. Then he put on the kettle and followed a set routine, choreographed to the smallest detail: the wash, the shave, the dressing, the tea-drinking, the breakfast and the washing-up had all the symbolic and stylised ritualism of a Japanese Noh play. Of course the seasons changed his timetable little by little: in winter he'd light a fire ready for his wife's later rising, and in early spring he'd spend longer in his greenhouse, planting and watering his seedlings, refilling the heater with paraffin ready for the evening to come. In autumn he'd hum to himself in the outhouse as he brushed and tidied the place, then he'd store his apples a finger's width apart in the loft, or prepare the apparatus – sieve and muslin, earthenware pot and jars, ready for his wife to make apple jelly, and he described its delicious clarity, with a sprig of rosemary as subtle as a coral reef in the bottom of each jar. But the mainframe of his existence remained constant, reassuring and habitual.

Each of our meetings was basically the same, but also slightly different every time, and by the end I felt as though I'd been to a particular play over and over again, many times – rather like that woman who's so addicted to *The Sound of Music* she's seen it thousands of times. Finally, I realised that Mr Barker played this performance every single day of his life, from his rising in the morning till the final curtain at bedtime. He staged 365 performances of his one-man show every year, with a bonus every leap year. I watched them, alone in the auditorium, and clapped silently after all of them. I could picture him in his dressing room soon after dawn, putting on his costume, applying the greasepaint; preparing his props – the pork pie hat and the ever-brown tie, his fork and his spade and his hoe, his ridiculous trainers for comic effect. This was not the National Theatre of Brent staging a Shakespearean play in five minutes, nor an Alan Bennett *Talking Heads* monologue, but a full staging of *King Lear*, daughters and all, since he had two of his own and I'd become the third. It was unnerving.

Each play, I realised, was a 24-hour re-enactment of his whole life: ninety-odd years condensed into a span between sunrise and moonrise, and it had to be completed or he would die. That was the nub of the matter. If he faltered, if he cancelled one single performance, the show would collapse and the curtain would come down for ever.

I saw it in his eyes. And sometimes it was a struggle, I could see that too, since old men get ill and they get tired… the trick is to keep moving – however slowly, however wheezily. Sometimes he sat on the seat by my side and chatted amiably; sometimes he indicated with his hand that he was out of puff and needed to recover.

As the heat of the sun dwindled this year, and the autumn arrived slowly, I noticed a slight shift in him, to match the sun's diminution. I had to wait for him more and more often; his arrival on the seat, on his way home from the allotment, was getting a little later – and more laborious – every day, or so it seemed to me. And he'd still be sitting there, occasionally, when I returned from the botanical gardens. He made light of it, saying he enjoyed seeing the kids go past, watching the world go by, and what was the hurry anyway, supper wasn't for an hour and 'the missus' didn't mind at all.

He talked about his wife in a cavalier 'her indoors' sort of way, but he boasted her accomplishments proudly: her landscape paintings, her poems, her housecraft.

I thought he was stuttering to an end in October. The play was faltering; he was beginning to forget his lines. He was taking too long to get across the stage, into position. Even *The Mousetrap* had to end eventually, I thought. But although his recovery periods on the bench became longer and quieter, he continued without losing a single episode. The day he faltered would be his last. Mr Barker's motto was: *The show must go on.*

I really miss seeing him every day, meeting him on that bench. It was so inconsequential, yet so consoling – talking about the little things in life, while maintaining life's steady beat, seeing the pendulum swing to its final point and then falling back again. My part in the play ended in early November, with a strange dry cough and a sudden loss of weight. Things hadn't been right for quite some time, but it's so hard to tell, isn't it? After the blood tests there were a number of hospital visits, then the diagnosis. An unexpected twist to the plot; a tragic ending. There's no real point in having any further treatment, so I'm going to soldier on behind the counter, waiting for my body to harden inside, and then I'll join the ancient oakwood and the yews in the churchyard.

I got a card from him only the other day, slipped under the door of the shop, complete with a neat brown fingerprint smelling of radishes. He said he missed our meetings, there's no-one to talk to nowadays about the allotment. His handwriting's well educated, stylish. A flamboyant and sensual *f,* with a looping descender. Why should I be so surprised? But I won't reply. What could I say? Come up and see me sometime? Come to my shop and see a few old women being served in silence? Because none of them has said anything much after the first slow wave of hesitant sorries. They don't know what to say, not to my face, anyway. They look at my wig and they wonder, I can see it written all over their faces

– they'll wash their hands carefully when they get home and wonder about the little white bus to Tesco's. At the moment they're still trying to be loyal. But then they all point at the mother ship and turn towards me afterwards… I can see from here that their teeth are stained with the story of my illness: their careful gossip has left a brown tea mark at the bottom of their cups.

The tealeaves have spoken. As for Mr Barker, I'll not see him again. He's a busy man – and the show must go on.

post office red

EVERY car accident has its own unique sounds, presumably. In the rock 'n' roll of a road crash, every performance is a 'classic' with amazing paradiddles from the drummer and great riffs from the bass player. Heavy metal. Crash bang wallop.

I was thinking this rather strange thought as I sat in the driving seat of my green VW Golf at about 3.30pm on Christmas Eve, 2007 – the time and date I noted later when I made an insurance claim. Fortunately, no-one was hurt since it was a minor accident and no other vehicle was involved. Even small reversals have their plus sides; there was that great feeling of being alive and unhurt after a potentially fatal misjudgement. The throb of my heart, the zing of the blood in my ears confirmed I was still on Planet Earth, still living the good life. I'm not religious so I didn't offer thanks to a god – but I nodded towards Blind Fate and gave an ironic smile of gratitude. I was forced, however, to stay right there in my seat until help came along because the car was wedged in a ditch with a muddy bank looming through the passenger side window and a small forest of blackthorns pressing against the window to my right. I was up against a hedge, and I could actually see an old blackbird's nest close by in the twisted branchlets. The car ticked and clanged for a while, then settled into a glum silence. So did I. Time travels so very slowly when you're going nowhere fast. Eventually someone came along and the curtain rose on an elaborate play, well-rehearsed in pretty well every human brain: here was an opportunity (at last) for a passer-by to be good and rather heroic as the mobile phone came out. As I sat there someone got a once-in-a-lifetime chance to dial 999 for real – and as he did so a whole heap of sensory experiences skidded into my brain: my eyes took in the cold muddy road, a wheel trim resting in a tree (and looking like one of those horrible torture wheels in medieval illustrations), globs of broken glass gleaming on the verge.

Police, lights, action. Firemen, lights, action. Out I came. Breathalysed. Negative.

You OK Mister?

Yes I'm fine.

But a passing doctor (yes, these things actually happen) expresses concern and insists I hop into his vehicle for a quick check-up. My eyes are a bit glazed, apparently. But that's my usual look, I joke…

His name is Jonathan and I make a faltering attempt at conversation while he looks into my eyes with his thingy. We sit there in his medical-smelling estate car: he says he'll take me to the nearest town once he's sure I'm not in shock. So we sit there in a lay-by, looking at the scene of the accident – a severe ninety degree bend in a country road, on a bit of a hill, overlooked by trees on our left and a house on our right. The house is tall and thin, rather gaunt and grey but in good condition, with clean windows offset by dark turquoise curtains. It's a farmhouse, I think, because it has a few tidy outbuildings with bright red doors and a small barn painted in the same bright Post Office red. There's a grassy yard in front of the house and an old Scots Pine, giant-bodied and gnarled, reminding me of an illustration in Grimm's fairy tales. There's a kennel but no dog. A cowshed but no cows. Pigpens but no pigs. I've seen this living postcard many hundreds of times, in fact it's embedded in my memory. I've even dreamt about it. Yes, this scene has a particular importance for me.

Nothing at all moves as we survey the scene. There is no evidence of life. Not even a dog-bark or a passing cat. Nothing. Not a dicky bird.

Maybe my gaze is a little too intense because Jonathan asks me if I'm OK.

Fine thanks. Really.

He wants to know what happened. I think he's playing for time, waiting for me to show any possible symptoms. Blood dribbling from my ear, whatever.

So I tell him.

I was looking at that house.

I sense his head turning to look at me.

Why? That's a nasty bend…

Yes, I should have been concentrating. But I was concentrating on the wrong thing.

Why the house… do you know the people there? he asks.

So I tell him the whole story.

Jonathan, I say, that house has been in my life forever and always. I passed it twice a day, as I went to and from school, for a decade. I've passed it hundreds of times since then too, and there has never been any change.

You mean it's always looked like that? he asks.

Yes, exactly the same. For the forty-odd years I've passed it, not a single thing has changed.

That's a bit peculiar, he says. The cars outside the place, haven't they changed?

I've never seen a single car parked outside the place.

But there's a garage…

Never seen the doors open, nor a car.

There's a washing line…

That's the first thing I look at, I say. That's what I was looking at when I lost control of the bloody car…

Children playing?

I've never seen one single sign of human life in that place, I say.

I don't know when I first started to look. It must have been during my teens.

There must have been a point in my life when my brain first registered this strangeness. A fulcrum in time when my young mind rang an alarm bell whenever I passed and told me to look at the place, to search it for any small signs of movement. Of course there must be hundreds or thousands of places I've passed during my life and I've not felt this imperative to stare: to look for a tweak of the curtains, or a dribble of smoke rising from the chimney. Even with holiday homes you eventually see *something* during a lifetime.

Jonathan breaks in on my thoughts abruptly.

I think I'll go and knock on the door…

He's also intrigued now.

I wouldn't bother, I say, if there was anybody inside the place they'd have come out when I crashed, surely.

Jonathan thinks about this.

Unless they were deaf, or old, or both perhaps.

I don't answer him, because my mind has gone off on a tangent. Do I actually want to see anyone move? Do I want to meet the perfectly ordinary human beings who may have lived in that house for x number of years, blissfully unaware of the story-line I've written for their home – or should that be *unwritten*? Because this thing I've got about the house is the exact opposite of a soap opera, isn't it? I'm making sure that nothing happens. I'm creating a non-story, an antithesis of *happening*.

Jonathan picks up on my thoughts.

Perhaps you don't actually want anyone to live there, or anything to happen, he says. And he adds a storyline of his own.

I went for a walk on the mountain behind my house last week, he tells me as a preamble to his anecdote. There's a seat halfway up so I had a bit of a sit-down to enjoy the view. While I was getting to my feet I noticed a scrap of cloth, about four inches by two, in the heather – light blue satin, I think, cut unevenly with scissors and frayed at the edges… I was about to throw it back on the ground when I noticed that someone had written something on it in biro. Chinese characters, a message in Chinese on a hillside in Wales. I was really fascinated!

Why didn't you take it to the local Chinese restaurant, they'd have translated it for you, I say.

Yes, I thought about that. I put it in a frame and it's on the wall above my computer because it looks nice there. After a while I decided not to take it round to the Chinese because...

It's my turn to read his thought.

Because you didn't want to know what the message says?

He laughs loudly and healthily.

Yes. It could be a shopping list or something banal like that.

I agree with him. Best to leave it undeciphered. A little bit of mystery.

Maybe it was a message to a girlfriend, or something. A last farewell note. Perhaps she'd taken it up there to have a good cry.

Yeah, it could be anything. Don't want to know, he says. I've already made up lots of meanings for it as I work on my laptop – mostly romantic, to tell you the truth. That's the way our minds seem to work, isn't it?

I agreed, and we chatted away for some time before he decided I was OK and drove to the nearest town, Llanrwst, which is where I live. When he dropped me off at my home in George Street he took my phone number.

I'll check up on you tomorrow, he said.

He seemed genuine and kind. I could imagine him being a wonderful father to four perfect children while keeping a whole community alive, or going out to Africa and ministering to a small shanty town until his hair went white.

When I said goodbye to him I never expected to see him again. But he was standing on my doorstep within forty-eight hours, his face all lit up with excitement.

Hope you don't mind me coming to see you like this, but you made me realise something the other day, he said as he sat with a cup of coffee rattling in his hands, crouching slightly forward in one of our front-room chairs, my wife's shadow hovering in the kitchen doorway. I've got a place just like yours – not so far away from here, actually. Never seen anyone move there either!

My wife gave me one of her looks, then disappeared into the kitchen. Is he all there? she asked when I went to tell her. You're going *where*? You're both as daft as each other.

But the fact of the matter was that we'd decided there and then to visit this place of his, which was somewhere in the valley, near Trefriw. I put on my warmest coat, since Boxing Day had turned out nasty, and off we went into a young gale. The trees were threshing about and the river was already running quite high as we meandered down the valley along the old road. Eventually we swung off the highway and parked up on a grass verge near a group of houses. There were three of them, 1930s style, with hipped roofs and iron windows. Two had been painted a bright white while the one in the middle looked run down and generally in need of some TLC. Jonathan handed me a pair of binoculars, as if we were a couple of coppers casing the joint, and said just three words: the middle one.

I took a good look at it. The curtains were ragged, the windows were dirty and the garden gate was half on, half off. I could see nothing unusual about it – the house was typical of many dozens like it in the area. Just a bit run down.

But Jonathan was absorbed by it. Been to that house on the left many times, bloke had a stroke three years ago, he said in a conspiratorial *don't-tell-anyone-else* sort of voice. I've also been to the house on the right a couple of times, but I've never seen a single movement in the middle house. And yet I get the feeling there's someone in there… after all, the holiday homes tend to be well looked after.

Perhaps someone died and there's no heir, I said. You get that sometimes – houses left to rot because nobody owns them and no-one knows where the deeds are.

And so we left it. He took me home and we said farewell. That was that, I thought. A bit of seasonal madness, really. My car was a write-off and I'm on the buses for a while, since I've got my OAP pass and there's no real need for a car of my own any more – in fact I'm thinking of doing without one now. Do my bit for the planet, now I've done my bit to wreck it.

So I pass that house of Jonathan's twice a week on the bus, on my way to Llandudno – I meet an old friend there for a chat and a pint, and if the weather's fine we go for a walk along the prom. Usual thing – we're old work friends so we chew the cud and keep each other up to date on ex-colleagues heading for the departure lounge. Many have already left for the world's only remaining place without a Rough Guide. As I pass that house of Jonathan's on the bus I take a good look at it. I even started carrying a camera so I could record any movement; as the bus approached the trio of houses I'd prime my digital Fujifilm and take a snap, in case there had been any changes.

Until a few weeks ago I'd collected 134 pictures of the house, all stored in a separate folder on my computer. A couple are blurred and a few are mottled with raindrops on the bus window but they all tell the same story – I never saw anything or anybody in the proximity of that house. Zilch. Until recently. Then, as I passed one day, I swung the camera to the window and took a picture which instantly told a story. I've studied it countless times. Picture 135 is different from the rest. It has a human figure in it, walking up the path, carrying two plastic carrier bags. Spar bags with six-pack and bottle shapes – a very old image in my mind. Some of my friends have been alkies; this was a morning trip for some recovery juice.

As the days passed by I began to wonder: should I tell Jonathan? Big, big question. After all it was *his* house – *his* mystery. On the other hand I was left asking myself: would I want to know about *my* house if he saw someone moving *there*? Would I want *my* illusions shattered by a standard digital photo sent by email, showing Mr and Mrs Normal and their two normal children in front of my lovely abnormal house? Or a lonely man walking up a garden path, feeling like death warmed up, convulsed with shame and morning sickness?

I chewed on this question until it was a mushy pulp. I worried it like a puppy with a slipper, I didn't let it out of my sight for an hour, day or night. I was so restless at night the wife made me sleep in the spare room. So I hung Picture 135 on the wall in there. She thought I was overheating in the upstairs department. It was like a scene from *Blow-Up* with David Hemmings looking at that 'murder in the park' photo over and over again. I didn't tell Jonathan or anyone else about the picture. Perhaps that was a mistake, because soon afterwards my eye fell on a headline in the *Daily Post*: **Doctor 'critical' after house incident**.

When I went to see him in hospital he was on the mend, though still virtually unrecognisable. His face had been stitched up, the bruised flesh criss-crossed with butterfly stitches. I asked him what had happened, and the plotline was pretty straightforward, as I'd anticipated: overcome with curiosity he'd visited 'his' house late one night, and since there were no lights on he'd tried the back door, which was open. While exploring the house in darkness he'd tripped over a prone figure and tumbled to the floor. Startled, the 'tenant' of the house had woken suddenly from a drunken coma, wielded and smashed an empty bottle frantically in the dark and (more by accident than design) had 'bottled' poor old Jonathan, severing the carotid artery in his neck.

Nearly copped it – thank God I'm a doctor or I'd be dead, he mumbled through his swollen lips.

The 'tenant' turned out to be an itinerant who'd been living there for many years: he'd got away with it because the neighbours thought he was the owner.

Ironically, when the itinerant made a statement to the police he said he'd watched the house over several weeks, while living in nearby woods, and after seeing no signs of occupation he'd forced the back door and made himself at home. Me and Jonathan laughed over that, we just had to.

I meet him now and again, and he's getting better. He was

never charged by the police; his profession saved him, I suspect, though I don't know what sort of story he told them. As for my own 'empty' house, the one on the ninety-degree bend in the country, I still haven't seen anybody moving there. And there's a reason for that. Since Jonathan's near-death incident I've given the place a miss – I still haven't got a car, and there's another road – with a bus route – to the place I visit; although it's a bit of a detour it ensures I never see *my* house again. People think I've changed my route because of the accident. But no, it's not that.

It's become strangely important that the scene remains undisturbed outside that gaunt little house with its red barn and tidy outbuildings. It's a painting on an easel without an artist to finish it off. And there's another thing. For some strange reason the thought has grown inside me that once I see any movement there I'll die.

blood

THERE is a place secreted in the hills of mid Wales which few people know about, and even fewer have visited. I suppose it's best described as a miniature version of the wide tableland which stretches for countless miles in the Chang-thang region of Northern Tibet – a place so flat and featureless it's been known to send men mad, overcome by their own smallness. But this place in Wales is no Shangri-La. Its long seclusion from the outside world has left it relatively unchanged for a thousand years, a bleak landscape flocked by countless sheep which drift in eternal silence below an old, forgetful sky. The shepherds who look after them have changed as little as the landscape; they while away their time in ancient ways, tending their sturdy speckled sheep, making a strong hard cheese in their mountain huts, and carving ornate bijou objects from soapstone with astonishing expertise: the finished article resembles a tiny catacomb, with perfect rooms and passage-ways, stairs and cellars within the stone. There are hardly any women, since all but the simple and deformed run off in their teens to become rugby wives in places such as Bradford and St Helens. It's an unforgiving terrain peopled by strong and unusual people – as the explorer and wit Valentine Zappa noted, it's a place where the women are monosyllabic, the sheep bipolar and the men trisexual.

Out of this place, one day, came a man called Gwynoro. He became a close friend of mine, despite medical protocol – I was his surgeon. He arrived in my operating theatre in great pain, due to a colonic tangle caused by eating too much of the local delicacy, not unlike haggis, consumed traditionally by rushlight to the wail of the Welsh shepherds' *brochbib*, a crude bagpipe, and the *crwth*, a primitive fiddle. When he arrived he was still dressed in the traditional garb – a sheepskin jerkin over wide black pantaloons, and I must admit it was I who ordered his wide-brimmed leather hat and puttees to be destroyed immediately, such was their appalling hogo. Thankfully he forgave me, eventually, but I mustn't rush into the story.

These people are hardy, and Gwynoro was young and fit, but he almost perished. During the operation he needed ten pints of blood, imported from Mexico as it happens, and this has a bearing on my tale because, about a month after he was discharged, Gwynoro started to behave in an unusual and intriguing fashion. I have to admit that I indulged him rather because he was such a charming and engaging character, unspoilt by the tricks and wiles of modern society. He kept us all in stitches with his simple, earthy humour and held us spellbound with the lore of his people, plus a thousand and one things we didn't know about the crafty and intelligent sheep he so adored (but only his own flock). Anyway, about a month after being sent home to the hills he returned, and the change was striking. Gone were the sheepskin jacket and hairy pantaloons; he arrived sporting a full Zapata moustache under a flamboyant sombrero, and he was clad in the wide breeches of the gaucho, complemented superbly by a pair of new Cuban-heeled cowboy boots (the leatherwork was breathtaking). I found him slumped in the corridor, with his hat over his eyes, and presumed he was having a siesta – but when I shook him it became clear he was in enormous pain, as if he'd taken a bullet from a gringo. He was back to see me because of a fresh digestive problem – he'd developed an addiction to chili con carne, and his guts were rotten again: even worse, he'd lost all interest in sheep, and had bought a herd of small and scrawny mules. Frankly, he'd been diddled and I was angry on his behalf. He was a sick man again, and I was mystified. What had caused this change in his behaviour? I consulted my colleagues, more experienced than I, and we formulated a theory. Of course, we all knew about cellular memory, whereby people who receive organ transplants often take on the memories, behaviour and habits of the donors. But not one of us had heard of cellular memory brought on by blood trans-fusions. Gwynoro was unique – and in making medical history he became a *cause celebre* in medical circles.

After his recovery we persuaded him to part with his mules, which we'd kept in a fenced-off part of the hospital grounds, near the psychiatric unit (an unfortunate choice, for reasons I cannot make public); they were sold to a former Welsh professor who did rides on Aberystwyth beach. While visiting them, Gwynoro promptly fell in love with the town and gate-crashed some of the history lectures at the university, where he learned all he wanted to know about Mexico's revolutionary history, and there's plenty of that.

This is a very interesting period in my life, amigo, he said to me one day, picking his teeth moodily with a cocktail stick. I'd been called into town to bail him out after an incident in the High Street late the previous night, when he'd fired shots into the air while shouting *Viva la Revolución* in the manner of a crazed *pistolero*. Fortunately for him he'd been firing blanks, otherwise he'd be behind bars to this day.

Something had to be done, and quickly. I set up a trust fund and, medics being a kindly lot on the whole, we soon had enough money to buy him a set of ornamental spurs and a plane ticket to Mexico, where we hoped he'd burn himself out and then resume his old life in the Welsh hills. Or maybe he'd make a go of it, estab-lish a new colony perhaps, like a distant relative of mine, John Hughes, who left Merthyr in 1869 and set up an industrial centre called Hughesofca in the Ukraine – now called Donetsk. Within a few years a colony of about a hundred Welsh families had been established there: perhaps Gwynoro could do the same, I conjectured. Little did I know my man. There followed a lull, which encouraged me to think that all was well. Unbeknown to me he was stoking up on tortillas stuffed with fresh green chilis – so hot and dangerous that the locals took him to their hearts, overcome with admiration, and dubbed him El Popo, the nickname of Popocatepetl, a huge active volcano near Mexico City. News came filtering through via the national newspapers that he'd become the leader of Mexico's largest trade union, and was agitating for land reforms to liberate the peasants. On October 1, 2006, a revolt broke out in Yucatan province and he was arrested. As the ringleader he was charged with insurrection and political agitation. With hindsight, I should have foreseen what was going to happen, it was all rather predictable, given Gwynoro's childish sense of justice, his hot-headed naivety, and his strange new blood. There were unexpected repercussions. A new cocktail called *The Red Hot Welshman* became all the rage in Mexico City and led to a number of fatalities.

Exotic blood transfusions took over from size zero, breast implants and Botox as the 'in' thing among celebrities, leading to some pretty amazing consequences: Paris Hilton learnt Welsh, became a pig farmer in Powys and wrote a seminal paper on moral philosophy, while Pete Doherty became a Sunday School teacher and part-time fireman in Abersoch, though he went off the rails when they refused him permission to try a new penillion style at the cerdd dant festival. Jordan formed a new pagan cult among the bosky groves of Anglesey, called the Mon Again Druids, and I needn't tell you what happened to Charlotte and Gavin – really, someone ought to have warned them about doing that sort of thing in Red Square on the coldest night of the year.

I'd bailed him out once, so I did it again. It was getting to be a habit, but I felt partly responsible. I flew out to Mexico (precipitating a substantial backlog of people awaiting operations, and forcing two Assembly AMs to resign), then attested at his trial that the blood transfusion had changed his personality etc, so he was deported with a warning never to bother Central America again, or he'd be starring in a real life version of *Bring Me the Head of Alfredo Garcia*. I took him home with me and installed him in a caravan, sited in a small paddock by my orchard. I'd used it as a study, and he turned it into a nice little home for himself. Touchingly, he called it his haciendavan. Poor Gwynoro was a broken man by now, and I felt a lump in my throat whenever I saw the shadow of his sombrero floating around inside the caravan – I think he even wore it in bed. I whipped him into hospital for a transfusion and managed to stabilise him on a fairly normal diet, though the red-hot chili sauce was never far from his hand; the smell of it hung in a sickly-sweet haze over the orchard, and my dear wife refused to collect the apples when autumn came. Then I made a fundamental mistake – I sent him on holiday to Porthcawl, hoping the change of air would help. I really should have known better. All went well during the holiday itself, but on the train home he met a Leninist-Trotskyite from Taffs Well (apparently they're all like that down there) and came home with his head stuffed full of new and exciting notions. He also brought his new friend, called Siencyn, and they set up a radical-syndicalist group called Meibion Marx, using the caravan as their base.

One night, while the neighbourhood was asleep, they rounded up every sheep in the district (using Gwynoro's ovine expertise) and branded them all on the (left) side with a blood red hammer and sickle. Next day we were hit by a furore unprecedented in Wales, with TV crews and helicopters ravaging the area, and gutter journalists offering substantial sums for any snippet of information. Some over-excited fool burnt down a couple of holiday cottages, and we had pandemonium on our hands for a whole month. Just when I thought the hoo-ha was dying down I was visited by a couple of heavies who looked like Pinkerton men searching for Butch Cassidy and the Sundance Kid, but turned out to be hoods from the US National Security Agency at Menwith Hill, the huge monitoring station on the Yorkshire

Moors. Apparently they'd picked up the sheep markings via satellite – there's wonderful for you. The smallest of the hoods was one of those smarmy super-intelligent types who regaled us for some time (in a false accent straight out of *Fargo*) with arcane facts about Welsh sheep: apparently our four-legged friends are unique in their tonal range, and had fooled the Menwith satellite system into mistaking their lonesome bleats for the wheel-screech of an antique Russian missile-launcher being manoeuvred into position near Gdansk. For a day or so, apparently, every warhead in Europe had been trained on a small field in Llanfihangel-yng-Ngwynfa.

The smarmy agent went down to the caravan to question Gwynoro and Siencyn, and ended up staying for a whole week. I got quite jealous and wanted to be there too – I could see Gwynoro's sombrero nodding sombrely as he listened, or wobbling manically as he made a valid point. Jealous? Yes I was. This journey with Gwynoro... was I starting to have feelings for him? Crazy, impetuous fool that he was, rabid village revolutionary, pocket Che Guevara, I spent more time worrying about him, caring about him, than I did for my own wife. I even wondered if some of his blood had seeped into my own system during one of the ops.

It was a four-berth caravan, and I moved in the next day. There was a downside, of course, there always is – I had to share a bed with Siencyn, who snored supersonically or abused himself throughout the night; there was no rest with him – the mark of a bona fide revolutionary.

What a great plot we hatched in our haciendavan, as the September monsoon enfolded us and the season of mists and mellow fruitfulness stained the orchard and the hillsides in a thousand tints of red and brown. Like most budding revolutionaries, I was now able to wax quite lyrical. This was our plan, and it was *magnifico*: we would steal back to the mid Wales plateau by dead of night and garb ourselves as traditional shepherds. One night, we did just that.

Gwynoro's hut was still there, but it was in a sorry state, slumped to one side, and the door was off its hinges; we ejected a family of rather irritable sheep, who'd made it their home. Gwynoro stood looking at it for a long time, with one eye crying and one eye laughing, as the Germans put it. But we tidied up and swung into cheese production; I used my medical knowledge to pose as a shaman and soon the other shepherds were flocking to our door in droves, to be cured of ringworm, orf, foot rot, all those common ailments which afflict civilised man.

One thing we all knew as we huddled over our evening repast of cheese stew: sheep were the answer. They invariably are. Our plan was codenamed The Menwith Manoeuvre, and now we swung into action. Waiting for the first moonless night, and working to our detailed instructions, the shepherds of the plateau penned all their sheep and branded them anew. Dressed in my shamanic skins and wolf mask, I'd told them to paint a runic sign on the sheep's flanks, to excite good magic (they were all in my thrall by now). But the sign was in fact the signature of our old friend, Mr Al-Qaida. Our plan worked perfectly: the Menwith satellites zoomed in on the sheep at first light, and by breakfast time the agents were arriving in carloads. We were able to deal with these small-scale incursions on a man-to-man basis, and the first day went well – I think we lost only two men to their sixty or so. The next day saw the arrival of the armoured corps, as we anticipated, and we were ready for them. It was Gwynoro who would claim the credit for the brilliance of our plan. Remembering that the shepherds were expert carvers, he ordered them to shape huge flocks of snowy white sheep out of cheese, and the results were breathtaking. Only when you touched them did you suspect the sheep weren't real. That wasn't all. Each of them carried a sizeable explosives charge, designed by Siencyn, who'd had a mania for that sort of thing since he was a small boy, running errands for Meibion Glyndwr on the streets of Taffs Well. Our false sheep were arranged in eye-catching clusters along the only pass into the region, and it was Siencyn who detonated them at opportune moments, resulting in another major success, and by the gods we were proud of ourselves by nightfall – the Americans retreated ignominiously: the battlefield was ours. To the victor his spoils, and we celebrated deep into the night, quaffing bowlfuls of sheep's milk followed by cheese stew and, for dessert, cheese fondue *a la Grec*. When dawn broke on the bloodstained fields, we knew that every single Cruise missile, every warhead the Americans possessed, would be ready to obliterate us from the landscape. And so we embarked on Plan B. It was audacious, and if we held our nerve manfully our names would live forever alongside such revolutionary luminaries as Garibaldi and Guevara.

During the early period, as we went about establishing ourselves as shepherds on the plain, I'd approached the Arts Council with a startling and original project. I planned to drive a flock of sheep, in the tradition of the old drovers (and following all the old drovers' routes) to Yorkshire. In a bogus and specious application bid I 'proved' that the speckled sheep of mid Wales were of ancient Celtic stock originating from the old Brythonic hills in the north of England, and my thesis was that the sheep would walk faster and faster as they got closer to home, and indeed would need no human guidance at all. The dimwits at the arts council swallowed it hook, line and sinker – soon I was a quarter of a million quid better off and the whole of Wales was primed, courtesy of a gullible and sentimental media, for the sight of a huge flock of sheep being herded along the A55 Expressway, followed by a posse of oddly-dressed shepherds. I'm glad to say, the police were most helpful. Our journey to the Pennines went remarkably well, though the short dash along the verge of the M6 (northbound) was dangerous and depressing. Once up on Saddleworth Moor, however, the sheep were in their element and they threatened to prove my 'theory' correct, such was their friskiness and general unruliness. Eventually we reached our destination, well aware that the Americans were still following us, missiles primed and loaded. On the last night of our expedition we staged an extravaganza for the media. After sacrificing some of our flock (not without a tear or two) we held a full eisteddfod, complete with a crowning and a chairing, followed with a feast held by rushlight to the wail of the *brochbib* and the *crwth*. Dressed in sheepskin jerkins and black pantaloons, with wide-brimmed leather hats and puttees, we were a formidable and emotional sight, moving even hard-bitten reporters to tears. But they were silent by the morning – we'd spiked their milkshakes with Rohyprol and, of the three hundred who revelled with us that night, only one was left standing by the morning. Meanwhile we'd been busy with the final – and most impudent – part of our plan. Before starting off we'd partly-sheared the left flank of each sheep, leaving a loose flap of wool which was held in place with a clothes peg. Underneath it we'd inscribed the tender flesh with the well known insignia, in a flowing Arabic script, of the Al-Qaida family. Now, as dawn's rosy fingers touched the east, we quickly removed the loose wool-flap on each sheep and pointing the whole flock towards Menwith Hill. Tears flowed as we waved them goodbye, but there was no holding them back now – they ran as if they'd seen the Promised Land. Alas, they would be in heaven sooner than they imagined. Within a few minutes they were in the shadow of the American tracking station, and soon enough the satellite system picked them up. The Al-Qaida insignia did its job remarkably well; almost immediately a welter of Scud and Cruise missiles filled the air with their hissing death-songs, and in no time at all the sheep and the tracking station were pulp and rubble.

We had little time to grieve, or to celebrate. Divesting ourselves of our garb, we swapped clothes with some of the sleeping journalists and milled around for a while, asking crass questions and prodding the dead sheep. Late that day we made our escape in a four by four with smoked windscreens, purloined from a hapless journo, and returned to Wales. We went back to the haciendavan and lay low for a while, but our revolutionary fervour was on the wane and sadly we took to quarrelling and blaming each other for the deaths of so many healthy and lovable sheep. Siencyn and the smarmy agent went their own ways, while Gwynoro and I went back to the hut on the plain where we spent the rest of our lives living as gentle rustics: tending our sturdy speckled sheep, making a strong hard cheese in our mountain hut, and carving ornate bijou objects below an old, forgetful sky.

yellow

I AM a nondescript European, podgy and white, with the sort of snowman's body all eyes flit away from on the beach. But once, briefly, I was yellow.

For a while I felt alien to myself and the world – as if I'd just landed on another planet. Or perhaps I felt like a Chinese coolie, shipped to the New World and cast among strangers, slaving on a new railroad in hostile surroundings: waiting for an arrow in the back, or a fatal bout of cholera.

It was a strange experience: wherever I went people looked at me surreptitiously but few said anything. Years later my friends joked about it – everyone seemed to have a *when you were yellow* anecdote, but they mostly kept shtum at the time.

It started in my eyes, this yellow pigment, and I began to wilt, as if I were an autumn leaf on the turn or a neglected houseplant.

Looking in the bathroom mirror, in a strange house in an unfamiliar place – I was living temporarily on an island – I saw my eyeballs change colour slowly, taking on a urine hue at their borders. Yellow on white: that eye-catching duotone you see when your piss hits the ceramic trough in a public urinal. It was a slow process: for days I thought it was an illusion. My visits to the mirror became ever more frequent and ever more pathetic; I stared and shifted in the pallid light, not quite believing my own eyes, but when I lifted my eyelids I saw confirmation of my fears.

I was turning yellow. There was a feeling deep inside my head that the dye was leaking from addled metal drums strewn around in a central depot deep inside my body, delivered there in dirty yellow lorries, and then dumped as poison in the still ponds of my surface life by tattooed mercenaries.

But to admit the truth, it was I alone who was the polluter.

Soon my companions in the house noticed too. The cuticles on my nails were next, little crescent moons turning cheesy yellow, and each morning when I checked myself, dreamily self-absorbed, the stain had spread further in a slow blush across my body. Death was doodling on my skin while chatting on the phone, making arrangements for my funeral.

When I walked around in public I thought of the Jews, forced to wear the Star of David in Nazi Germany. Suddenly I felt a strong sense of empathy with them; I felt as though I were wearing my own personal yellow star – my skin. I'm not trying to make a connection, god forbid, my condition was trivial in comparison. But that is what I thought of then. My sanity changed colour about that time too. I'm told that madness has been linked with the colour yellow. And I remember an advertising man telling me during one of those mystifying workplace conventions that yellow is the best colour to use if a black and white advert needs bringing out – the human eye is drawn to it quicker than any other tint.

So I went to see a doctor – who saw at a glance that I was a living advertisement for my ailment. No prizes for guessing what created this new yellow me. Two bottles of vodka a day chased down with gut-rot cider – the fabled White Lightning – on top of hardly any food at all had battered my liver into submission. Within hours I was in hospital, watching real living people as they really really died.

There's a phrase, *frightened to death*. But during that episode I was frightened to life. Frankly, the shock of that yellow malfunction made me realise how awfully mortal I was, and I ran for my dear little life. Sheer cowardice. As I'd suspected all along I was a yellowbelly, literally and metaphorically. I've not had a drink since December 28, 2001 – and I'm an average white man again nowadays. Incidentally, vodka birthdays are much more meaningful than real birthdays. December 28 shimmers in my cranial calendar as no other date ever has: it's the birthday of my twin brother who came out of my side, into the world, about fifty years after my own birth. We talk together often about December 28: he has a morbid interest in the lifetime I led before that date.

The years passed and my yellow period faded almost out of memory. One doesn't meet many yellow people in public, not the lurid yellow of the jaundiced, anyway. Then, one day, I came across a yellow person in a very public place. I was standing on a platform at Crewe railway station, waiting for my connection, when she walked in front of me. My emotional response was immediate and strong: I wanted to go to her. The instinct was very powerful – magnetic. I wanted to tell her that I too had been yellow once upon a time. But of course I didn't. I say *of course*, but we don't trot up to absolute strangers, normally, do we? For a start, there might be reasons other than alcohol for her hue. Hepatitis caught on holiday perhaps, or kidney stones. So I stood and watched her, fascinated, as if I were a rare bird watching another of my kind coming in to land on an otherwise lifeless island strewn with the hot dry guano of thirst. I reasoned that she wouldn't want to be bracketed with an ageing alcoholic. She might be ashamed of her colour, wouldn't want anyone to draw attention to it. And decorum, bloody decorum. Christ, the decorum of humans in public places, passing each other without a word or a nod. Urbanites in particular treat every passing male as if he were Hannibal Lecter in the last frothing throes of avian flu and rabies combined.

So I stood there, ogling her, studying her yellowness, controlling the impulse to step out, walk towards her and say *Hey! That happened to me once!*

She was about half my age – in her mid-twenties – and distinctly underweight. Hardly any shape to her, just a plank in pencil jeans and slip-ons over white socks. She was about five foot seven and wore a faded parka with a fur-trimmed hood which was a bit too big for her, flapping and tenting around her elfin face. What I could view of her flesh was bright yellow. She had eyebrow rings and a stud in her nose, typical urban memorabilia, over a thin, purplish mouth. And like the rest of them she was obsessing into her mobile phone – as if it were an occult altar, a pentangle in her palm. She was chain-smoking cigarettes and trembling, from the cold weather or the cold turkey – or both. Fresh out of hospital, I thought. Two young males buzzed around her, also in parkas, Mod relics or sub-stream chavs. But she wasn't jaded – she seemed quite animated and lively. Of course, she could have been on the bounce back up after a couple of cans.

It's at times like this that a good old-fashioned imaginary conversation comes in handy.

Soon I was standing next to her (in Never-Never land), chatting amiably. I don't know about your imaginary chats (don't fib – of course you have them), but mine are incredibly wise and the whole wide world would be an earthly paradise within days or maybe even hours if only people listened to what I have to say.

Our conversation starts on a banal note, both of us breaking the ice. Rule Number One is – treat a drunk carefully at first. Don't rush the person.

But people who have been through a yellow period – and the accompanying spell in a hospital or psychiatric unit – usually identify fellow travellers quite quickly. No doubt about it, there seems to be a recognition system, as if we all had zebra stripes or spoke with a conspicuous accent. So I'm enjoying a close-up chat with this girl almost immediately. In my mind's eye, of course.

You're a flattie girl, aren't you? I inquire.

Flatties are the half-sized bottles used by distillers – quite distinctive and comfortable in the hand, less likely to slip. Lots of sensual curves. Comforting groove down the back of the bottle, like the cool furrow running along a woman's spine. The flattie is user-friendly and easier to hide, though prone to slide away in a hedge or a rabbit hole.

Me, I'm a full throttle man with a liking for the cylindrical litre bottle, triple distilled for ultimate purity. I don't normally respond to ceramics or glassware, passing those piles of Portmeirion or Nantgarw or Lalique in museums without a second glance. But the vodka bottle could stroke me like a cat again if I let it. The feel of it in the hand, the crack of the seal as the top is released. The hot perfume of the first kiss.

Of course certain races simply can't take alcohol. Take the Eskimo, or the native American Indian – genetically indisposed to it.

Like the Japanese and milk, I hear her say. Doesn't suit them, makes them sick.

Having warmed up – ah! the sublime plunge into heat with that first sip – we move onto familiar territory.

Sick in the mornings? I inquire.

Every bloody day, she replies.

I sympathise with her. It's very unpleasant, the end game. You desperately need more firewater inside you so that you can feel human again, but the body can't process the alcohol and throws it straight back out again. I can still remember the taste of the vodka coming back up, warm and phlegmy, passing through my fingers. The hollow, empty retching.

Did you itch when you came off the booze? she asks.

Christ yes, I reply. Worse than wearing a hair shirt – like being wrapped up in that stuff they lag roofs with, makes me scratch just thinking about it.

On and on we went, worrying the same old subject, two little puppies with an old slipper. But it's not the same, talking to yourself, it's never as good. You can't beat the real thing – a good head-to-head with a total stranger on a railway platform: pigeons flickering to and fro, the Tannoy sending disembodied messages

41

to the otherworld. Detached Christian-looking people trundling their trolley-cases devoutly from the newspaper kiosk to Calvary and beyond.

You can't beat a meeting of like minds in unexpected places. Birds of a feather. Fellow travellers. I've picked them up all over: I call it cottaging because it's just the same but without the sex. I love the stakeout, the silent patient watch, the thrill of the encounter, the quick exchange, the retreat into anonymity. Much more sophisticated than pestering or moidering or ear-bashing – it's the cerebral equivalent of two spies exchanging microfilms on a ferry crossing the Bosporus. Instead of a one-night stand with a ten-second orgasm, it's a ten-minute encounter with a clunking psychological orgasm guaranteed to last all day.

So I'm standing at Crewe station, a spaghetti nexus for travellers, a focal point for hordes of people on the move, and in this inpouring and outpouring of humanity I've been deposited next to a yellow girl. Destiny? Don't be ludicrous. Chance, nothing more. Statistics allow for this sort of thing, in the way they predicate against my winning the lottery. The laws of chance were drafted by a despot with a quirky sense of humour, probably a retired tax inspector with a huge store of Ken Dodd jokes.

Still feeling the need to swim out to this girl and grab her, drag her in from the human tide around her, I turn again to converse with her on my brain-platform.

Her flattie's almost empty and she's beginning to sweat on the next one; her mind's already clouded with logistics. She exerts her brain day and night, there's a noise like the railway station's arrivals and destinations board going cha-cha-cha-cha-cha metallically as she counts the bottles in, counts them out, worries about being late, worries about never getting there on time.

What would I say to her anyway, if I spoke to her for real?

I hope you don't mind me telling you this, but I was yellow too, once. Looked like a bloody banana, actually. Poisoned by a Russian agent, Miss Smirnoff by name. The bitch ruined me. Met her in a bar and fell for the oldest trick in the book – went back to her place and they filmed us having a fabulous time. Best lover I ever had. When I woke they'd filmed my soul, sold my body to the national health. Dreary business. How about you?

Or would I saunter towards her, theatrically, and say: *I've been there too kid.*

Our eyes would meet and we'd both know the truth about each other, immediately, without saying a word. *Not bloody likely.* And if she listened to me, wouldn't I sound like a born-again Christian trying to sell her a miracle cure?

But I wanted to go to her, yes, and I wanted her to recognise me for what I was, quickly – someone who was trying to share an experience, to show some compassion. But was there one single thing I could tell her that would change things?

No, said a little voice in my head. Nothing you could say would change the course of this girl's life. Except two words maybe. *I survived.* And that would sound a mite triumphalist, wouldn't it now?

I conceded the game. She knew and I knew that the yellow people already know which train they're going to catch – up or down the line, heaven or hell, freedom or slavery. Usually they don't have much time to decide which one to board, and some say the ticket was bought long ago, way back in childhood.

I ended my 'conversation' and returned to my studies on the platform at Crewe station.

She was still there in front of me. I could still step up to her. It could be done.

Perhaps she would want to talk – it's often easier with strangers. A quick exchange. Perhaps I could tell her, as un-evangelically as possible, that it wasn't as difficult as she might imagine, staying above ground. And worth it, dammit – life could be very sweet when compared to the war zone of addiction. If only for a year or two.

Be kind to yourself, I'd say. *Don't punish yourself any more.*

The pigeons cooed some more and the Tannoy gabbled some more too – in fact I made a connection between its announcements and the message I'd intended to give this girl – equally garbled, more likely to induce panic than composure.

When I lifted my eyes from the pigeons she was moving towards the lip of the platform and a train was chuntering towards her. It wasn't my connection, so I watched her do the standard black and white feature film exit, the *Brief Encounter* wave through the window to her mates, without all the steam and romance.

I almost walked to her even then – had it been an old-fashioned train, with pull-down windows, I think I might have. But I didn't. Then I lost her, and in the ensuing vacuum my brain instigated two wayward meditations on the colour yellow.

First, I went back to my childhood, and it was a morning in summer, soon after dawn, with the early sun flooding onto my bed and songbirds singing outside. I was a little boy who wondered why each window attracted the sun, my fingers trying to catch it – without a thought of what would become of me later in life, when the sun and I were older and weaker.

Next I thought of an incident which happened when I was a gardener, briefly, at a stately home – it was a summer holiday job and I hated it. Plagued by mice in the walled vegetable garden, we set traps – or rather the head gardener did, because I managed to avoid the task. Traps were never really my thing, though I managed to end up in one myself eventually. Don't we all. But despite the fact that I wouldn't set the traps it was me who examined them first each morning, fascinated, driven to discover...

And in one of them I found a mouse, still warm but limp, the eyes glazed over. I turned it over in my hands, this newly dead and still lovely thing. It was a yellow-necked field mouse, with a bib of cadmium yellow. Dead and most beautiful.

That day on the platform at Crewe I caught my connection and returned to Pembrokeshire. For the greater part of a long and tiring journey I was followed by the reflection of the sun in the carriage window, hot and buttery. I had met the only yellow girl I was ever likely to meet at a railway station, and I'd missed my opportunity. I still think of her, often. I wonder to myself idly – is she alive or dead? Happy? Lost? Waiting at another railway station?

I hope she chose the right train. But I have to face up to the truth, because that's what I try to do every day after my fling with Miss Smirnoff. You see, there was only one genuine reason for wanting to talk to her, and it was this: I wanted to tell her my own story, not to listen to hers.

A story I've told to so many people in so many places. That's the legacy of survival: the wish to tell your story, always, to anyone, at railway stations – or pretty well anywhere for that matter, when you're far away from home.

wine

I AM a methodical man – a modern professional. I'm an accountant or, as outsiders refer to my line of work, a bean counter. Every working day I bring order and meaning to Nitromo's spreadsheets; every night I sleep on sheets made of French silk in my waterside flat, already paid for. Thank you Lord for making it all add up for me. There is someone special in my life, at last, and I am content. My parents and family live on another continent and I see them once a year, at Christmas time. I am thirty-three and fit, though last year I had a health scare (rather personal); fortunately, I was alerted to the condition by an article in my paper, the *Daily Mail*.

I have a small group of friends, mainly from the gym and the church. Generally I live a well-ordered existence, which makes me happy. However, an incident happened recently which made my life rather difficult for a while. My friends in the Bible class have lost interest now, thank God, but my employers insisted on a course of counselling and my superior invited me into his office for 'little chats' every Friday afternoon for a month or two. All was not well. This is the nub of the story.

On my birthday, which falls (unfortunately!) on Boxing Day, I was given a new address book by one of my fellow choristers in the New Jerusalem Choir. It is rather nice, bound in soft calfskin leather, and each section from A to Z has a fronting page which tells the story of a famous saint: for instance the letter A features St Adrian of Nicomedia, patron saint of soldiers and butchers, while the letter Z features St Zenobius of Florence, who could bring the dead back to life, and is shown reviving a small child run over by a cart.

One Sunday morning after church I began transferring names and addresses from my old address book to the new, with diligence and pleasure, in my neatest handwriting, using my favourite pen. It's a Parker, and I use turquoise ink for all my personal correspondence. Whilst transcribing I noticed that many people in the old book had already disappeared from my life, for one reason or another. This made me sad, but I continued. I also noticed, for the first time, that I had no friends or relatives in the O section, nor a professional contact either. The O pages were completely blank in the old book, and remained so (of course) in the new book. I especially like the illustration which fronts the O section. It features St Omobuono 'the good man' of Cremona, who gave all his food and drink to a beggar one day and, on refilling his flask in a stream, found the water had been changed into wine – a miracle. St Omobuono died suddenly in a church, which seems appropriate – I wouldn't mind going that way myself!

I suppose I'd better admit I was a bit perturbed by not having any contacts in the O section, which remained bare. So I took more notice of people's names when they introduced themselves to me. I scanned the church membership register but there was no Orwell or Owen sufficiently well known to me, and it seemed un-Christian to seek someone's friendship merely to have them in my address book. A few weeks passed by, the issue became less important, and I almost forgot about it.

Then, one Friday afternoon, I did a Christian Act. I try to do one every day, but often that's impossible due to my lifestyle, since I can go for weeks without meeting anyone who needs help. My friends are mostly well off, and they rarely disclose their problems to me, since I am a bit green in these matters, having led a rather uneventful life. I don't think I'm particularly selfish – just inexperienced.

The Christian Act I refer to became possible while I was travelling home for the weekend, having completed an exhausting but highly successful audit at Nitromo's regional office in the pretty city of Chester. I was guaranteed a bonus, and I felt good about my work, which after all is as essential as a doctor's or a politician's if the country is to run smoothly. So, while entering a slip road in the environs of the city, I spotted a hitchhiker by the side of the road. I scanned him as well as I could, given the time limit: he had short hair (no dreadlocks!), no visible tattoos, was relatively well dressed, and had a newish-looking red rucksack propped up against his knees. I made a snap decision and picked him up, since I needed to do something good before church on Sunday. Fortunately he didn't smell, and seemed sober. I thanked God in the sky above for my good fortune, since I don't normally pick up strangers in this way. After I established that he was going in my general direction, we made small talk about the weather, the state of the country, the usual topics. He asked me my name: I said Paul. I asked him his, he said Oggy. Apparently he never uses his real name – everyone knows him simply as Oggy. He said he was unofficial. What he meant by that, apparently, was that he doesn't exist in the eyes of the state – he has no home, no National Insurance number, no birth certificate, no passport, no documentation at all. Zilch. As you can imagine, I was intrigued, and felt an urge to report him to someone – but to whom? – as soon as I got home. I didn't, as it happens. Call it Christian charity. Besides, I was tired and hungry. Oggy told me a terrible, disturbing personal story, a testimony of abuse and deprivation which moved me deeply – and which moved everyone else when I repeated it at Friday evening's Bible Class. It was nice to capture their attention, because quite frankly they were boggled by the story I told them. I tried not to embroider it, but maybe I added a detail or two, I'm not sure. I was rather surprised at myself, because I enjoyed telling the tale. I'm normally very reserved and taciturn, since I'm a man of figures and sums rather than verbs and nouns – but there was little doubt, I was able to command their attention and stir their emotions with Oggy's desperate story. I'd slipped him a twenty-pound note because he said he had no money to buy food that night, and he wanted to buy a present for his sister's handicapped baby daughter.

We agreed at the Bible Class to collect money in a china moneybox, shaped like a sleeping cat, which was about to be cleared out of the attic by Rachel Turnbull (Registered Class Member Number 101, I seem to remember!). We called it Oggy's Moggy and set a target of £250, I agreed to look out for poor Oggy and present him with the money, or if I failed to find him, we would send it to Shelter. I didn't tell them about the empty O pages in my new address book. But his name began with an O and I was tempted to put Oggy in my new book's blank O section. Instead I put it in my old book, as a sort of practice, to see what it looked like.

The following Friday we met again for Bible Class and every-one wanted to know more about Oggy – had I seen him again? They all seemed disappointed when I said no, so nobody paid much attention to me after that; indeed, I felt depressed by their reaction, as if they were reproaching me silently for letting them down. They wanted to know everything about Oggy, and I felt responsible. So on Monday evening after work I headed straight for the slip road where I'd met him, to see if he was there. But the cupboard was bare. No Oggy. I felt my heart sink down to my boots. I went on Tuesday again – same story. Wednesday and Thursday – no Oggy. So on Friday I took time off in lieu and spent the whole afternoon cruising around the slip road area, hoping to catch him.

By four o'clock I was weary and feeling a bit paranoid, in case the CCTV cameras picked me out and the police came to arrest me. By five o'clock I was ready to give up, but decided on a last sweep of the area before heading for home. As I turned into the slip road for one last recce I expected to see nothing more than the dirty grass verge again, but this time I was in luck – a patch of red caught my eye (hallelujah!). It was Oggy's rucksack. Eureka! It was him sure enough: he was there by the side of the road, waiting to be picked up again, his left arm held aslant in a hitching pose. I squealed to a halt and made a big show of being surprised.

Fancy meeting you here again! I said genially as he piled into my BMW. This time he ponged a bit, I noticed, and I definitely smelt alcohol on his breath. He was less together than he was the first time we'd met, but I turned a blind eye (to his language especially, it was much too colourful for the Bible Class!). Dear God, what a week he'd had. Poor Oggy had bought a present for his handicapped niece (poor little girl, what with only one eye working properly and terrible epilepsy, but so precious, so special) then the poor little mite had been rushed into hospital with meningitis. While they all cried and prayed by her bedside (I was glad about that) a thief had broken into the house and 'nicked' all the girl's birthday presents, plus all the money they'd saved to send her to Lourdes (Oggy knew who'd done it, he'd get the b******). There was even more bad news after that; I ended up choked with emotion and close to tears. This time I gave him sixty pounds and presented him with a surprise gift – a mobile phone we'd bought for him (Ruth Godwin's idea – not too grand, bog standard and no camera) so we could keep in touch with him. He was delighted (well made up guv) and he shed a couple of tears himself when I dropped him off where he asked, the car park of a McDonald's. As I drove off I saw him take a bottle out of his pocket and toss his head back to drink its contents. Poor bloke, he needed something to steady his nerves after a week like that.

The first thing I did when I got home was to put Oggy – 07933 703 940 in neat turquoise writing in my new address book. I felt pleased I'd solved the problem of the empty O section, and I hummed in the shower as I prepared myself for the Bible Class. During tea I rehearsed my talk to the club – and to be truthful I prepared all the information on my computer in PowerPoint format. It looked rather good. I put on a newly laundered suit and tried to look my best (as if I was briefing an important new client!) when I joined the rest at the Bible Class.

Meeting Room 2 was absolutely full when I walked in, I was amazed. It took half an hour to register twelve new members (I was particularly impressed with Rachel Forman, Registered Class Member 199!). After prayers we got down to business – nobody wanted to do the usual stuff because they all seemed to be there for the latest news on Oggy. While my laptop warmed up I gave a brief but poignant talk on how I'd found him again, after days of searching among the down-and-outs of Chester (this wasn't actually untrue, technically, and they'd never have understood the bit about cruising around, since some of them already think I'm gay). I told them that Mary (the little girl) was on a life support machine and the next few days would be critical, so they all had to pray extra hard!

I felt a warm, almost moist wave of compassion when I began my PowerPoint presentation on Oggy, complete with a picture of him, which I'd taken on my mobile.

He's so handsome! whispered the new girl, Rachel Forman.

And so rugged too, added the girl next to her.

I must admit I hadn't noticed his looks, and I was slightly miffed that the girls were obsessing about something so superficial. Surely we were trying to save his soul. The collection that night was gi-normous – over two hundred pounds. Oggy's Moggy was stuffed full of cash when I took her home to be emptied. Rachel Forman phoned me later and we had a nice chat about the evening, so I invited her round on Saturday morning. When she arrived we spent ages talking about Oggy over coffees in the kitchen (her reflection looked really nice in my smoked glass table-top), and for a while she put her hands over mine and held them emotively while she discussed Oggy. I was exhausted and a bit trembly when she left a couple of hours later.

After that, things began to spiral out of control. The whole church became involved, and one Sunday I was asked to address the congregation after morning worship. I got a bit carried away, said I was going to offer Oggy a home with me until he was back on his feet. (Whatever made me say that? Was it the way Rachel Forman looked at me and held my hands in the kitchen?)

I phoned Oggy but couldn't get hold of him – I suppose I was slightly relieved about that, but the story had its own momentum by now. When I addressed a crowded meeting of the Bible Class one Friday I fell into the pit of sinfulness: I told no lie, but I told no truth either. I said I would live among the down and outs of Chester for a week if everyone in the church gave a tenth of their wage to Oggy's Moggy that month. Rachel Forman began to talk in tongues and went into raptures – afterwards, in the recovery room, she called out my name and said I was a saint.

And so it came to pass. When I managed to get hold of him, Oggy was all for it. He was there waiting for me when I went to get him, on the slip road, and when I showed him my spare room he tested the bed with a happy grin on his face. All went well: he had a bath and then wore some of my clothes while I put his things through the wash. I gave him a spare key and told him to come and go as he pleased, so long as he took his shoes off by the front door. Meanwhile, I prepared – with a downcast heart – to leave my own home and sleep in a cardboard box (or whatever else these people use) for a whole week. It was at this time, when I was spoken to by Satan himself, that I weakened. Any number of escape routes opened up in front of my eyes. I could accuse Oggy of some unmentionable act or crime and get rid of him, perhaps – but although I'm a weak man, I'm not a bad man, So Help Me God.

So I made a plan. I knew it would cost me money, but it was the only solution.

Oggy helped me along the way by confessing on the second night – after seeing off a whole bottle of expensive malt whisky in my 'welcome' cabinet – that his stories were a fiction: they were how he stayed alive. There was no sister, no 'special' baby in hospital. Every day for the past five years he'd hitched from his sleeping place – a railway station – to Chester and back, telling stories. He had a gift, he said. Within minutes of getting into a car he could tell what sort of story the driver wanted to hear. I'd been easy, he said. And he was right, I'd been a pushover. But Oggy wasn't a bad man either – he wasn't doing anyone any real harm. Merely redistributing wealth, he said, and practising one of the oldest professions – storytelling.

It was a joint decision, in the end. We came to a mutual understanding. He'd always wanted to go to Glastonbury: all I had to do (and it wasn't much, given my resources) was to book him a ticket and take him there with some spends in his pocket. And then he would disappear out of my life for ever. A few weeks later he was gone, and I have to say I rather miss him (spiritually, you understand, not physically!). In return he gave me two very positive and life-enhancing experiences, which'll look good on my heavenly CV. He left me a story, which I've sold to Reader's Digest (without mentioning the Glastonbury bit!) and which I've told to countless people all over the world. And he's still in my address book – I call him sometimes, but he's never there.

Lastly, he found me the love of my life. It's like a fairy tale – as if Oggy had imagined it all and told it to someone in a car on the road to Chester. Tomorrow I marry Rachel Forman at the church where we met. It will be a day of joy and celebration (and we'll honeymoon at Glastonbury!). Rachel knows about Oggy. I told her the truth. And that was fine by her, she said, holding my hands in the kitchen and making me tremble. She said she loved me, and she forgave me. Rachel Forman wants to be my wife for evermore.

Glory to God on high – and praise be to St Omobuono of Cremona, who gave all his food and drink to a beggar one day and, on refilling his flask in a stream, found it full of wine.

red

IT'S THE hottest day of the year so far and the town lies squat on the ground, a scorched pancake swimming in a syrup of lethargy.

A dying jellyfish stiffens slowly on the sands and a tiny aneurysm drifts within it, a bubble trapped inside its spirit-level skin. A fat old man (who may be me sometime in the future, I'm not sure) lies breathing softly on a hot and tousled bed. His apertures suck the air for oxygen, and the rolling dunes of his body shine with sour sweat. Seeping through the tinnitus of summer he hears ghostly echoes, disembodied hoots and honks from the traffic, and a steady beat which may be the clack of the Chinaman's wok as he prepares food in the take-away, five doors down from his flat.

Someone arrives suddenly by his bed. A nurse – she wants to puncture him again. His arms are already strewn with violets and bluebells. To her it's blood, to him it's ichor. When he was a young god he exchanged the clear liquid of his vigour with lovers, many. Now his lifeblood is dark and turgid. The wok clicks and clacks in the distance, but it's not the Chinaman – it's different, a mechanical noise. Where is he?

I want to send a message to this old man. A final memo from me to him, on a day unknown, wet and windy or dry and dusty, I don't care. A mental note that will arrive during his final few seconds, when his breathing rattles to an end and his eyes puddle into two small plastic jellyfish.

Slowly, he twigs what's going on around him. They've moved him to the hospital. A trading post – he can hear them doing business over his body, bartering. Soon his family will hand him over, swap him for a morning off work and a jarful of ashes, lumpy and grey. The ritual is underway. Someone will throw in a posy of flowers, too, and a couple of damp handkerchiefs. In another room, out of sight, the crucibles are fired up: they're preparing to melt him down.

The wok's clack-beat is suddenly irregular. No, it's a machine. Systolic, diastolic. Someone's heart. It's struggling, it's in crisis. Is the old man on a sweaty bed in his final throes, is he about to depart? There's a deathly silence.

Listen old man, this is the last story you will hear. Are you listening?

As the nurse skims towards your bed you will hear her soles squeak on the chessboard floor tiles – she will come to you as your body loses its own pattern, begins its slow descent towards ground zero. Moments before the rictus I will be with you for our final exchange. Old man – this is my message, which will be your final thought. When the nurse comes to tattoo more purple on your chest with her electric machine, don't look at her eyes. Listen to her soles, squealing like two frightened little pigs. Then you'll remember…

A day in December, long ago. Grey and gruesome after weeks of rain, saturated, a dead cat floating in the water butt, fur all matted together. You were nearly thirty, late twenties for sure. Quite handsome, still in good shape. It was late at night, with cold hard rain. A party going on in the background. Someone was playing an acoustic guitar, someone else was banging spoons on dirty crockery.

There was a house in New Orleans, they call…

God, those parties: raised voices, the usual menagerie of drunken shrieks and laughter. A glass shatters on a floor somewhere and a hoarse collective *hooray* fills the smoggy kitchen. But you were relatively sober. Why? Perhaps you wanted to keep an eye on her. You always did have a small-town streak in you. Bit of a jerk, really, staying off the booze just to keep tabs on her. If you expect it to happen it will, boyo. Sure as eggs. She ran off in the end, didn't she? Women don't like that sort of thing, being watched, doubted. You took a long time to learn. Anyway, round about midnight you heard a squeal of brakes outside the house. Just after the band left. That's right, you've remembered. There was a band there. Hardly anyone noticed them shuffling off because the party had skidded out of control by then. Christ, it's flooding back now – it was her birthday, nearly everyone legless. The band left, and then you heard the bang. Trademark sounds of the twentieth century: tyres screeching, metal crumpling, glass breaking, then a lone disc of metal – hubcap perhaps – tinkles on the tarmac at the end. It was the same that night so long ago, wasn't it old man? Are you still with me? Can you hear me through the seeping hiss of summer? Cover yourself man, your gooseskin flanks are naked for all to see. Pitiful. What's that white residue around your slack old gob – a high tide mark, foam? Medicine perhaps. Don't go to sleep, you won't ever wake again. Concentrate. What happened next?

You ran out of the house, yes ran, you old fool. Haven't done that for a while, have you? There was someone with you. Tall, dark, on the periphery of your social group. Peter? Paul? Don't start searching your memory, for chrissakes don't start the ABC thing now, we'll be here for ever. Is that the idea? Stuck on a hospital ward for eternity going *ABCDE what the F was his name*, the tall dark boy who came after you through that massive front door, across the wooden footbridge clank clank clank, across the gleaming black pavement and into the road? Can't remember, won't ever remember again. Gone forever. He's a silhouette now, can't even remember his face, can you? Nice bloke, going out with one of the girls. Good manners, no trace of any dark matter swirling around him. Wholesome, that's the word, he was nutritious. One day a middle-aged woman will snuffle into her handkerchief and say he was such a lovely man, he was the best daddy in the world. Could be happening right now: hundreds of weeping people, biggest funeral ever seen, popular figure, doting husband, greatly loved father and grandfather. Not like you, old man. So forget him.

What's that noise… is the Chinaman slapping his wok again, five doors down?

No. It's closer now. Systolic, diastolic. Dum-dum, dum-dum…

The drum is beating again outside the trading post but this time the drummer's right by your ear. They've wired you up, old man – to a machine. Your private spokesman is describing physical carnage and chaos, that final helicopter flight from Saigon. That faltering, diminishing beat is your own heart, loud-speakered out to those who can't enter the stadium of death. And the medics, traders in turmoil, dealers in decay, are all around you, striking deals with your mortal friends. When the music stops you'll be taken away. Swapped for a plastic sweetie jar full of the greyness extracted from you, your honeycomb shattered. Your body will be hot-wired by a gang of po-faced funeral directors, driven around then torched. Yeeee-haaa.

But let's stay in the past for now. Let's go back to the accident outside your door, the rolling hubcap, the deathly silence immediately afterwards. You and the nameless, faceless one are standing by a motorbike which is lying on its side in the road. It's raining slantwise across the orange streetlights so you pull your collar up and study the scene. There has been an accident. A man lies unconscious in the road, near the bike, which is still hot. You can hear end-of-performance, off-stage noises – clicks and clacks, the sound of a cleaner in the wings, sweeping up broken glass.

The bike's a 250cc two-stroke, you can smell the oil. But the engine is no longer running. The man-boy in the road is wearing black leathers and a full-face helmet. Peering into the visor (because you've been taught not to touch this prone figure) you espy that he's wearing a scarf or a facemask, covering his mouth and nose. Bad news. You also see the band driving off into the night in a big black Mercedes van, their eardrums still too stuffed with noise to hear anything real. Finally, as your dark acquaintance runs into the house to call the emergency services, you notice a trickle of thick black liquid inside the biker's helmet. The bad news gets worse. Let's leave it at that for now, old man – you're exhausted. Have a little rest while I try to recapture the scene.

At this point I can afford to think out loud, since you won't remember a word I say.

You're in a side room at the local hospital, it's a hot and wind-less day, and your rickety old brain cells – in their piss-stained pyjamas – are having a final dribble up yonder in the Cranial Rest Home for Retired Gentlefolk. By the side of your bed there's a bleeping monitor, which you keep mistaking for the Chinaman's wok five doors down from your flat. Your thin and purple lips are embellished with a white scum-line. You're alone. That's worrying. If indeed you are me in the future, old man, scrawny right flank exposed to the stares of passers-by (clutching their Tesco flowers and their pathetic fruit tokens), then there's much to concern us both. Why is there no-one at your bedside? No concerned chil-dren. No worried wife/lover/brother/other. Nobody at all, old man. You must have been a bastard. A sod. A selfish prick.

Me? A sod, a selfish prick? Let's leave that one alone, let's not go there. Let's go back to the crash scene, quick. Feed me another morsel from the past, oh great and masterful brain, before you slip into your tartan slippers and forget which pills you took today, before you fall down the stairs, tangled up with your last and worst dancing partner, Fraulein Zimmer.

No, let's not go there either. For chrissakes, organise yourself. Control your thoughts. Try to think clearly. Focus. We're trying to guide an old man through his last moments on Planet Earth, goddess of creation and gluer of all dust and particles into semblances and forms. We're at the site of a fatal accident, kneeling in a shallow puddle of water, by the dying man-boy you met four hours earlier as he leapfrogged joyously and youthfully up the steps of the Labour Club (helmet in hand, smiling and nodding to you as he bounded past, his buckled leather boots leaving a trail of muddy prints on the hallway floor). You happened to think, as you passed, that his prints would irritate the hell out of the fat Italian cleaning lady who mopped that floor every Sunday morning, her gargantuan, filthy-looking mop trailing stringy bits which reminded you of the puppets' hair in *Rosie and Jim*.

Kneeling by this poor boy in the rain, you realise slowly that you have to do something. His treacle-blood is seeping between the facemask and his skin, onto his lovely white neck. You remove the helmet as gently as you can, then you peel the mask downwards, away from the mouth, an unfurling of clementine peel from the fruit, his skin a pale pith in the lamplight. Somehow you remove your coat and fold it into a pillow under his head. Do you hold his head off the cold asphalt as you juggle with your coat? You can't remember. It was the black leather jacket you always wore, presumably. Blue jeans with it, always. Now, with cold air flaying you alive, the full scale of the tragedy becomes clear. He has a hole in the side of his head, above the right ear, and his hair all around it is matted with congealed blood. A car drives up and stops. You ask the driver to keep guard, then you run into the house.

The party is still going on, they haven't a clue what's happened. You push your way through a horde in the hallway, up the stairs past snogging couples, towards the linen cupboard on the first landing. You kneel by it, open its (pine) doors and grab sheets and pillowcases, newly-washed. Rising and turning swiftly, you race back down the stairs, noticing as you do so that you left dark wet footprints on the green stair-carpet as you went up them. Then you struggle through the shouting, laughing, smooching, smoking, drinking crowd in the hallway and run back into the road. Kneeling by the boy, you place a pillowcase over the wound and fold a sheet around his head to keep it clean.

Your knee is being jabbed by chippings, so you stand up. Eventually, an ambulance arrives. They take him away. The rest is a blur. You can't remember what happened to the bike – who took it away? What happened to the sheets? Your coat? No idea at all. No, that's not quite correct. We can piece something together, using pictures. There's a photo of you somewhere, sitting astride your own red 250cc Suzuki, wearing that black bomber jacket. You've forgotten her name, the girl sitting behind you, grinning into the camera. But you haven't forgotten the jacket, emblem of your youth. After doing some crude mental arithmetic you realise that the girl on the bike behind you came after the girl at the party, the one who ran away because you didn't trust her. So the jacket survived the accident. You must have lifted it off the road as the ambulance jangled off into the distance.

But wait – there's something else. In that photo of your precious little red bike (fastest 250 on the road, you told everyone you met), the young superman (you) sitting astride its black plastic seat is wearing light brown boots. You can see one of them clearly, resting on the gear-change. Lace-ups, with a horseshoe ridge around the uppers. Mud and sand used to collect in a little man-made dustbowl above your toes. Crap and gunge met there daily. Why should those shoes be so important to an old man in his dying moments, as the cardiogram tires of playing its childish monotone, the same old beat? Those cheap Polish shoes will be the last image in your head. And why? Why will you remember a cut-price pair of light tan boots, whose eyes began to disintegrate as soon as you bought them? Aha, you've remembered something. Their soles were made of crepe, a spongy material. Never bought a pair like that before or since. Odd bouncy soles as if you were walking on a rubber mat. People looked at them when you passed, their eyes drawn to the unusual lightness of the crepe sole. Creamy and porous.

And what did they absorb on the tarmac that winter's night, what exactly did they suck up as you squatted by a young man's deathbed? What was the stain you took through the house, leaving livid red footprints all along the green hallway carpet?

Was it water, was it mud?

No, old man (who may be me in the future) it was blood, which had been watered down on the road's rainskin. The soles of those boots looked like the lower half of a sandwich, peeled away, with runny red jam sucked in by the bread.

Those footprints you spread through a large Victorian house, which has also been eradicated since, demolished and reduced to memories, those cartoon footprints stamped on the stairs were red, the colour of blackberry juice on your fingers after an hour's picking.

So, we come to the last few moments – yours, not his, since he died almost thirty years ago, a few minutes after reaching casualty. He would be a middle-aged man, now, fretting daily, probably, about the safety of his own children. You can't remember much about him, but if you tried very hard (and if you had enough time to spare) you might remember the fresh, slightly acne-pocked face which passed you on the stairs of the Labour Club, some four hours before he lost control of his motorbike and slid uncontrollably into the back of a black van containing four musicians, one of whom would die years later in very similar circumstances.

But you won't remember any of that, nothing at all.

The drums are throbbing again, but the beat is faltering, weakening. The deal is done.

They've traded your earthly remains (worth little, if anything at all) and you're off to the atomic shredder. Personal pin number rendered unreadable, proteins sundered in helixes of smoke, your code destroyed for ever.

In an act of metallic irony your own son frolics every night with his own little killing machine, a souped-up Ford, around the wasteland by the sea, where the factories once stood, and to mark your own passing he will be given a morning off work – though he will take a whole day and get a written warning, which he'll crumple and throw over his shoulder onto the back seat of his dangerous little car. In addition, he will receive the condolences of a small group of people and a death certificate. No inheritance, no fine pictures, no heirlooms. Finally, he will receive a jarful of dull grey ashes and a small collection of memories which on certain occasions he will replay swiftly on the miniature screens of his mind.

That's it then. The last few seconds are here. Wait for it – the countdown begins.

10, 9, 8... and your very last memory, what will it be? A face perhaps, looming out of the fog of your departure: the face of a young man-boy bounding past you on the stairs of the Labour Club one winter's night long ago, his dark hair pushed down flat by his helmet and his red woollen face mask pulled down below his chin, making him look gypsyish, slightly dangerous, interesting to girls.

7, 6, 5... will it be a last welling of compassion and pity for his poor mother, about to outlive you both, who lost her own real life that night, who still lives in a limbo of waiting?

4, 3, 2... will it be a pang of wonder that you yourself cheated death so many times?

No, old man, who may be me in the future, it's none of these. As your jellyfish eyes cloud over and the monitor emits its final beep, your senses will be attracted to a loud squeal, a tortured rubbery screech coming from the shoe of a nurse as she turns towards your bed and starts to run.

The scrape of her shoe on the plastic floor-tile will remind you of a pair of boots which you once owned. And as your inward eye rests on those light brown boots, made in Poland, as the defibrillator drops down towards your chest, you will remember one last thing: a man in a café asking you about the blood on your shoes, and it was days, months, years after the night of the accident. You kept them, you still used them. What sort of person were you? Poor? Heartless? And since you won't remember throwing them away, and since you won't remember giving them to anyone, as your breathing rattles to an end and your eyes puddle into two small plastic jellyfish, you'll ask yourself a final question: whatever happened to the boots with the red crepe soles?

violet

LET ME take you back to that hot summer in France, more than thirty years ago: I can still smell the coffee and the drains, even now. Dry little dust bowls in the cherry orchard and soil trampled into fine talcum, blown onto our feet in cool puffball clouds. Blue ceramic skies, fired in a vast kiln, vultured with black dots now and again, and all around us a drug-crazed landscape warping and shimmering in a constant mirage, pale and unreliable. Four of us living in a barn with no windows, sleeping on the republic's last remaining iron bedsteads, queer and crooked; feathers wafting in our sleeping quarters, floating on the stale air: blown in downy raspberries from a hole in my lumpy mattress, drifting also from a troupe of dowager hens in the entrance – hens which studied us, trying to learn our language, guarding us (contemptuously, I thought) from their sentry box in a fan of hot yellow sun in the doorway. When we clapped and flapped they treated us to a Gallic shrug, or the closest a hen can get to one. Mistrals and dog day afternoons: a huge, violent Alsatian darted from a lonely house on the road into town and bit my bum; for weeks I worried about rabies, waiting stoically for hydrophobia to drain me. I pictured myself in a hospital, tended by the nuns of Loudun, making desperate gurgling noises – sucking the last few drops of water in all of France into my arid intestines.

Chris went to Marseilles to buy a knife. We were all of us fateful about that knife.

I remember the shape of its blade, and the face of the old dog which loped around the yard. He's been dead for years now; buried under a tree probably, but I can't imagine old Bruyes, the farmer, crying over anything, least of all a dog. I have a picture in my mind's eye of its skeleton, white and curved in its last sleeping position under the dun soil, with young rootlets threading their way through its bones, fanning bronchially in its rib cage. We all liked that dog: regulation black and white, short haired and fatalistic, it was called Lucky.

We went up to the orchards early every morning to finger-vacuum the cherries; there was a knack to it and a pro could make £100 a day, even then. The best pickers were a gypsy family who lived in an opulent motorhome the size of an articulated lorry. I met the father collecting snails from the dank verges one evening at dusk and he invited me round for a meal; I was sorely tempted because his plump, post-pubescent daughter – unblemished by any formal education – had been making black olive eyes at me and I was still young enough to consider all the openings that came my way. Never could eat snails: said No. Looking back, those people lived wonderful lives. No taxes, picking money off the trees in bucketfuls, browsing, moving leisurely from one crop to the next. Wish I'd married that girl now – she was straight from a French *Darling Buds of May*; we'd be fat on snails, slouching around in white vests swelling around our Pyrenean tums, always brown, sleeping sweetly on the shores of the Mediterranean, perfumed with garlic and happy ever after, me drowsy with wine.

Anyway, to cut a long story short, Lucky copped off with a poodle one morning in the orchard, early on, soon after sunrise in fact: the dirty dog must have been thinking about it all night. Still a few drops of dew on the leaves, delicious strands of coolness inside the branches. But the poodle was twice his size and he had his work cut out. He stuck to his task dogfully, though. At first he got a rousing reception from the onlookers, beating their buckets, shouting *Allez Lucky!* and *Vas-y Lucky!*

A circle of about twenty, mainly French but some Spanish, looked down on him as he prepared to hump away among the cherry trees – making wood, as they say. Only one of them said nothing at all, a slip of a girl, small and slim, boyish, brown as a berry in a simple country dress or tabard made from felt in a burnt carmine brown. Simple but effective. Short black hair, fussless, freckles, olive skin, pumps, small breasts and violet eyes which never looked at Lucky or at me. No, not once.

By eleven o'clock they were still making a fuss of Lucky, stuck to his poodle, stuck to his task, bobbing away on his scrawny haunches as we reaped the cherries. The red ran from the trees, lipstick smudged from lip to cup. Among the ladders and the stepladders and the buckets, somewhere by the weighing machine (ancient, rusty) he pumped and wheezed but my little French tomboy never cast a glance at him nor me, oh no, not a single sideways look. Such bloody insouciance. Not even when two little boys started playing with a scorpion under my tree, moving around it in frog hops, prodding it with sticks, not even then did she show a flicker of interest; little girly shoulders and apricot hips, slender, a body without a flounce or a bounce, that's all I saw of her all morning – and she in the next tree, a short monkey-dash away.

By lunchtime they were getting fed up of Lucky and his extravagant, illicit shagathon. His eyes had puddled into two small dribbles of yellow candle wax pooling in a smoky Parisian bordello. Dinner time came so we left him to it, climbed aboard Bruyes' van, one of those archetypal Froggie things rippling with corrugated iron and confessional windows. Someone had crammed half a dozen seats in the back long ago; I'm not joking, that crate might have ferried people from the Bastille to the Place de la Concorde when the tumbrels were full. Come to think of it, was that cherry juice running freely on the floor, or blood?

Mademoiselle Violette stayed up there in the orchard with

Maupassant's ghost, teaching sang froid to the sparrows and nibbling croissants with perfect élan, her pretty little nose in the air.

When we arrived at the farmhouse Bruyes went into a rage and fired an enfilade of frank nasal insults at Jo, one of our group, the fourth musketeer, who'd slept through the morning in our dormitory and now stood romantically in one of the empty windows, framed by it, playing a violin to one of the hens which was perched on the sill, listening to him intently with its head cocked to one side. At this point a train of storm clouds appeared over the horizon, thanks more to Bruyes' language than the weather. We munched our baguettes in a sweaty sub-tropic of stormy promise, the air charged with electricity which tickled the fine hairs on our legs with waves of frisson. A row of gofers appeared in the caravan windows: our gypsies were peeking at the sky too, their faces wimpled by the chintz curtains. Dinner over, Bruyes' dreamless nap finished, we returned to the orchard, a cartoon cloud of Roadrunner dust following us *meep meep* all the way up to the greenery where Mademoiselle Violette napped against the bole of a tree and Lucky shagged, still, clinging tenaciously to his poodle life-raft but half dead by now, a drowning rat drenched with sweat. *You dirty dog* said nearly everyone in French or Spanish or English or Welsh, disgusted by his antics. Some threw their buckets at him but Lucky continued, his sex storm unabated.

My little French tomboy turned her back on me once again and made love to her tree; cherries fell, clouds rumbled, people pointed, Bruyes grumbled; come four o'clock a few heavy drops of rain splattered and pocked the dust, bullets falling back to earth after a half-hearted uprising by revolutionaries in the far corner of the plantation. Lucky had finally attained nirvana but the couple were still inseparable, so to speak. They both looked pretty shagged out by now, two marathon runners clinging to each other feebly on the finishing line, stooped and breathless. Suddenly, people melted away from me and even Lucky made a run for it, divorced at last from his paramour – the parting was quite painful,

I believe. I legged it though the trees and was just in time to catch them firing up the van, trying to escape without me. I clambered aboard as the heavens opened. A synchronised mass of identical raindrops, rubber-capped, muscular, Olympian, dived down together into a newly formed swimming pool then rested after the plunge on our windows, swimming in a slow back crawl along the glass while they recovered.

Oh joy, oh rupture! Who was next to me in the van, burnt carmine dress rucked and pressed against my hot little hip, but Mademoiselle Violette. She looked into the far distance, to a point just beyond Venus, to anywhere except my face as we rolled out of the cherry orchard and started homewards, the storm enfolding us and sluicing us with water; for a while we sat in a *plein air* car wash, battered and pummelled by thunderous rain. Hot mists of sexuality wafted from Violette's body and I came close to levitating on garlic fumes and lust. In front of us, Lucky rested his weary head on Bruyes' shoulder and regarded us with two bloodshot eyes. We eyed him back with mixed feelings; admiration mainly, with a *soupçon* of revulsion stirred in. Violette stroked his head briefly but he made no response, too enfeebled poor thing. I watched her little brown hand ripple over his head and felt giddy, my skin crackling with the static of base animal desire, craving her attendance alone in the cherry orchard where we could roll in a warm crimson mud made from dust and juice, savages, naked and wanton among the roots of the forest; I imagined leaf-shaped weals and cherry-stone indentations on her perfect little bottom, moss green stains on her divine buttocks.

Shocked by a huge rush of adrenalin my heart shivered: a sparrow's last wing-flutter as the cat's needle-mouth stitched it into the tapestry of death; I came close to madness, nearly dropped to my knees, nearly fastened myself to her perfectly-formed leg, came close to pawing her burnt carmine dress pitifully, whining, making a complete bloody fool of myself in our metal tumbrel. I hid my shame with my hands, wrested my eyes off her juvenile breasts and quelled the uprising which had swept through my head, travelled down my chest, past my febrile heart, a peasant's revolt sounding drums and clarions, firing shots in the air, waving banners, seditious and streaked red as it plunged downwards into the gorge between my legs, mutinous, making me tremble, leaving me with toothless *tricoteurs* in the van, ready and willing *toute de suite* to enact my trial and execution in the pouring rain, my blood spreading along the farmyard floor, watered-down vin rouge running through the hens' talons, through Lucky's sodden and bedraggled paws, into the drains.

Ready to face my fate, ready for the zing of the speeding guillotine, I fingered my neck and prepared a brief but moving farewell speech, referring dutifully to my family and declaring my love for she of the violet eyes. In a calm but plaintive voice I told a seething horde in the, by now, hushed Place de la Concorde that although my love was but a few hours old, and although I was staring death in the face, I was the most fortunate man alive since I had tasted a *coup de lumiere*, a grand passion of the highest and noblest kind, indeed I was happy to go to my death that very day since I could rejoice in the knowledge that no other love, ever, in the history of the western world, had exceeded or could possibly emulate mine etc, etc.

I cast meaningful glances at Violette while I delivered this panegyric to the tumultuous masses as they seethed on the blood-soaked cobbles; they would spare my life forthwith and promote me to the position of the First Republic's chef d'amour, giving me her hand in marriage, as one would expect, *naturellement*.

Thud! would sound the guillotine behind us as we threaded our way through the crowd, towards the Left Bank where I would become an existentialist and she a painter, lovely fingers streaked carmine, burnt umber, French grey, violet, living dangerously and sleeping fitfully under an intense Parisian sky, playing chess moodily by the Seine; we'd drink coffee and share unspoken moments of *tendresse* following endless nights of tempestuous passion, her ardour pinned in butterfly beauty on the rumpled white sheets of our garret bed.

While I delivered my mute speech to the masses a commotion spread through the van and for a moment I thought we had joined a frieze from French history c1789, since everyone had turned to face the back of our tumbrel with excited and flushed faces – as if Marie Antoinette herself was in the cart behind us, clutching an exquisite silk handkerchief to her powdered breast: some of our company pointed, others exclaimed loudly. The air had cleared a little, enough to let us see the road snaking behind us, and a sight of tremendous beauty met our eyes, truly amazing: shimmering masses of ball lightning were descending from the heavens and bouncing off the ground like so many footballs at a pre-match practice session; they reminded me, for a moment, of the torsos of snowmen, made in winter by little boys with snow-encrusted mittens, begun with a snowball and rolled until too large to move; rough-hewn, lop-sided, fluffed all over with puffy snow – and just like fat snowmen's bodies the balls of lightning shimmered down to earth, wobbling, jellies on the run, luminescent, evanescent, space-glowed, alive, frightening, getting closer, threatening, magnificent, unforgettable, and exactly the same colour as Violette's eyes! *Vraiment!*

I tugged at her sleeve and when she looked at me I pointed to her eyes and then at the balls of fire behind us – and yes, yes! she afforded me the briefest of Mona Lisa smiles before returning her gaze to Venus, before returning her heart to the icy hospital container where it had lain until now, frozen, waiting for a suitable donor.

We escaped, but only just. It grew darker, we fell silent. All the way home we said nothing, none of us, silhouettes in the tumbrel, returning to the Bastille. We disembarked and petite Violette disappeared from my life for ever. We four musketeers left for home the next day. Our working holiday was over; it was time to return, to live normal lives again. Chris and Jo went on ahead together, heading for la Manche with an eight-inch Bowie knife in Chris' rucksack; a shiny new knife with a mouthful of wolfish, serrated teeth. We looked at it silently for a long time before he sheathed it.

On the morning of our departure I went down to the village café-bar to say goodbye. I don't know what happened exactly, but I think I drank too much strong coffee on top of a bad hangover; in the next few hours I came apart. As I started hitching with Tim, he and I the last two remaining musketeers, I descended into a frightening abyss, bitten by the black dog. I became panicky, shaky, very depressed.

France being France, no-one wanted to give us a lift and we stood at the roadside for hour after hour, dust creeping up our jeans until we had white puttees. Eventually a 2CV rolled up and I breathed a huge sigh of relief: I just wanted to get out of there.

I was about to get into the car when Tim's hand hauled me back. I had just enough time to see what he had glimpsed before I dived into the car's shady interior: a gigantic hulk of a man with long unruly hair, shrouded in a big black coat, straddling the back seat and playing with a flick knife. We moved away from him as fast as we could. I believe that Tim saved my life that day. Had I been alone, exhausted and emotionally vulnerable, I would have jumped in, I would have chanced it. But without doubt we were intended for a shallow grave somewhere deep inside a forest.

The years passed by and our trip to France became a fantasy; when we met occasionally in pubs we talked about the good old days, as you do. About old Bruyes and Lucky, the storm, the cherry orchard, the vigilante hens, the violet thunderballs. We remembered different things. Tim remembered his frequent trips up and down the ladder because he ate too many cherries and they made him want to wee all the time. Jo remembered all the tunes on the jukebox in the café-bar. Nobody else remembered the girl with the violet eyes, nobody except me. But we all remembered Chris' trip to Marseilles to buy the knife.

So it was with an awful sense of fate that we all happened to be sitting in separate pubs, independently, when we heard the news. A man had been stabbed in the next town; he was dead. He hadn't been stabbed with the Bowie knife he'd bought in Marseilles, but it was Chris who'd died. And although he hadn't been named as yet we all thought of him and no-one else, straight away, when we heard the news.

From that day on I have believed in fate – not as something preordained, but as a collection of possibilities and probabilities heaped inside two buckets and balanced on the fulcrum of an ancient weighing machine somewhere just like Bruyes' orchard, see-sawing throughout the duration of our lives. In a matter of seconds only, when the weight of the world tipped one way or the other, it was Chris who was taken down to the guillotine and it was I who was spared.

chocolate

HE remembered the room as rather old-fashioned, even then, dowdy and cluttered and squashed, with frayed seats and dusty corners. People still smoked at work and took their sandwiches with them in tins or plastic Tupperware containers which released personalised wafts of cheesy or fishy smells into the air. Old Tom had died on the job many years previously but his gunmetal sandwich box was still used to hold the tea money – and still it percolated old aromas into the atmosphere. Anwen the older-than-sin cleaner had scrubbed it many times and even kept soap in it for a while, but it continued to exude Tom's spiritual dinners, as if it had been an amphora containing rich wine set aside for Odysseus' long-awaited return. At lunchtime a no-nonsense programme of cheese and tomato, fishpaste, or ham and mustard hit the airwaves. Tastes were simple, exotica rare. Some people were still described as poets or intellectuals with awed reverence. Doctors were saints and politicians were damned clever, to a man. That was a long time ago and he struggled to picture it in his mind. But a few memories lingered on in ghostly isolation.

From the window to his left, glued shut by countless layers of old paint, he recalled a view over slate rooftops aslant, more often than not shining with fresh rain, their purples and mauves coming to life under the constant showers which varnished them.

On the windowsill squatted a big brass plant-holder, Victorian and vulgar with embossed nymphs or caryatids rippling the metal and dead flies clogging a dusty necklace of spider-silk inside it. Within this bulbous, Brasso-profundo monstrosity reclined an aspidistra or suchlike, brought back to life periodically after bouts of neglect, its long crooked stems naked without the leaves it had shed during enforced droughts.

Morgan had started as a junior in that office, indentured. Now, in the conservatory of his rather grand home, he chuckled to himself and said the word over and over again. *Indentured.* He sat passively with his useless legs tucked under a crimson rug, under strict orders not to move. *Indentured*, he said again to the plant by his elbow. A contract of employment – a thing of the past, like him. He tried to formulate a pun about dentures, for his own were loose and hurtful, but his mind refused to grapple with the words. He toyed with the crumbs in his lap, feeling their texture under his fingertips, and then he returned to the past again. After his indentureship he'd qualified and gone on to consolidate his career in the little office at the top of the stairs – the only room in the world for him then.

Mags brought him a fresh cup of tea and busied around him, tidying his newspaper. He'd been ordered to drink plenty of fluids, so she sat in the wicker chair opposite him, across the table, nagging him silently into taking a few sips. Time slipped by and when he next looked up she'd dropped off to sleep under the heat of the glass. He studied her, dispassionately. Again, he went back to that office where they'd met for the first time, more than fifty years ago. He tried to recover the pungent smell of the printer's ink and the hot lead, fresh white paper and beery masculine smells in the compositing room. When she was taken on suddenly – the firm was going through a period of prosperity – there had been nowhere for her to sit so she'd been given a spot on his table, after he'd been consulted in the corridor outside by his boss, in whispers. He knew he had no choice, though he was used to having the table to himself. It was a large but surprisingly light affair made of ash with a square section of inlaid baize in the centre. A typewriter had arrived on it one Friday afternoon, and the following Monday morning Mags had been ushered in to sit behind it. He'd bumbled to his feet, as was the custom then, and stammered a welcome. Small talk wasn't encouraged, so he glanced at her whenever he thought she wasn't looking in his direction, as subtly and indirectly as he could manage. As the days passed into months the paraphernalia of office life gathered around her, partly obscuring her from his gaze. She became a fixture at the end of his green baize table. He was able to study her in the soft slatted light which lit up the aspidistra and wove a delicate pattern of blind-slats and green plant-shadows in her chestnut hair. She took responsibility for the plant immediately and it prospered; she was quickly popular, and he sometimes felt envious of the easy rapport she shared with the other staff. One day it occurred to him that the distance between them across the table was somehow too formal, almost ceremonial – just as configured as a boardroom table, or even the round table at Camelot.

One damp Sunday afternoon, fresh from chapel and inspired by something the visiting preacher had said, he decided to make a scale map of the room where they worked.

He went in early on the Monday morning and measured the place as accurately as he could with his feet, planting his shoes one after the other in a slow caravan across the desert of the office floor. The preacher had talked about dimensions: in particular, the cubit as the distance between the elbow and the tip of the middle finger, an ancient measurement quoted in the Bible as it described Noah making his ark. The preacher had pumped himself up and hit a state of *hwyl*-inspired excitement delivered in a singsong voice, his spade beard waggling with emotion. He'd finished off with the fathom – the six feet or so between fingertip and fingertip when the human arms were outstretched. Nowadays, thought Morgan, he'd have mentioned the Angel of the North. Why did the human race have to fathom everything out, the preacher had asked, why couldn't people leave every-thing in the hands of God?

After pacing out the office Morgan had taken his measure-ments home, inside his lunchbox. On his way from work that Monday evening he'd bought some graph paper at WH Smith and pushed it under his coat hurriedly, while he was still in the doorway, damaging it slightly. In pencil at first, and then with coloured pens, he'd drawn out the floor plan and added (in black) each arc and interstice. Once this was done he'd noticed that his own seat fell on an interstice while hers didn't, lying outside any of the black lines which connected all the other points of the room. Armed with this information he studied her avidly, day by day, watching the shafts of light criss-crossing the room and meeting in sunny places, doubling the yellowness where they met. He watched the sunshine as it candyflossed her hair, or threw her profile in shades of peach and butter. Sometimes the sun made her eyelids luminous, finely webbed with her blood-lines. At such times she seemed scented and feminine and vulnerable. On other days the soft down on the back of her neck glowed and burred in the summer light, and during those moments she seemed vigorous and robust. Then she was gone, leaving for another job as suddenly as she came.

Morgan watched her now, in the conservatory, waking up slowly. The profile was still there, though more etched of course, with deep lines fingernailed into the clay of her face. She stood up slowly, patted down her hair and her clothes, then took their cups away, chinking all the way back to the kitchen. He fell back into his reverie on dimensions and intersections.

The next time they'd met was at her home. A senior reporter by now, he'd been sent to another sloping terrace on another sloping hill because she'd done something remarkable enough for the rather stuffy newspaper he worked for to take notice: she'd qualified as an architect – the region's only female architect, astounding everyone around her, especially the men in suits (himself included). They'd sat in her mother's immaculate front room, on either side of the household's best oak table, every doily in its allocated place, and an aspidistra plant between them, so that she'd had to move it – thus ruining her mother's elaborate arrangements.

It's the same plant, she said with a smile. The one in the office.

He studied it dutifully, a quarter of cucumber sandwich poised in his curled right hand, hovering over a white china plate – curiously shaped, square with cut-off corners – in his left hand. No crumbs yet. The cucumber reminded him of the aroma in old Tom's gunmetal tin, but that was a coincidence, surely. She was talking to him, he watched her mouth move, fascinated by the slender shadow under her lower lip. What was she saying? The plant – ah yes, she'd taken it with her from the windowsill in the office – a killing field for plants – and replaced it with another, more adaptable bit of office vegetation: a cactus. He hadn't even noticed.

It transpired that she'd grown attached to the aspidistra, and he could see – in between nibbles of cucumber sandwiches and then home-made chocolate cake – that it had thrived in its new home. He inquired about the cake. She'd made it herself, and by golly it was delicious. He complemented her on her many talents – he meant it, he was really quite impressed, as he told his mother quietly in the kitchen back home. During that hour in the front room Mags had relaxed in her chair, allowing him to admire her openly. She'd seemed friendlier, warmer and more open. He could see more of her, physically, than he'd been able to in the office when they worked together – her typewriter had blocked most of the view – and now he was forced to avert his eyes from the swell of her bust in her Sunday best, a scalloped Irish linen blouse. As they chatted after the interview, which went well, he tried to memorise the dynamics of the room: its planes and focal points, its radii and tangents. At home, later, sleepy and charmed, he'd made another map, this time a rough-out on foolscap paper. Again, she'd sat just outside a line in the nexus of connections.

But they'd sat easily together, and there had been a gentle rapport, he thought. He was puzzled. In his mind's eye he went over the meeting again, dissecting the scene: her stance, her posture, and her position in relation to his own body in that room. Had she been closer, physically, was that it? But his mental arithmetic discounted the possibility. She had seemed closer – perhaps his response had been more subjective and emotional. A subtle angling of their bodies, perhaps, had synchronised their orbits.

He closed his eyes in the conservatory and slipped into a daydream. When he opened them again Mags was standing in the doorway, and he looked at her again in the way that old people do, as if she were a marble statue. She was a half-shadow in the doorway, hands on hips, her trademark stance. She seemed to be disappearing into the shadow – and the stoop he'd noticed recently, was it getting worse? She asked him a question.

No, he didn't want any supper yet. The blanket was overheating his knees, he noticed, so he took it off laboriously, folded it unevenly, and draped it over the arm of his chair. She tutted, but left him alone to his thoughts. She was baking a cake, he could smell it. Chocolate. Her tour de force, feted by her friends at the Townswomen's Guild, and all those other societies she belonged to, in which the sisterhood filled the hours – like spare rooms – with junk and said to each other wordlessly, *let's not give up hope just yet.* To every person God gave a special gift, and Mags made divine chocolate cakes. A strange gift to receive through heavenly providence, he thought. He never touched so much as a crumb now. The consequences were too dire.

They'd met again, only days after the interview in her mother's front parlour, which on reflection had more of the royal levee about it than a simple act of courtship. Morgan closed his eyes and rested his head on the back of his chair. He could remember the phone call almost word for word: his shyness mingled with excitement, his fearfulness and stammering. He'd asked to see her again, to clear up a few things, but it was a ruse, they'd both known that. They met in the tea rooms at the top end of town, near the funicular railway which took tourists to the top of the limestone cliffs. He was in his best suit again, his only suit, a bit shiny around the bottom but she said nothing as of yet. She was dressed quite racily, he thought, in a pencil skirt and a flimsy peach blouse: he could see her bra straps, but he said nothing as of yet. A little black hat and crimson lipstick... by god she was a looker, gathering admiration from all around; he was puffed with pride as he sat beside her on his slightly shiny bottom.

He'd worn his rugby club tie – not a player but a good secretary, vital role really – and he'd tried to impress her with his knowledge of words: his special gift from the man above. After all he was well on the way to becoming an intellectual, and he read poetry before going to sleep, though only socially approved material, Dylan Thomas and RS Thomas, no outlandish stuff. What was the connection between *funicular* and *funambulist*, he'd asked her as they drank their Lapsang Souchong. He'd pointed towards the railway, for some unfathomable reason. Amazingly, she knew. A funambulist was a tightrope walker, and *funa* was Latin for rope. He was visibly astonished.

Then she'd poked fun at him and he'd blushed. The women around them all noticed him blush, and he blushed again. But the meeting went well, and by the end they both knew that something was on the cards. Her shapeliness and intelligence did it for him. And as for her? Oh, there was his boyish interest in everything around him, and his blushes perhaps. What with nobody much else on the scene and time running against her she might as well get it over and done with – she agreed with her mother on that. Her parents' marriage had been sturdy and strong like a cast iron stove but there hadn't been much love or finesse. Mags and Morgan might be lucky, and it was all down to luck in the end, wasn't it? Look at all those arranged marriages in Persia or wherever, the success rate was round about the same.

Within a year they were married.

Often afterwards, in the first flush of love, he'd made a mental map of the tea rooms and tried to correlate all the planes and parabolas. Mankind so loved patterns, he thought. Circles and cones, checks and diamonds. In the tea rooms their bodies seemed to sit in harmony, as if they were celestial bodies reaching a perfect Pythagorean pitch. Perhaps that's all love was, really – a geometric formula based on the distance between two bodies at any given time, a day when patterns met and matched, melding a marriage of shapes which pleased all around.

Mags was in the doorway again, almost completely in shadow now. Was there anything he wanted?

He sat for a while, watching the building's shapes fade into dusk. There was nothing he wanted. Only his youth again, a big soft bed and an hour or two for dalliance. For astonishingly, unexpectedly perhaps, their physical union had been an unqual-ified success, on both sides of the bed. Nights of tumultuous, unending sex. Years of consummation, shared orgasms, relaxing cigarettes passed from hand to hand; he could remember the taste of her lipstick on the filters. Yes, their sex life had been top drawer. The stuff of dreams. It had saved their marriage on more than one occasion.

As she left him he opened a book but put it down quickly; almost all his concentration had gone, dissipated with the years, along with all his energy. Drifting off to sleep again, he thought of their life together – their homes, their children, their fading hopes. Because their mental patterns had never really matched. That day in the tea rooms he had sought to impose a pattern, to connect the lines and intersect the radii, but he'd had to admit it later, at first to himself and later to others, their marriage had never been more, really, than a physical palliative to both of them. He'd shuffled the Morgan shape and the Mags shape all around like a pattern-maker, but they had never truly matched, except between the sheets – and that was good and certainly important but it wasn't quite enough, not over a lifetime. He was tired of thinking these thoughts over and over to himself. Should he tell her? But she already knew, surely. What was the point of an autopsy?

As he drifted off again, Morgan thought about the chapel and its neat little cemetery, yews and graves in tidy rows. Because there was one decision outstanding: when he'd suggested – as was natural – a joint grave she'd gone strangely quiet.

Let's talk about that another day, Morgan, she'd said.

Whoever lived longest, it seemed, would decide on the final pattern.

In the conservatory all shapes and lines faded into darkness as he snoozed in the company of an old but tumultuous aspidistra plant. The smell of chocolate pervaded the whole building. And his final thought as he drifted away was that his very first map of their relationship, drawn on graph paper, had put that plant in a perfect isosceles triangle between him and Mags as they sat in an old newspaper office at the top of the stairs, the only room in the world for him then, when he was young and ready for love… so many years ago.

purple

MY Great Aunt Mary died recently.

She was a mountain dweller – and a sizeable mound in her own right, a formidable matriarch who wore a hefty Paisley-patterned apron and Wellington boots for six days of the week (we thought she slept standing in them, at the kitchen sink) and a black coat plus floral hat on the seventh. The hat was a statement, never to be understood by mortal man.

Like most farmers' wives of old she had never been seen eating, but spent almost all her life preparing food for an extended family of bipeds and quadrupeds: she didn't seem to care much who got what; I wouldn't have been greatly surprised to see a lamb at the dinner table and a greedy child nuzzling a bottleful of milk in the yard.

I can see her now, waddling towards me across the farmyard, carrying two large pails of pigswill, making one of those ancient noises used on farms to call the animals; experts say these *chucka-chucka-yaaa* noises are probably the oldest in the human repertoire. On workdays she wore a headscarf which accentuated her chubby red cheeks, and the plentiful hairs on her chin seemed as natural as her husband's. Standing in the kitchen with an industrial-sized rolling pin at the ready, her heavy apron held together with a broad leather belt, she had the air of a tired and greying Bedivere or Gawain girt ready for the Battle of Camlan.

She smelt chaotically of bacon, soap, beef, custard, suet, manure, flour, iron, blood, hay, toffee, udders, mothballs, bibles, babies, henhuts and butterchurns. To be frank, the apron was a large rustic corset which – like an African dictator – tyrannised a small country of flesh and held in thrall a continent of smells. It was hardly surprising that she was surrounded almost always by a ring of open mouths, as if she were a bird with her chicks at the nest. Out in the yard she was immediately surrounded by concentric rings of animals: pet lambs, calves, hens and children, all waiting to be fed with soft brown eyes full of love and gastronomic expectation.

Never in my wildest dreams did I ever imagine that Great Aunt Mary – who'd sown, weeded, reaped, washed, prepared, cooked and served up more food than all our celebrity chefs put together – had a dark secret. My first intimation of it came at the wake, when my Uncle Dafydd, himself a spindle of a man (bachelor, raconteur, expert wielder of crook and billhook) made a comment about the size of the coffin in relation to the size of the little girl who had very nearly starved herself to death in the distant past. I barely registered his words, but they returned to me when I received a dusty, battered case – a Victorian portmanteau – containing Mary's personal documents. The job of sorting them was allocated to me partly because no-one else wanted to do it, partly because I had just finished my A-levels and had a whole week in which to kick my heels, between the final exam and shearing day. Since we lived in the hills there was no town to paint red, nor did I have any tiles to spend the night on, except in the dairy, so I knuckled down to the task every evening, after the daily chores. As I did so a year in the late adolescence of a young girl came sketchily to life, but only after I'd sorted the paperwork into piles: letters, newspaper cuttings, certificates, postcards, and so on.

The most striking clue to her story was a newspaper cutting about Sarah Jacob, known as 'the Welsh fasting girl'. I'd never heard of her. There were many similar tales, apparently, about young girls who survived miraculously for long periods without eating. There were magical or religious connotations. Some of them developed stigmata, but the medical profession dismissed them as frauds or hysterics. Their symptoms included paralysis and staring fits. In Mary's childhood, women were encouraged to nibble daintily on the rare occasions they ate in public, said the article. And to have a 'clean' body (inside and out) the fasting girls controlled their food intake rigorously to increase their 'spirituality'.

Sarah Jacob, who died on December 17, 1869, aged twelve years and seven months, convinced a vicar she was authentic. Her story became widely known and she was sent gifts and donations. But doctors were sceptical and she was sent to Guy's Hospital to be monitored by nurses, who were told to give her food if she asked for it. Poor Sarah went into a steep decline, but her parents – convinced she was genuine – refused to halt the test, even when told their daughter was dying, as she duly did.

When I started to excavate Mary's past I tried to be methodical, but the piles of paper had an antic life of their own; finding a linear story seemed impossible. So I changed tack: I sifted though all the papers again, putting aside anything touching on the Sarah Jacob story, or on Mary's illness. Eventually I was left with nine documents, not including her birth and death certificates. After fiddling about with them well into the depths of the night I seemed to have a plot, but I still couldn't be sure. This is the sequence, as I established it:

Document A: Mono postcard showing a view of Carno in Breconshire, date unintelligible, addressed to Margaret Jones (Mary's mother).

Sorry to hear about Mary, we are praying for you. Try a little bread and milk with sugar but no butter. See Mrs Henry Williams Hengae, her angelica works well with the stomach. Weather up and down, lost a field of hay last week. Gwynfor bad with his rheumatics.

Yours, Ceridwen.

Document B: Sheet of sun-yellowed paper, much-folded, many dirty fingerprints, with an embossed letterhead – Capel Hebron. Message (translated):

The Deacons met on Sunday evening to consider your request. We cannot supplicate to the Lord on your daughter's behalf, it is His will that she lies in bed afflicted, for she has been meeting William Evans the cobbler's son at the mountain gate while pretending to go collecting bilberries. We are also informed, regrettably, that you have consulted Vicar Pritchard, and it is therefore our wish that neither you nor your family attend this chapel until the issue of your daughter's passion and sickness is resolved.

Yours truly, Edwin Williams, Deacon.

Document C: Small card, in good condition though foxed, showing a mono etching of a church on its cover. Message:

Further to our conversation, the Bishop informs me that Bell, Book and Candle is inappropriate in this case. I will intercede with the Lord on M's behalf every day in my prayers, for I truly believe she has seen the Lord's Shining Path. I beg of you not to rely on the ministrations of the woman they call Morfudd Hên, and to trust in God, for He is Good. M's exultation has uplifted my heart. I shall visit you again on Sunday pm to see how she is. Do not press food upon her, our Lord will nourish her Spirit. I will look into the possibility of lustration.

Yours etc, Vicar Pritchard.

(I looked up lustration in the dictionary and it was defined as 'to make somebody or something spiritually pure by means of a special religious ceremony'.)

Document D: Note on plain paper, with traces of pearly candle wax:

Further to my diagnosis – infantile hysteria – I confirm there is nothing more I can do. Encourage her to eat small mouthfuls of dry bread or biscuits often. Insist on her drinking clean drinking water from the well, frequently.

Yours, Dr Jones.

Document E: Dilapidated letter, almost falling apart, bearing evidence of frequent reading, again headed Hebron Chapel. Translated:

The Deacons met on Sunday evening to discuss your daughter Mary, and our great disquiet over her visits to the mountain with her people. We are told by Deacon Robert Morris that Mary has seen a wondrous sight, and many go with her, a large crowd wishing to see the object of her jubilation, though no-one but she has witnessed it yet. Deacon Robert Morris informs us that the multitude grows daily, and a light shines in their eyes. He says they sing hosannas and rejoice, waiting to witness Mary's wonderful vision. We warn you it is sinful to worship false idols.

'Beware of false prophets, which come to you in sheep's clothing, but inwardly they are ravening wolves' – Matthew 7:15

'Whoso boasteth himself of a false gift is like clouds and wind without rain' – Proverbs 25:13

'Ye men of Athens, I perceive that in all things ye are too superstitious. For as I passed by, and beheld your devotions, I found an altar with this inscription: TO THE UNKNOWN GOD. Whom therefore ye ignorantly worship, him I declare unto you.' – Apostles 17:22.

Tell your daughter to cease her false witness with immediate effect, or the Lord will fall upon her.

Yours truly, Edwin Williams, Deacon.

Document F: A summons issued by the Caernarvonshire Judiciary ordering Mary and her parents to appear before Caernarvon Magistrates following an incident on the mountain-top known as Mynydd y Gweledydd during which the Riot Act was read; they were charged with failing to disperse after the reading of the aforementioned Riot Act by the Chief Inspector of Police.

Document G: Letter on lined paper, blue feint, stamped in the top right corner with a franking machine: Holloway Prison. Translated:

Dear Mother and Father, they are treating me well here and I have a cell of my own, the doctor and chaplain come to see me every day and I want for nothing except to see your dear faces again, and old Shep I miss very much too. How is Abel, are the hens laying? Have you finished with the hay? I am sorry I am not there to help. I cannot see the mountain from here, but I am allowed to pray as much as I like, and I read my Bible all through the day. I am excused duties. I can see the sky and it is blue today, with clouds in it, and I think of what I saw on the mountain that day, and when I think of the Miracle I saw I am allowed by God's Grace to walk again under the clouds on Mynydd y Gweledydd. They leave food for me every evening at bedtime, bread and cheese mostly, but by morning it has gone, the mice I think.

Please write to me soon, I am your obedient and loving daughter Mary.

Document H: Letter on plain A5 paper, yellow with age. Carno written in the top right corner and underlined stylishly. No date:

Mary arrived yesterday evening under the escort of the local constable. She was dusty from the journey and looked weary, but not particularly undernourished, though lean about the face. I believe she will make a full recovery, with the help of our 'mice'.

I agree, a year spent with us in Carno as a servant will do her no end of good, and allow the past to recede. She says she still reads her Bible daily, but she has ceased to speak in tongues and is passive in company. She went to bed without a murmur, and is still asleep as I write. Will let you know as soon as something happens. Gwynfor's rheumatics worse, almost unable to walk some days. Lost a hen to the fox last week but the cattle are doing well on the new ffridd and the drovers took twenty with them to England last month. Things are looking up!

Yours as ever, Ceridwen.

Document I: Grey exercise book, lined blue feint, with many pages removed or torn out; rusty staple marks on the paper.

Some pressed flowers, secured by stamp hinges in the opening pages, together with a sketch of a planned sampler. A dozen pages of verses from the Bible (probably learnt by rote for Sunday School) and Welsh proverbs, all written childishly in pencil. After a few blank pages, the following passage, also in pencil, entitled My Own Testimony. Translation:

This is my Witness, may God punish me if I lie. In the presence of my father and mother I have sworn on the Bible that what I say is True.

There is a place I go to collect bilberries with a quart pot, every Saturday afternoon in summer if the weather allows. This place is about a mile above and to the left of Y Gors Ddu (the black bog). It is on the northern flank of Mynydd y Gweledydd, the mountain I see from my bedroom window. It is not true what they say, that I go there to meet William Evans the cobbler's son, I met him there by chance once when he was crossing the mountain to visit his Uncle Huw Gorseinion. One day I was on the mountain picking berries, alone, when I heard a sound which was not the sound of the lark or the curlew, it was a great and wonderful sound, as if a great bird or an angel was arriving from the sky. I did not collect any more berries, I listened to the angel flying through the sky and its wings beat the air around me, blowing my hair and caressing my ears. I was not afraid, though the noise was strange and unearthly. I left my bilberry can by the sheepfold and walked along the sheep path to the top of the hill which is next to Mynydd y Gweledydd, and I sat on the white rock known as Maen Efengyl (Gospel Rock), overcome with amazement. The sound of the angel roared in my ears and I covered my head in shame, for I knew the Second Coming was upon us. After a while I lifted my eyes to Mynydd y Gweledydd and there were three tall angels standing there, shining brightly in the sun, I was speechless with emotion. And when I looked again the angels had changed into the three crosses at Calvary, and our Lord was crying Eli, Eli, lama sabachthani? in a sorrowful voice, and the purple of the heather was His blood upon the ground. I ran from that place with all the strength I had left, because I thought the Lord had come to judge me, and to

send me among the damned in Hell for consorting with William Evans
the cobbler's son, when I had only met him by accident. I cried to the
Lord as I went, 'I do not love William Evans because he is spoken for
and I will put aside all desire for him'. Then I fell in a dead faint.
When I awoke I was in my bed, and the mountain was still there in
my window. From that day all desire for food left me for three years. I
was sustained by God's love.

This is my sworn testimony. Mary Jones.

And so ended the strange story of another Welsh fasting girl, as I
had pieced it together in the attic of my home. Mary had
evidently turned some sort of corner at Carno, living as a maid
with her aunt, and had then returned to a relatively normal life in
north Wales. But my amateur detective work wasn't over yet,
because I decided to visit the site of her vision, Mynydd y
Gweledydd. So one fine summer's morning I took a plastic
container – to hold bilberries – and walked up from Mary's old
home, an old Welsh farmhouse, squat and small-windowed, along
the exposed granite road which leads to the mountains.

It is steep and windy, tufted in the middle with grass and clover
and wild flowers.

Eventually I arrived at the mountain gate, where I enjoyed a
sandwich while I imagined Mary's meeting there with the
cobbler's son, so long ago. Presumably she'd made the journey in
clogs and a long dress, which must have been hot and exhausting
work. Then I followed the map route I had worked out beforehand, and found a sheep path – perhaps the same as Mary had
taken – to the top of the hill next to Mynydd y Gweledydd.
Strangely, I too began to hear a whooshing sound as I progressed,
and I began to feel quite peculiar because Mary's experience was
being duplicated, seemingly – the noise was getting louder with
every step, and indeed it did sound like the wings of a huge angel.
When I arrived at the white rock, Maen Efengyl, I immediately
saw the cause of the noise – three massive wind turbines churning
the air on top of Mynydd y Gweledydd, all chopping the breeze

like crazed kung fu fighters. I sat on the rock and looked at them in wonder. In a way they could be likened to three white angels, but they certainly hadn't been there nearly eighty years ago, when Mary was a young girl. Had her vision been a presentiment? Or was it pure coincidence?

I mulled, cynically, on the similarities between wind power and god power: both served only a tenth of the population, relied on a lot of wind, and their powers were greatly overestimated. Whatever happened to Mary on the hill would never be explained. But in a way her vision had come true. She had indeed seen a second coming. As I wended my way down the mountain I thought of the portly lady I had known, whose life had been dedicated to food. The irony was tragi-comical, just like Mary. And as I walked down the mountain road I felt the presence of both Marys, on the one side a young and impressionable girl with a quart pot of bilberries in her hand and a stream of prayers coming from her mouth; and on the other side the Mary I knew, plump and resigned to her fate. I arrived home in a sober mood.

I remembered something Mary had said to me once in the kitchen as she filleted and diced some meat – just a few words muttered in passing.

Look at this fat, Euros, she said, looking at me sideways, desolately. So much fat in the world... it's sad. Because fat is a form of grief, Euros. Yes, fat is a form of grief.

white

WE drive to Capel Curig in his black Sierra and park behind Joe Brown's.

I feel a pang of guilt whenever I see that car. He cracked the front bumper on a gatepost when we were turning round on a narrow pass last summer. We'd strayed in the wrong direction – my fault – and it was my idea to turn in that gateway. Smack.

Of course, he didn't give a toss – the bang, when it came, hardly registered on his Richter scale.

We go east, walking into the Carneddau Range, and the trail out of the village swings to and fro, a childish squiggle on the landscape. In the thin wintry light our shadows are two exclamation marks searching for an end to the sentence; our boots press wayward commas onto the path. I follow in his footsteps, slowly but steadily: there's no hurry to complete a story we've been creating – but not writing down – for nearly a hundred years between us. We both trashed our bodies some time ago and now we're in the restaurant at the end of the universe, waiting for the final bill. Tweedledum and Tweedledee in anoraks. Noddy and Big Ears doing a hoodie thing.

Creeping licentiously along the hyena flank of Pen Llithrig y Wrach, on a stony path, we are no more than lice drumming a surface vein, seeing if we can tap it. Then we walk along the edge of Llyn Cowlyd, a cavity left over from a huge molar extraction, and the peaty water is thin brown blood, staining the lake's gums.

He is the thinker, I am the notary: he plots the course and I carry the charts. Many years ago he taught me the art of map-reading, turning symbols and contour lines into a vision of the world. He is (and always has been) the hierophant, the explainer of mysteries. A fabulous draughtsman of the unseen. My own interpretations, in comparison, are crayon squiggles on a playground wall.

It becomes a day of reference points. At the eastern end of the reservoir I decide to tell him the secret inside me. It's been there for a long time now and I want it out in the open. I want it exhumed and reburied. This is for my sake, not his. He would rather not know, I'm certain of that. I look around, and realise that this isn't the right place. Right time, wrong scenario. Somehow, I'll know where that is when I get there…

Around us there are abandoned, crumbling homesteads trying to keep their footing, drunkenly, on the edge of the seeping marshlands. Miraculously, they still have names – *Siglen* (bog) and *Brwynog* (rush-covered, sad). Never were two ruins more aptly named. They are senators representing hundreds more like them, leaning into puddles crookedly like aeroplane shadows, all along the length of Wales' hinterland.

There is an old story that fairies called at one of these farms near Cowlyd late in the nineteenth century, asking if they could enter the house to wash and dress their baby. Having done so they left, leaving money as they'd promised. They also left the lotion used to clean the baby. It was found by a servant girl, who examined it. As she did so her eye itched, and in rubbing it she transferred some of the lotion from her finger to her face. Later, when she went to Llanrwst Fair, she saw the same fairies stealing cakes from a stand, and confronted them. They asked her which eye she saw them with, and when she told them, one of the little people touched it quickly. She never saw them again. But they still dance, frolic and sing on the flat meadows by the River Conwy every moonlit night. That's what people say.

It's hard going. We head for Moel Eilio, probably the least visited hilltop in the Carneddau Range. Visitors are rare, there's no recognisable path, so we practise a pantomime waddle through the vegetation. We raise a woodcock, and then, euphorically, two black grouse cocks, samurai with twin vermilion wounds in their sable helmets. We struggle for words in the springy heather, in the way that middle-aged people do – standing in an ever-darkening hangar we survey the antique engines of our lives, dismantled and left lying around in bits on the ground. We clean each semantic nut and bolt with a rag, wondering where each meaning came from, glad we'll never have to put it all back together again.

We search our corroded lexicon for words to describe the wattles on the blurred, escaping birds, and he conjures scarlet, alizarin, ruby, carmine and cerise. But there is no point to this naming of the parts: it's no more than a walk to the garage every so often to start a vintage car. To let it idle for a while.

Carnedd Llewelyn's clefts and ravines are veined with snow; the mountain's ancient skin is blemished by burst capillaries running in cobweb filaments down the slopes. But the dominant theme is black: the mountain has used all its dark arts to win a secret, nocturnal battle. Below us, Cwm Eigiau trifles with our senses. We are two tiny krill lodged in the corner of the valley's gaping whale-mouth, two miles wide.

We talk, fitfully, as we walk. It's an old friendship; conversation comes in staccato bursts, then we are muted again by the vastness; each mountain is a crashed comet, reminding us to be small. We pick a path through the bog and I regurgitate a bolus of information about Dafydd ap Gwilym and one of his jocular poems. While riding to a love tryst one starless night, Dafydd and his horse stumble into a peat bog and he vents his spleen on all things peaty and boggy. He's particularly upset because the tumble has fouled his best pair of courting socks.

Hopping from tussock to tussock, it's more than likely that I too will get a bootful of cold bog-juice sooner or later. I feel like a kid trying to follow the timetable, wandering from lesson to lesson, trying to keep up. A raptor ripples above me and I pause to watch it. Time loses all meaning, retreats through a gap in the soundless clouds. This cwm also struck the ancient tribes as timeless – it was home to the Owl of Cwm Cowlyd, the oldest owl in Wales. When the owl was asked where Mabon was, it answered: *If I knew, I would tell you. When I first arrived here this great valley was a wooded glen, but a great race of men came and the wood was laid waste. A second wood grew and was also laid waste, and a third also. And as for me, why, all that's left of my wings is two little stumps. From the first day to this I have heard nothing of the man you seek.*

I've fallen back again, the usual story: he says something just out of earshot, so I have to catch up with him and ask him, bronchially, to repeat himself. He plucks a name out of the air: Francois Villon.

The name means nothing to me, so he fills me in.

Dead six hundred years, he says. Murderer, thief, drunkard. In and out of prison, condemned to death more than once. Wrote witty, ironic, melancholic poems about his life in the medieval melting pot, where all human flesh was rendered:

Remember, imbeciles and wits,
Sots and purists, fair and foul,
You girls with tender little titties,
That death is written over all.
Famously, he wrote: *Mais ou sont les neiges d'antan?*
But where are the snows of yesteryear?

We cross the shallow valley between Moel Eilio and Cefn Cyfarwydd. Blocking our way is the pipeline taking water from the reservoir to Dolgarrog's hydroelectric station, owned nowadays by Innogy (my, how they must have wet their knickers thinking up *that* name). The pipeline – a catheter plugged to Cowlyd's bladder – is black and big enough to walk inside, crouching. I cup my ear against it, trying to hear the water rushing through. Nothing: no sound at all.

Ducking under the pipeline we meander along the valley floor, following the sheep paths through the morass, gambolling occasionally from tuft to tuft. We have all the paraphernalia of middle-aged walkers: rucksacks, phone, compass, hypothermia blanket, map. Our age is written in the rucksacks' inventory. Gone are the days when we came here in t-shirts and pumps, still bleary, puffy from last night's revelries...

There's sunshine on our side of the Carneddau, but I can see a wagon-train of cumulus clouds approaching Carnedd Llewelyn on the other side of the range. I feel wistful and disconnected. Snow is the closest we get to walking in our dreams, or on another planet – the closest we ever get to fairy dust and magic.

This is a story of reference points, so I'll take another bearing.

The first is this: many years ago my daughter fell ill with a minor illness. Tonsillitis I think – certainly, it was nothing serious. I stayed at home to look after her, and let her sleep on into the morning. Snow had been forecast, and as I sat by the window, looking out on the bleak landscape of winter, the sky became a bowl of cold porridge. Suddenly we were inside an old eiderdown of swirling, obliterating snow. I watched it, wondering if I should wake my daughter to see it, or let her sleep on. The snowstorm continued; I prevaricated. The snowfall stopped, and I still didn't know what to do; languorously, I sat there looking at the blinding landscape as the sky cleared and a blue cupola replaced the porridge bowl. It was then that she woke up, arriving soundlessly by my side in her red winceyette pyjamas covered in teddy bears. I became conscious, as her eyes moved from the snow to my face, that I'd made a mistake. Only a small mistake. But I realised, the moment she looked at me, that I should have woken her when the first flakes were falling.

We come to a large outcrop of quartz on the brow of Cefn Cyfarwydd. Heather stalks lunge at my legs as I pass, conger eels darting hungrily from their hidden caves. We sit on an eruption of quartz, frozen toothpaste escaping frantically from a cracked tube, and as I lift my eyes to the mountains I observe the cloud-train over Carnedd Llewelyn, hiding it behind a white curtain, as if enacting a silent, courtly masque. Their magic is revealed after they've passed over the peak: they have spread a white cloth of snow over the top, and it gleams now, a linen shemagh on a sheik's head, glinting in a Saudi sun. I goggle at it, as if I were a fish which has seen the silent, shimmering hull of a dredger pass over to deposit its ballast on the ocean floor.

We approach the dark cockscomb of Creigiau Gleision, the highest point of our walk. The lake lies far below us, a cat's saucer of milk, frozen, and the drop is sheer enough to make me nervous. The wind sharpens and attacks my ears. Perhaps we should head for home, I suggest, fearing the snow will come to encase us too.

I focus on a second trig point in my mind, and a sharp pang of memory arrives like a contraction. I remember one of Kate Roberts' stories in *Te yn y Grug* (*Tea in the Heather*). Four-year-old Begw is sobbing uncontrollably on a stool by the fire, her shawl trailing in pools of melting snow: she has woken up to a winter wonderland after an overnight fall of snow and she has opened the door excitedly – only to find her beloved cat dead on the doorstep. Her mother accidentally reveals the truth: it was her father who locked out – and killed – her little pet. To me, this tale of cruelty is a huge footprint in the snow: I want to know more about the yeti who was her father.

Along comes another contraction, and my memory finds a third trig point.

I look down on one of the ruined farmsteads, and I see a scene from the past.

Down there, in one of the roofless outhouses, with its bent walls and its broken slates, I see a boy of about ten, dressed in ragged clothes and Wellingtons, one of them leaky. His knees are red raw and scarred from countless falls. There are painful weals around his calves, which are chafed hourly by the Wellington rims (he hasn't learnt to turn them down, yet). He's dirty, and he clears a steady stream of snot with his sleeve. He wears no underpants. His clothes are cast-offs, and he has whitlows on his hands. There is a pad of hard skin on the thumb of his right hand, because he still sucks his thumb as he approaches his teens. He is tough, and already solitary.

He is small and lean, wiry and strong for his age. He masturbates almost constantly, and he is cruel to animals. He shoots sparrows with an air rifle and blasts pigeons and moles to pieces with a shotgun. When he's allowed to he ranges far and wide, climbing trees, making hazel whistles, building dams.

He is almost wild, though he's literate because he reads his father's musty books by candlelight every night. There is no water in the farmhouse, no electricity, no toilet. He is already an expert ploughboy and he knows a great deal about sheep – about their oppressed lives and their frugal cunning. He is from another age.

He has just caught a young female goose in the farmyard; the chase has left him with a jagged beak-shaped scar across the fingers of one hand; bubbles of blood cluster around the weal in ruby droplets. He has been attacked by the gander. He carries the goose into the outhouse and tries to strangle it, but fails. He's not quite strong enough. Carrying the goose by its legs, upside-down, he goes to another shed and returns with a hatchet. He rests the goose on a broken-down manger and arranges its head on a wooden truss, then slashes at it. He misses repeatedly, then loses his temper and lunges at the goose. Eventually he kills it and removes its head. Blood spurts on his trousers and his Wellingtons, coating his hands in warm crimson paint. He sits on a three-legged milking stool in the outhouse, which has virtually no roof remaining, and he plucks the goose, starting with the soft belly feathers, fine and still warm. The feathers stick to the blood on his fingers and to the mud on his Wellingtons. He is not impervious to beauty: a strong sense of futility and pain and melancholy wells up in him as he mangles the loveliness of the bird. He looks as though he has been tarred and feathered. It starts snowing. By now the goose is cooling. The feathers are harder to pluck. The boy's fingers are weak and sore as he pulls desperately at the large wing-feathers. He almost disappears in a cloud of snowflakes and feathers. He is intensely miserable, not because of the death of the goose, but because he will have to kill and pluck many more before his tasks are finished. He will have to singe the birds and gut them and truss them for people who will complain about his ineptness – the torn gooseskin, the quill-stumps left inside the wings.

When nightfall comes he will gather a handful of wing feathers and take them into the house, where he will make quills and write spidery words in a scrapbook, his sentences scratching the paper with birds' footmarks...

That little boy is me.

Tired now, exhausted almost, we descend into Capel Curig silently; I have told him the story of the geese in the snow. All the stories have been recited already, some of them many times. Night is almost with us and the white of the mountain peaks is fading into darkness.

We both become warmer, calmer and more reflective as we click our way through the church gate and enter the village. Our boots scrape on the tarmac, and we lift our feet a bit higher, suddenly conscious that we're weary. We dump rubbish, collected on the walk, into bins: I think of all the debris gathered in my brain, unwanted but unbinable. We are silent now as we watch the light fade around us, the delicate shade-by-shade disappearance of the natural world. Other shapes emerge – man-made shapes, doors and windows, angular and harshly lit. We become two moth-men, our shadows flitting around in the orange glow of the sodium lights.

We buy chocolate in the shop and browse around Joe Brown's, fingering the ropes and crampons. Then we sit quietly in the black Sierra, listening to the river pulsing through the mossy boulders below us. But my mind is much further away than we've been all day – at a lost and defunct trig point, far away in the ceded territory of my past.

He is my friend and companion, this man sitting in a black dented car. I want to tell him about the night I slept with his wife. About the day of the funeral, too.

I want to tell him that I wasn't able to think the right thoughts that day – that instead of thinking about the tragedy and the pain of death, I had thought about the night we had spent together in my bed. I would never be able to tell him how wonderful it had been. In the crematorium, when I looked at the coffin on its rollers, I had thought little of the pain in my friend's mind and body; I had imagined her shape as I had seen it that night in its nakedness and sexual greed. I had thought of her hands as she held me, the curve of her back and the sway of her hips as she left our bed. That is what I thought, not what I should have thought.

And when she died I felt nothing but guilt, and the absoluteness of death. I did not think of him at all.

I hoped perhaps that when I told him part of this story, when I took this story from the cold storage of my memory, he would understand, in that big, big way of his. My friend. But I couldn't. Not here, in a car by a river. Not in Wales, perhaps. The time had felt right. But the place… I was beginning to realise that location was going to be more important than timing. And I couldn't find the place. Was that because my guilt was associated with a place?

I would have to wait.

The moment was lost. That unfading memory of what happened must stay within me. Buried under the snows of yesteryear.

orange

I LIVE in a village six miles from the sea. Good jobs are scarce, winters are long.

Our skins are yellow and our feet always wet: we float forever on a cosmic water-bed in which hydrogen and oxygen atoms copulate torridly, endlessly, in sweaty threesomes to make yet more water babies.

Our poverty is typical of western seaboards, from Galicia to Cape Wrath – where the buzzard mews and the bagpipe keens so do men get drunk, women falter and babies sicken.

Our valley is a fresh green leaf veined along the centre with a broad central river joined at various points by six smaller streams. We live under stones by the water's edge and we spend much time sheltering, since the hills around us attract rain as old people draw memories. I need tell you nothing about myself: if you want to find me ask for the man who plays snooker with Mr Smart.

There came to live among us one day an Englishman. There was nothing very remarkable about him and he lived quietly in one of the roadside terraces which remind me, in some obscure way, of a game of Monopoly which has gone on for far too long. He formed an attachment to the many slate tips which linger around gigantic holes bored into our homeland by the mythical beasts of the past, and he spent much time clambering among them. Englishmen, as you know, fall immediately into two divisions when they come to

Wales: they either caramelise their essential Englishness, stiffening slowly into withdrawal and aloofness, or they pour themselves into the communal pot and add a slightly new tang to the local broth.

This Englishman did neither, which drew our eyes towards him.

There were certain things we noticed. Although he let slip one day that he was in his seventies he had the gait of a young athlete: smooth, rhythmic, fast, and seemingly effortless. He reminded me of a messenger in an eastern fable, seen first as a dot on the horizon, moving unerringly towards me in a whorl of dust, arriving clear-eyed and resolved, his outstretched arm holding a message of fantastic truth.

His experiences had been almost too many for one human lifespan. He told us stories about Russia: Moscow grieving under the snow, samovars, journeys on a tiny ship ice-trapped in a vodka sea. The silver birches had been babushka brooms sweeping time under the vast carpet of the steppes; he had met Uncle Vanya weeping among the cherry blossoms, seen the onion domes of St Petersburg moonbeamed and mystical; he could recall furtive attempts by a Soviet naval attaché to draw him into the Lubayanka's web.

Then there was India: the flight into paradise with Osho – cock-crow dawns in the ashram with a new name tart on his orange tongue; all the streams of his multifarious life merging in a great delta of knowledge and joy beneath the bodhi tree.

His many lovers emerged, one by one, to form a ghostly line into the past, each bearing a casket of remembrances; this one he'd wooed whilst reporting for a shipping magazine (look, there she is in the background, blinking into the camera); another had read his poems in the pallid light of a London street-lamp – they had met on Hampstead Heath, at a funfair; and still they came, young, amused, intrigued by his enduring vigour, travelling through his eyes to another dimension.

To us, the rough-hewn local boys, this dimension was fenced off, like the slate shafts dotted around us. We could never enter, not because he wanted to exclude us, but because we couldn't unstick ourselves from the slate's Velcro grasp; we were stuck to those purple hills as burdock burrs cling to a cow's underbelly.

He initiated a drama company and new names rattled on our rusty tongues: Brecht, Chekhov, Foe; our young people were fired by the plays he staged in a crumbling chapel. He invited the cognoscenti to his home and they appraised him over the fine wines he drew from his cellar. Inevitably he inspired envy and his enemies sprinkled his winter lawn with frost, killing his crocuses; inexorably he made many friends, who waved to him on the streets, sea fronds caught in the warmth of his Gulf Stream current. There was a lover, too, who tuned his summer lyre.

And then he was gone.

He simply vanished. No-one saw him go (and this was a great feat, since few people can depart completely unnoticed in our realm).

After a day or two people began peeping through his windows, but there was no movement. He had taken a few possessions but his wines, paintings and books had been left behind. We decided that we'd never see him again. His threshold gathered grime and his windows dust. His plants straggled and waned, his gutters grew cluttered and his gate fell unhinged. At some point, I can't tell you when, his lover moved away.

Months passed, a year became two. I got a job in the quarry sawmill, slicing massive slabs of slate into windowsills and lintels. I made good money and got drunk every night. I played snooker with Mr Smart and fathered a child but forgot its name.

One night, without any particular motive, I broke into the deserted house.

I've told you now – do what you will. I've forgotten why I did it. Drunk maybe, or still consumed with interest. I hadn't been part of his circle, but I'd watched his dusty dot speed towards us from one horizon and disappear towards another. I took nothing, merely nosed around, picking up books and putting them down again, looking at his paintings; then I lay on his bed, wondering which poems he'd read by candlelight to his couchant Aphrodite.

I slept briefly on a flamed Byzantine coverlet worked with silver and gold thread; by now the cottage was tinged with abandonment and a musky smell fumed my nostrils. I got up to leave.

By the bedroom door my boot clanged against a cupboard and the door swung open. I rummaged inside but my hand hit on nothing; I was about to turn away when a gentle rolling sound came from within the locker and an object trickled to the edge. I caught it as it fell towards the floor.

At first I thought it was a goose egg, but it was heavy and clearly made of stone; when I polished it with my sleeve I saw glints and swirling striations, a weave of sparkling, brightly-coloured minerals. It was similar to the magical obsidian stones of the Aztecs and Mayans, brilliantly hued, perfectly shaped and finely polished. The temptation proved too much: I stole it.

I know – it's true, I lied to you earlier when I said I took nothing. But it was nothing much, was it? Who cares about a bit of stone? For pity's sake, we're surrounded by the damned stuff, choked by it, entombed, trapped in it like a body left to rot in a cellar. No-one worries about a little bit of stone.

Fearful, however, of being caught with it in my possession I hid the stone in a gap in the wall of the sawmill by my workstation and damped some moist earth over it. Occasionally, when I was left alone, I would dig it out and polish it, watch the light catch on its glinting surface. Then I would bury it again.

We were busy. I made more money, I got drunker every night. One day, as we strove to meet a big order for gravestones, I uncovered a strange enigma as I sliced through the soft blue-stone. Through the water-sprays which cooled my saw I spotted an irregularity in the slate after my spinning blade had cleaved it. My workmates gathered round, one by one, wondering why I had stopped, and watched me as I hosed down the divided slab in a shower of rainbow droplets and dust, which dimmed the light around us. I turned off the saw and others switched off their tools also. The din ebbed away and a silence of sorts fell upon us. When I'd removed the dust and debris we stepped between the slabs and looked closely at what I'd seen as the blade hummed through it: a perfectly-shaped bubble in the stone – a rarity beyond memory, probably unique. They touched this unnatural vacuum, my workmates, running their fingers around its smooth concavities.

It was then that a thought struck me and a pulse ran through me, a jab of icy pain which filleted my mind. A heavy wire net tightened around my flapping brain and held it aloft like a terrified fish waiting to be dropped into a hold; my body ran hot and cold, I gulped anxiously. The thought which came to me in the sawmill – when I saw that indentation – came to you also I'm sure, as it came to Mr Smart, instantly. But none of you can imagine the dread which filled me when I realised that a power beyond my control was now forcing me to act on that thought, a force which moved my feet away from the slate slab, towards the hole in the wall by my workstation.

I knew I was making a terrible mistake, but I couldn't help myself. The frisson was too strong; I had to find out, and I had to do so in front of everyone, because my mind had decided to gamble wildly: it had become a drunken speculator chancing all on one throw of the dice. The rewards were too high to resist, the kudos too great.

A single high-pitch buzz filled the cavern in my head... was it the Celt in me, unable to resist a chance to mythologise, en-fable myself? But if I was right, how they would laud me! What glory would be mine!

I scrabbled at the earth around my stone egg, keeping my elbows still so that no-one would realise I was burrowing; I tried to look like a priest at his altar, preparing to turn with the communion. Hurriedly I cleaned off the soil and polished the stone with my quivering fingers. Then I turned and stepped slowly, purposefully, towards the slate. The other workers watched me somnolently. There was almost perfect silence by now, except for the tic-tic-tic of my saw as it cooled, and the occasional scrape of a boot on the floor. When I reached the flaw in the slate slab I lifted up my secret stone, allowing it to glint in the half-light, and then I applied it to the empty bubble in the slab. It fitted perfectly – an eye couldn't fit its socket better, more naturally. There wasn't a hundredth of a millimetre between the slate cup and my stone of many colours, nestling like a lapidary baby in its Neolithic womb.

It didn't take a genius, said Mr Smart chalking his cue that evening, to realise I'd made a monumental mistake. Whatever possessed me, he asked. Had I taken leave of my senses? The stones should never have been matched – couldn't I see that their morganatic marriage was too dangerous a liaison?

I'd realised all this, and more, in the first few moments of my madness, as the saw blade still spun above the rent in the metamorphic mass I'd sliced in half for an hour's beer money up there in the sawmill's gloom.

The repercussions were many. As Mr Smart foresaw I became a legend. I was apportioned fabulous powers. The villagers showed great reverence to me wherever I went; chairmen asked me to join their societies, to talk on this, to adjudicate on that. Children asked me to mend their toys. Young girls asked me to foretell the names of their husbands. Farmers asked me to cure cows and bless infertile mares. I was invited to manage the football team, open fetes, end feuds, patch friendships, restore libidos, enlarge organs, cure damp...

The days went by, one year became two.

By then I was a joke. They scorned me, reviled me openly. I'd been unable to do anything asked of me: no dream had come true, no disaster averted.

I drank even more heavily and I lost my job. I lost my home.

I became desperate when Mr Smart found another snooker partner.

One night I broke into the house again. No-one else had been there, and nothing had been touched: the Byzantine bedspread still held the imprint of my body.

In the same way as the nearby rivers met each other,

unavoidably, and in the same way as my two stones had merged, I too had reached a point of resolution, and I found myself nestling in the cupped hand of my nemesis. Change was inevitable; I could no longer continue on this lonely course towards disintegration. I took my stone egg and a few possessions, bundled them into a satchel, and disappeared into the night. Somewhere I had to deposit the cause of my troubles, that lovely, accursed stone. I also knew, instinctively, that I was a mere courier; that the stone would dictate where its next home would be.

The Englishman had talked of London. He had mentioned Edmonton more often than anywhere else. I had no money, so I hitched along an arterial motorway, floating past many tributaries, onwards in the great stream which flowed southwards.

Eventually I was flung on an alien bank, an ugly place where I found somewhere to cling to. I begged by day, putting the stone in front of me: for some strange reason it drew people towards it. I told my story to them and they gave me money. By night I slept under an archway, with others, my beautiful stone bulging inside my clothes, warm against my belly.

The days went by, one year became two.

I failed to find the Englishman. Every day as I sat with my stone I studied each face that passed, but his was not among them. I made enquiries about Osho and the sannyassins, but they had left India: I was told they had settled in a valley in Oregon. The Englishman, I felt sure, would be among them, moving as a nomad does from one spiritual tent to another.

I hit upon a plan. Every evening I combed the public houses around me, listening to accents. I wormed my way into conversations, put my stone on the table, and told my story. I listened for North American voices, and I talked to many before I found someone from Oregon. It took many encounters with Oregon people before I found the right person: he was slight, he was in his seventies, he was quick, and most importantly, he was prepared to help me. I invited myself to his hotel room, bought two bottles of the finest red wine, and told him what I wished of him. Fortunately, he was intrigued. He too had travelled through the steppes and had stood in Red Square; miraculously, he too had been among the orange people. He agreed to help me, and I told him my plan. We drank the wine and talked late into the night, then I left him.

I left the stone with him too. I returned home, but this time I followed the lesser tributaries as I moved slowly towards my motherland.

The days went by, one year became two. By now my disgrace had dimmed in everyone's memory and I was accepted back into the fold. My journey was seen as an expiation, and since I had seen things which no-one else had seen I was accorded some dignity. I got a job in the sawmill again and fathered another child, but this time I not only remembered his name I also treasured him. I showed him to everyone I met and extolled him to all who would listen. I played snooker with Mr Smart.

For many nights, as we stooped over the green baize, we conjectured about the stone egg. Was there a meaning to it all? A message perhaps? Mr Smart thought he saw an allegory, but it faded as soon as he tried to express it in words.

I learnt to accept the events which had overtaken me.

My own life swelled and ripened. I sought out the first child I had fathered and learnt her name. Gradually I was allowed to become part of her life. I put the stone egg to the back of my mind; it paled in my memory.

And then, one day, the Englishman came back. No-one saw him arrive. My daughter, on her way to school, noticed smoke curling from his chimney.

The next week saw much activity: new curtains, a freshly-washed doorstep, a tidied garden. Within a very short time the house looked as though it had never been abandoned. Callers were amazed: the Englishman behaved as if he had never left.

He was much the same: fleet of foot, clear-eyed, sharp-witted.

And although his physical movements were fast and fluid he held within him a lacuna of calm.

He had gifts for everyone he knew: toys for the children, books for the readers, baubles for the vain. Of course, I expected nothing. After all, I hardly knew him. But one day, as I passed with my two children, he waved from his front door, gestured me to stop, and disappeared inside. Soon he was back, striding towards the low wall which separated us. Standing between two radiant bursts of crocuses he smiled, stooped, and chatted with the children before handing them each a gift. Finally he stood up straight and looked at me with his clear grey eyes. He handed me a package also. He asked me to open it later, when I was alone.

There was no meaning to it, I'm sure. These coincidences do happen, I'm told.

But that night, while the children slept, the seven rivers roared, and the stars quivered under the leaf of heaven, I opened the packet and found a wooden egg, of exactly the same shape and dimensions as the stone egg I had passed on to another in a London hotel. It was beautifully polished and the grain swirled in lovely patterns. I put it on my mantelpiece, tentatively, hoping that no new calamity was approaching me.

None did.

My wooden egg still rests there, and no strange indent has appeared inviting it to nestle within. However, I must tell you one strange fact. Although the wood, honey yellow and serene, almost orange, is quite distinctive, it was some time before I could identify it.

Mr Smart was the one who recognised it. Bending over the snooker table one night, in a pool of light, he paused over his shot and remarked, in passing, that my wooden egg was made of Oregon pine.

black

I AM waiting for a woman.

On a chilly day in December, with a drunkard wind reeling along the alleyway, fumbling at my door.

I am tired of waiting. Dirty raindrops liver-spot the window – the panes are old and the horizon pitches up and down in grey waves beyond the glass. The tide wanders in and out in senile drifts, fractious and lost.

It's going to be a black day, and I'm glad.

My day's work is already done. I have been in my study since the small hours, as always. I lit a candle shortly after three and began work immediately on my manuscripts. I love silence and shadows, the naked dance of the flame. This is how the past speaks to me. I write to you from the monastery of my books, where so many words are sworn to silence. As you foretold, the day has come when I must review my own past. Time, the great despot, is about to overrun my mind; it has already subjugated my body. Never one for solitary pleasures, I want to share my experiences; this woman who comes to me every week, on Sundays, is my confidante. We share the same intimacy as lovers, without the coda; I am prepared to forgo the finale because each culmination draws us a little closer to the last. Together, we have viewed the antics of others coming and going on the great bed of life, but we have never been lovers. I am worn and depleted now;

the force has left me. But it was you, I think, who told me that real love – immortal love – sometimes arrives after sensual pleasure has departed...

She is here. I walk out of the house, slowly, into the wind; it paws me insistently and tries to knock my stick away. I say nothing as I enter her black estate car, then we set off for today's destination, the Conwy Valley. As we drive onwards the roads flood into shallow silver canals and the town becomes a temporary Venice; I glimpse a sudden flash of bright red disappearing down an alleyway. We pass a floating café with faces looming out of a vaporous mist, then we travel in silence, through the rainworld. Eventually we yaw into a side-road and hiss uphill towards the foothills of the Carneddau mountains. Our objective is the lake at Llyn Geirionydd, in summer a hellhole overrun with tourists, now a tub of freezing peat-water. We cower in a forest siding, waiting for the great sky-dog to lower his leg, to stop pissing on us. Through my window I watch shark-grey clouds swimming overhead as a wet-nosed wind pushes its cold muzzle into the day's underskirts.

I need information from this woman who sits quietly by my side. Her body is useless to me, but she is mentally rapacious: she is my go-between. Saturnine by nature, she is dressed sombrely in the sables and duns of winter. She has information for me, written carefully on lined notepaper. On Wednesday evening, during our discussion on the telephone, I imparted my regular weekly instructions; and as usual I sensed a shiver of anticipation at the other end of the line. I wanted to know more about Gwladus Ddu, born to the Welsh prince Llywelyn Fawr eight hundred years ago. Black Gwladus fascinates me unduly. She seeded many illustrious descendants, among them two American presidents: George Washington and Franklin D Roosevelt. She got her name, probably, from her dark eyes. I have a mental picture of her: she has long straight hair, black as coal, and paper-white skin. A beauty of the old Welsh courts, haughty and coolly intelligent; skilled in the social arts, adept in company, dressed in golds and greens, booted in expensive cordovan leather. Beautiful and accomplished; ill-starred in love: destined to be pared off with cruel, aggressive lordlings, the bastard sons of warrior kings. Secretive. Kind to her dogs only, and to her faithful old nurse.

I lay my fingers on the woman's arm and thank her quietly. She has obtained some excellent information, which will be the thrust of a new entry in my manuscripts. I have already uncovered an unusual fact about Gwladus' parentage. No, the name of her father was never in doubt – it's her mother who's in question. Some say her mother was Tangwystl Goch, who later bled to death during a premature childbirth, brought on by a fall. Others, the majority, say her mother was Joan, illegitimate daughter of the English king John. Why do I pursue such inconsequential things? I have wondered many times. The thrill of the chase, perhaps, with a different quarry: discreet facts instead of indiscreet acts.

A rip in the clouds reveals a blue chemise – the sky – so we coat ourselves, stooping into hail-needles as we circle the water, anti-clockwise. The lake laps avidly, hawking spittle onto the shore… and I recall another lakeside, a place from my youth. In my mind's eye I see two figures standing by the fringe of the lake, near a small group of stunted weather-beaten trees.

I watch them quarrel suddenly, violently. She turns her back to him with a supple movement, evening shadows moving along her spine as she runs away between the trees, still naked, and to my eyes she is still porcelain white. I'm stupefied by the nectarine viol of her arse. Her companion calls; she stops and turns. Forty years apart, young man by a blue summer lake and old man by this lake now, we admire the girlish upturn of her breasts, the rosebud nipples. He raises her lace camisole, waves it, hides it behind his back, provokes her, presses it to his face, inhales her absence. There is summery silence in the heather, then a bee glides by. The drone sways drowsily and she's fooled by his little drama: she returns to their love nest in the springy moss… sun-drugged, they continue their intimacy, stroking each other's skins, rekindling the fire. Her final cry threads between the silver birches and fades into the lake's lapping waters...

I pause on the lakeside path, touch my companion's shoulder, and we stop.

I share the memory. She turns away from me and continues along the path.

Slower, I must go slower. I want to recover all those valuable episodes strewn around my brain, littering the floors of remembrance.

Having circled the lake slowly we wandered onwards, conversing freely and agreeably on various subjects touching our lives; upon reaching a certain point of vantage, with bosky slopes on either side, she called a halt and hushed me into silence. Craning to listen, we heard a bell tolling in the distance, the gentle sound alluring, so we walked towards it, summoned by its appeal. Insistently, the muffled metal called us – and drawn by its magnet we found ourselves among a merry band of people, chattering sweetly as they filed through a gate. It transpired that we had arrived – miraculously – in time for the Christmas service at the lonesome little church at Llanrhychwyn, marooned since the sixth century in the upland fields of this sequestered parish. God's little acre in a kingdom of sheep and silence. Miniature fields and strips of bracken pleated into a recognisable national costume. Since this was the only meeting of the month, our chance encounter with all these people was indeed remarkable. They were in festive mood, cheerful and gregarious, a troupe of mastersingers on their way to a morality play. There was but one choice for our pagan souls: we would never get closer than this to God's little kingdom, so we entered with the rest, in the spirit of the occasion, which was greater than us all. I smelt soap, and face-powder clinging in fine chalky particles to the women's face-hairs, lavender and eau-de-cologne mingling with the fusty smells of the rudely-awakened church. Some of the girls looked back at me over their shoulders and nudged each other, giggling. My partner indicated with her eyes that they were smirking at my yellow-dyed hair, which makes me look younger and more vigorous than I am. I made a lewd gesture to them and I heard a stifled giggle. The bell-ringer wore a seraphic grin but he seemed sinister, a gargoyle knotted to his rope, rocking in a hunchback sway; he continued for a long time after we had all sat down, until the cleric's nod. I sensed the age of the building in the odour of its shadows; I nudged my companion and whispered a suggestion. Dutifully, she jotted a note on the lined notepaper she always carries with her when she's in my presence; and I felt smug, briefly, knowing that I had another page-in-waiting for my magnum opus, the great work I will be remembered by, *A History of Shadows*.

Sitting on a stone bench built into the wall, my feet rest on the grave of a woman who's been dead for three hundred years. Swathed in their simple music, hidden from their collective gaze, I fantasise over her once-young flesh…

She giggles from the shadows behind the font; my mischievous maid, freckled, wild strawberry stains on her hot mouth. Her milk-maid's hands are cracked and calloused but they shan't touch me much. I can smell the cowbreath in her hair. Ducking down, I unbuckle my shoes and quietly slip between the pews, the cold stone pressing against my bare feet, shocking, sensuous, my toes meeting folds of her still-warm clothes on the chilled slabs. My flesh prickles with excitement and my blood surges in a high tide which fills all those unknowable creeks and inlets along the shores of my body. Circling her half-hidden shape I see a hint of her, a suggestion, a swell of hip, shoulder and black hair tumbling. Coming up behind her suddenly I encircle her with my left arm, pressing her to my body while muffling her cry with my right hand…

My companion elbows me, almost savagely. Has she guessed what I'm doing, with my wanton mind? Probably. She knows me well enough. But what of it? The maid is dead, I cannot take her. More's the pity. Look at them all, trying to be righteous. Every man kneeling in this chanting-room would join me in the act, given a chance. The shadows of the cloister echo with confessions, and as we all know my friend, confessions are the best aphrodisiac.

This is the oldest church in Wales, according to some. It felt old that day: we, the congregation, were sown in rows like corn, rising from the stony soil, but the church's past rested profoundly on me, a heavy boulder pushing me back into the earth.

They sang, they prayed: I listened fitfully as I sat on the stone bench; the cleric extolled the spirit of the bell, and my mind drifted in and out of the service. Dressed in his holy vestments he stood in a beam of weak wintry sunshine, and his words flowed melodiously. They were well-construed words, finely-wrought, seductive and powerful; mesmerised, almost drowsy by now, I felt the phrases pillow my head, lull me with their wonderful, sooth-ing power. While my mind was being stroked I must have nodded off, for I was woken suddenly by my partner, nudging me discreetly. When my thoughts cleared I realised, with a flush of hot realisation, that the cleric's voice had seduced me. As I fingered my hair into place again and adjusted my garb, I noted that he had used the very same devices that I had used on many occasions to sway women and entice them into my bed. I smiled at him as we departed, saluting a true equal. He smiled back innocently, little realising my true thoughts.

As we left the church I recalled, in the genial hubbub, that this church was once the spiritual home of Gwladus Ddu's mother, Joan of England, before Llywelyn built another church at Trefriw down below us, to save her the long walk uphill. He must have loved her. Remembering my companion's notes, I recall these words: *I gave my womb to politics like every king's daughter. There is no room for love's disorder in ruling a family and a land.*

We headed homewards, as the day declined. Her heavy black vehicle looped downwards into the valley and we turned towards the sea which looked – at a distance – like the polished surface of a vast marble floor: in the last light of day a couple of boats seemed no bigger than broken toys, abandoned by children who'd been called suddenly to bed. We were both silent, because on the steep hill leading down to Trefriw we had seen a strange and ominous sight – supernatural, chilling. What we saw, coming towards us, was a crooked man, in the later stages of life yet ageless, with a gnarled face and mystical eyes which saw everything, yet nothing. He was dressed in black, in the manner of an eighteenth century peasant, with a white collarless shirt buttoned or studded tightly below his prominent Adam's apple. His dark hair was slicked backwards without a parting, glistening in an old-fashioned and defunct style, which gave him the appearance of a Corsican fisherman taking his catch home. He was clean-shaven, but his skin showed the craterous evidence of acne, or maybe scarring from smallpox. His face was angular, aesthetic, with shadows where his cheeks were sucked in thoughtfully.

His trousers were mud-spattered around the rims and his boots were old, black leather, slightly tipped up at the front, hobnailed and battered with use, yet in good repair. He seemed not to see us in passing, as if we were beneath his attention, undeserving of his acknowledgement. He carried an enormous hessian sack on his back: stooped under its weight he passed us by, as if we weren't there, as if we were stones or weeds by the wayside.

He was not of this world. He would frighten any living person who saw him.

My companion said he was the Gatherer of Sins.

We park up at a spot overlooking the Menai Straits. A pot of reddish-orange paint has been thrown at the horizon westwards, so we sit awhile admiring the sunset, recreating those few minutes in time when the Gatherer of Sins passed us by on a hill, far away from anyone. As usual, we share a last few thoughts. As I have said, we have nothing to hide, though others might misconstrue this weekly rite of ours. It is, after all, the behaviour of small town adulterers. She talks to me quietly, enumerating and annotating the main points of the day, the main conclusions. A red tinge spreads over the land. Curlews sadden the shore.

I consult my companion's notes, trying to check the facts. It is easy to imagine Joan of England standing outside the car, shivering in a white linen nightdress, looking out to sea with a grotesque image in her mind: she has just seen the Marcher lord William de Breos hanged by his neck in the village behind us – at Abergwyngregyn, the estuary of the white seashells. Joan had a home here, with her husband Llywelyn. During a visit, during the long dark night, de Breos was apparently discovered in Joan's chamber, an unthinkable crime in medieval society. He was hanged in front of eight hundred onlookers.

We listen again to the curlew's haunted cry on the long shore and I picture the scene: a hemp rope creaking tautly from an oak branch, the sudden silence, the dangling body, the barking of distant dogs. One thing was certain, I tell my friend; we would never know the truth. But as a libertine I have my theories.

Tired, both of us, we drive back to my home and I leave the car with hardly a word.

Before I retire I spend a few minutes in my study, ordering my new material on Gwladus Ddu, she of the dark eyes, so that I can work in the night. The wind is back, rattling my windows, invading my bedchamber. The piss-dog splatters my panes again. I light a candle and undress, ready for the night ahead. Alone in my bed there is nothing to do but sleep, fret, or rekindle the past. In the night I will be visited again by the gaunt man we saw carrying his sack up the hill near Trefriw. He will stand at the foot of my bed and he will talk to me, as he does every night now. He will say to me in his quiet voice: I am the Gatherer of Sins: it is your own transgressions which occupy my sack. I will return when you least expect me: I have already passed you on many hills in many lands. You will recognise me, standing in the shadows, with a quaking heart. I am not the fifth horseman, nor the first day of the apocalypse, nor the first child killed on the first day of every war: I am here, I am now, I am always and for ever. I am everywhere, I am hidden in dust, in fire, in presidential semen. Do not try to avoid me or to cheat me: this would be futile, for I am the Gatherer of Sins and therefore the greatest sinner of all. I will reap you as your skin rubs the cold stone floor, in the immeasurably short moment before your final breath clouds the cold air. But it is not for depravity nor immorality that you will be punished, no, nor will I rebuke a single soul, not once, in the whole span of time, for the brief pleasures they have winnowed from the world's troubles. You will be punished for living. And you have lived long and you have lived well. Farewell for now, my friend. Wait for me in the shadows, for I am the Gatherer of Sins.

transparent

ON THE morning of his sixtieth birthday, as he looked in the mirror, he decided to fall in love for the last time.

The decision came suddenly, as he fingered the stubble on his jaw and prepared to shave – a chore he loathed, but which he completed dutifully every morning in the cold gloom of the bathroom. His face had to be smooth, as soft as a baby's bottom, and completely kissable, before he left the house. Finally, he'd dab himself with some *Loverboy* aftershave, sent to him in an act of futile irony by his ex-wife on the first Christmas after their divorce. He'd used it every day since, because it was the first present from her he'd ever really liked. He was completely unaware of the double irony.

Falling in love again: the thought had lain dormant for some time, but now it kicked like a baby inside his still reasonably flat belly. In recent weeks he'd watched his own daughter fall in love for the first time, and he'd loved the feeling it gave him, watching her eyes brighten, her complexion clear; she'd buzzed around him with the golden pollen of love clinging to her body, glowing softly in the sunlight. The birthmark on her left cheek had faded and almost vanished, or so it seemed to him as he watched her. Sometimes he felt an urge to go to her council flat and peep through the window, to witness her strange new capacity for love. Of course he didn't, but he yearned to see love's colours around her body, inside the room, irradiating the glass in her windows. He imagined a nectarous scent wafting from her door every morning when she opened it to the world.

Now, in the bathroom, as he filled the basin with lukewarm water and spread shaving foam over his wet face, he started to enlist the qualities he would like in his new lover, as if he were ticking boxes on a dating agency form. He was too old to be fussy, but nevertheless he began to build up a photofit picture of his ideal woman – a blueprint as it were, because he was a builder after all, and he was still at the planning stage.

She would have to be slim and smallish, almost boyish, but with all the female bits in all the right places. He was drawn to tomboys, and if they had light red hair and green eyes all the better. He seemed to remember the term *Irish Sheelagh* being used to describe his dream woman in the local newspaper's Looking for Romance page.

Next on his mental list, as he drew a disposable razor from the window shelf and damped it in the water, came humour: he liked women with a bubbly sense of fun and a lively disposition. So, as he lifted the razor to his right forelock – he started in exactly the same spot every morning – he was in a position to begin his advertisement in the newspaper: *Pocket Venus/Irish Sheelagh, lively & GSOH, wanted for…*

And so he dreamt on as he scraped his upper right cheek, clearing it of foam and beard, and after swishing his blue plastic razor in the sink a residue of bristles drifted on an island of foam, making him think of tiny tree stumps in a miniature avalanche.

That night he started to sleepwalk, for the first time in his life. He woke up stiff and sore, naked and curled in a foetal position, in the hallway five floors down from his flat. His first memory of the day was the postman stepping over his body, on his way to the postboxes…

Day 2: Still bleary-eyed, and greatly troubled by this new development in his life, he stood in the bathroom, dressed by now, looking in the mirror and slapping shaving foam onto his face, dabbing it carefully over his upper lip. He wasn't particularly shy, and the whole village knew he'd nothing to be ashamed of in the trouser department, but he didn't want to go a-wandering at night again because he didn't want a dodgy reputation, like that fat little writer with bulgy eyes who'd allowed his dressing gown to open, more than once, as he opened his front door to the paper boy.

Should he use the same razor as yesterday? He swished it in the water and started off on his right cheek, as usual. Trying to steady his hand, he thought again of his quest for love, and his shopping list. He liked intelligent women, but how to put that across? Clever? No, that wasn't right. Smart? Bright? Professional? How about Educated (bit snobbish) or perhaps Curious? That sounded too much like bi-curious, which he assumed meant people who wanted to try a bit of AC/DC, and he certainly didn't want that. He decided on Inquisitive, which covered a multitude of sins. He didn't want a happy-clappy, so he'd put in Secular, and he didn't want an ice maiden, so he'd put in Warm. So far he had: *Warm, inquisitive Pocket Venus/Irish Sheelagh, secular, lively & GSOH, wanted for...*

That night he walked again, down the stairs, through the hallway, up the high street and into someone's garden near the newspaper shop. He was woken, naked again, by a milk float growling and clinking along the road. Fortunately, covering himself with his hands, he managed to return home unseen. He was acutely cold and had nettle stings all along his left hip. Disturbing.

Day 3: Very worrying, he muttered to the mirror as he cut a swathe to his chin with a new razor. Some of the foam strayed into his mouth as he talked to himself, so he pulled a face and spat it out. What was going on? Should he go to the doc's? No, he'd leave it for a day or two, it was bound to stop. Mind turbulent and agitated by thoughts of love perhaps. Something below the surface, like the silver below the glass in the mirror (which reflected a red-eyed wreck). He got thinking about mirrors. Why did they need glass? Who cared, he thought moodily. He scraped away at his top lip, vertically then laterally, contorting his face into all sorts of shapes to help the process. He'd done that hundreds of times now, didn't have to think about it. But today he nicked his upper lip (always problematic) and he was forced to start the day with a twist of toilet paper stuck there to staunch the flow of blood. Sitting on the toilet, brooding about his impending love affair, he added a few more items to his shopping list. He and this virtual woman would have to share some interests. He liked pubs, so he'd put Pubbing. And Holidays Abroad because he'd had a good time picking potatoes – and girls – during a spring in Jersey when he was much, much younger. And Cinema because he often took out a DVD on the way home, to help him go to sleep. How about Walks on the Beach? They all seemed to like that, and it wasn't too strenuous.

Warm, inquisitive Pocket Venus/Irish Sheelagh, secular, lively & GSOH, into Pubbing, Holidays Abroad, Cinema, romantic walks on the beach, wanted for...

That night he sleepwalked all the way up the high street, along the same route presumably, and woke up in a bus shelter at the bottom of Mount Road. He smelt of piss when he got home and had to take a shower. Someone saw him, he thought. A face at a window, a curtain falling from someone's hand. Time to seek help? No, walking home naked might revive his reputation. People had talked of retirement. But you never retired from Love. Not him, anyway. This time he wanted the real thing, not make-believe. A final grand passion, a French kind of thing. It was possible, surely. You often read about two old codgers in a home, over ninety both of them and shaking so bad you'd think they were having it off on a washing machine, getting married and saying it was lovely, just like they were young again.

Day 4: This was getting out of hand. He would sleep with his clothes on, under his light summer duvet. He'd die of cold or shame if it went on much longer. Aching all over from his latest nocturnal jaunt, he cleared the stubble from his left cheek and thought of something he'd read in the paper, something about your beard growing a lot faster if you'd had sex the night before. He hadn't noticed anything, not even after his record twelve bonks in one night with the two German hitchhikers he'd picked up in the pub. Three in a bed. Wonderful times. He felt himself stiffen slightly, just thinking about it. He finished the shave without incident and dabbed some *Loverboy* on his neck. Not much left. He'd have to pop into his ex's salon, creep past all those Dalek hairdryers, ask her where she'd bought the stuff. Perhaps he'd try it on with her. She'd given in a couple of times. Better than when they were married. Strange, that. Could he be bothered going to work? He was bloody knackered. Didn't fancy a day in bed, not on his own, so he ate some cereal and walked downstairs, whistling through his teeth, thinking of his shopping list again. Dreams. Pie in the bloody sky. What did he want out of this? Sex? Yes, but he could always get that with Sharon Shagpot (so called because there was a Sharon who wasn't a shagpot, or wasn't yet, anyway, despite his best efforts. Perhaps she was a lezzy.)

No, he wanted Tenderness and Understanding, a Meeting of True Minds and all that.

How would he put it? Soulmate, that was the word. And she would have to be a non-smoker because he'd finally given up on New Year's Day and it looked like the only resolution he was ever going to keep, because he had to – his chest was beginning to rattle in the final stages of coitus, and that was no bloody good at all, because Sharon Shagpot had started to giggle one night when he was about to finish. You couldn't have true love and an asthmatic wheeze when you were on the job, it was ludicrous. He snapped the front door behind him and added another category: Healthy. He didn't want some old crone with her teeth in a glass and a face like cold putty after she'd scraped a grand's worth of slap off her face. So far he had: *Warm, inquisitive Pocket Venus/Irish Sheelagh soulmate, secular, healthy, n/s, lively & GSOH, into Pubbing, Holidays Abroad, Cinema, romantic walks on the beach, wanted for...*

He went to bed in his clothes, remembering beforehand to remove building debris from his turn-ups. Thank God for that, he said to himself the next morning, after his head had cleared, because he found himself lying on his back in someone's garden shed halfway up Mount Road. He'd stared at the timber ceiling in the way he stared at bedroom ceilings when he woke up next to a strange woman in a strange house, wondering how the hell he'd got there. Now, as he crept stealthily out of the shed, and wended his way home, he thought he saw a pattern. His sleep-walks were taking him somewhere. But why? And where would he end up? Was his mind trying to lead him to his true love, surreptitiously? Maybe yes, maybe no...

Day 5: He swept upwards with the (same) razor, up his neck from beyond his right earlobe to the ridge of his jaw, and swore loudly, because the razor was blunt and it scraped his skin. The water in the sink reddened, and he slowed down. Pausing, he peered into the mirror, trying to see through the glass, to the silver beyond, or whatever they put there nowadays. An old mirror, so silver foil? He'd ask someone in the pub, there was always someone who knew that sort of thing. He washed his face with cold water to stem the flow of blood. Part of him was disappearing down the plughole. Bits of him disappearing into holes everywhere, all the time. Perhaps black holes in space worked like that too, sucking in... what? He sat on the bog and strained. He'd no *Loverboy* left for tomorrow, unless he added some water and swilled it round. Could you do that? Try it. Bugger. No bog paper. Bugger. He waddled into the kitchen, clenching his buttocks, looking for old newspaper. None. He looked in the breadbin. Lucky – some soft wrapping paper left over, mouldy crust still inside it. Back to the bathroom, thinking… how would he describe himself? Builder? No, wrong message (though some of them liked a bit of rough). Divorcee? No, wrong again. How about BHM – Big Handsome Male? That'd do. And what was that phrase he'd seen somewhere… DDF. Drugs and Disease Free. Well he was, wasn't he? Hopefully. Sharon Shagpot had given Will Wasted a dose last Christmas. Perhaps he ought to put No Strings Attached, but that wasn't true, he wanted to be tied down, didn't he, if only for a bit? He'd put LTR – Long Term Relationship. Perfect. Now he had: *BHM, DDF, seeks warm, inquisitive Pocket Venus/Irish Sheelagh soulmate, secular, healthy, n/s, lively & GSOH, into Pubbing, Holidays Abroad, Cinema, romantic walks on the beach, for LTR…*

That night he walked further than ever before in his sleep, to the top of Mount Road. He woke on a hard wooden bench, and he panicked when he came to, because his hands had turned orange. He realised, slowly, that he was under a streetlight which was still shining down on him. He walked back home and took the day off.

Day 6: He slept all morning and woke himself with a huge snorty snore. His mind took ages to clear. He had a stiff neck and a headache, so he lay there for ages, drifting in and out of consciousness. Eventually, around noon, he rolled over in bed and studied the empty space by his side. He wasn't used to the daytime sounds in his bedroom. A soft wind moaned in the guttering outside, and his alarm clock seemed extra loud as it ticked away the seconds. He contemplated the future. Did he really want someone – the same someone – in that big empty space by his side every morning when he woke up? The same face? Same smell? Not always womanly. Personal smells. After a while she'd mumble *gerroff* and wiggle away whenever he pushed against her bottom in the early morning.

He got up and stumbled to the bathroom. Could he be bothered shaving? He looked deep into the mirror, to a point inside the wall somewhere, as if he were staring into one of those 3D pictures which appeared suddenly if you got it right. Nothing happened. He rubbed the sandpaper of his jaw and imagined a row of men, all dressed in red lumberjack jackets and big brown boots with metal toecaps, rubbing a plank with their chins to sand it down. He must be tired or something. So he sat on the bog with his head between his hands, doing nothing in particular except listening to an occasional dribble of wee whispering into the pan.

After a hasty wash he put his coat on and walked down the stairs, heading for the pub. Checking his pockets as he went, he realised he'd virtually no money on him, just loose change. He re-ascended the stairs gloomily and conducted a desultory search in drawers, pockets, in his usual hidey-hole under the wardrobe. Nothing. So he took all the cushions off the couch and wiggled his hand in the crevices. A couple of quid only. Still, it was enough to start off with – he could always bum a fiver here or there. He couldn't ask for any tic at the local because he already owed a tidy sum to the landlord.

That day he got absurdly drunk, too pissed to do any courting. Unknown to himself, because he was on a different planet by now, he staggered home at closing time and ate a Pot Noodle and a crust with mould on it (he was too pissed to notice). A whole day had gone by and he was no nearer love. He hadn't even thought about it.

That night he rose from the couch (he never made it to bed) and walked out of his flat, down five flights of stairs, up the high street, up Mount Road, along Jubilee Walk, and into a small muddy paddock. When he woke, deep into the next day, his nose encountered farty smells, rich and fruity. Turning over, his eyes searched the gloom. Who had he ended up with? And why was there so much straw in the bed? It took him a while, but eventually he identified a small fat mountain pony sharing her shed with him, wearing nothing more than a halter, her thick winter coat covered in dry mud.

He went home.

Day 7: He stayed in bed for most of the day. At six he went down to Flat No 1 and sold Mrs Williams a hard luck story; managed to scrounge twenty quid off her. Back in his flat he had a wash but gave the shave a miss. Looking for paper to write a shopping list, the only thing he could find was a cardboard wrap-around from a microwave meal, but it already had something written on it: *BHM, DDF, seeks warm, inquisitive Pocket Venus/Irish Sheelagh soulmate, secular, healthy, n/s, lively & GSOH, into Pubbing, Holidays Abroad, Cinema, romantic walks on the beach, lots of laughter and true love. No time wasters please.*

He tore it off and used the rest of the paper to make his list, then headed for the pub. *Time I had a break from work,* he told Psycho in the reassuring glow of the bar lights. The rest was a blank. He never got to the shops, probably never made it home either. That night, asleep or awake, he walked through the high street, up Mount Road, along Jubilee Walk, past a paddock and up a cul-de-sac. When he woke it was two in the morning and he was in Sharon Shagpot's front garden, slumped against her front door.

Day 8: Don't ever do that to me again, said Sharon. She'd got the kids up and sent them off to school, then made two big mugs of coffee. She'd run out of fags but found some in his pocket, which was strange, because he'd made a big fuss about giving up. Now she was standing by the big double bed in her bedroom, looking down on a grossly hungover man, unkempt and unshaven, discovered on her doorstep in the night after some feeble knocks and a shower of chippings on her window. As usual, his motives had been transparent.

I don't want you coming here in that state again you silly sod, she said, standing over him, her blotched knees swelling from underneath her nightgown.

He studied the swirls of steam coming from the mug by his bed. He'd use one of her Ladyshaves, as usual, and go to work whistling through his teeth. Later.

Come back to bed, he said in his best husky voice. I love you.

They listened to the sounds of the morning – rain pattering on the window, cars swishing through roadside puddles, lorries' peep-peep-peep reversing on the industrial estate.

You're still pissed you dirty old sod, said Sharon Shagpot.

Then she got back into bed.

sepia

STRANGE things happen at night. When I slip out of sleep in the small hours my room's lost its shape – doing a Goth thing, moody and broody. All the noises which came in during the day through the windows – thrown in like rubbish, littering the place – have disappeared, muffled under layers of soft black crepe in my wardrobe. Without looking I know it's about three. Dead of night, and time sits around like a bored psychiatrist. So I try to drift off again, spread a little fog around my mind, throw a blanket over those nocturnal thoughts, pesky as parrots.

That's when it happens. Not always, just now and then. Suddenly I go away, into the darkness, as if – in the click of a shutter – I move from inside a camera to the outside world, and I'm flying through the chill of the night. It's happening in my mind, but it feels real. The first time it happened I went to a place I know well, but during a time of day – I mean night – when I'm not normally out and about. I'll describe it to you – the first time was best.

I'm standing outside the old pilots' cottages by Llanddwyn Island, on the isthmus of land reaching out to the defunct light-house. The windowpanes are spangled with cold silver and there's a moon-sheen on the land. In the distance, in Newborough Forest, the owls swoop and call. The sea whispers sleepily in the beyondness. My naked feet and the hem of my nightie are damp with dew.

My knees brush the vegetation under the window and a moth flits upwards through my hands; I see it pass across the moon. There's an odd shape huddled not so far away and it irks me. As I fret over it, waiting for it to move, I remember there's an old cannon in that spot. These sea cottages have been turned into some sort of museum, but they've never been open when I've visited the place. So I peek through a window, as I do in daylight when I'm here with mum and dad and my baby brother. It's much darker in there now, a sort of washed-out colour, as if I'm looking at an old photograph. There's a picture on the wall but I can't see any details. The rest is smudged out in shadows, except for a bench set against the far wall, to my left. I crane to see what's there and I see two human shapes squeezed together shoulder-to-shoulder with their legs splayed out wide, like me and my friends when we're having a lark at school. I catch them having a giggle, and one of them puts a finger to her lips when she sees me. The silence is deafening now, I hear the blood rustling dead leaves in my ears. Every time it's the same – slowly I realise that one of them is me, when I was smaller and thinner, the time my hair was quite long and curly. My face is white, but that could be the moonshine. My eyes are dark rings, tired and ghoulish, sparkling as they do when I've gone a bit hyper. And the person I'm sitting with is an angel, every time the same one, a bit bigger than me but not much, and I'm nestling in one of his beautiful wings. He's a very light blue all over and he shimmers, it's magical and nice. My feet are getting cold in the grass but inside I'm warm all over thinking about the angel.

Then it all ends, and I'm back in my bed.

Perhaps a few weeks pass, or a few months, I'm not sure how long, then there's a next time.

This time I go to a different place, high in the hills, where there's hardly any greenery, just rolling brown country with bogs and hillocks covered in dead brown grass, starved of food. I've never been to this place before, but I think I know where it is. My dad described it to me once, after my bedtime story – it's somewhere from his childhood. I think his eyes misted over. Thinking about that place made him feel all nostalgic and sentimental.

So I'm lying in bed, it's three in the morning again, and I'm bobbing on my dream raft when – zip! – I'm taken through the night again, fast as electric, and I land outside a shack or cabin up there on the moors. There's a wind blowing in noisy gusts through three or four old trees, tall and stooped over me; their leaves surge and hiss and roar. No moon this time, it's almost totally dark, and very cold. I press my body against the wall of the cabin which is made of big rough boulders. It makes me think of the homesteads in the Wild West, in picture books, with animal skins drying on a rack outside and smoke coming from the chimney; there are eyes staring from the undergrowth maybe and a face streaked with warpaint – the sort of thing you see in books about Hiawatha or Pocahontas. I'm shivering because I'm in my pink Naughty Girl pyjamas and nothing else. This shack I'm standing by has a rusty tin roof held down with hawsers pinned into the walls, and there are rows of white in the corrugations – hailstones. The walls are rough and uneven, with moss here or there on the stones and a rickety door wedged shut, but it's not a tight fit. Shafts of yellow light escape between the gaps. Not all the fire smoke is going up the chimney – some of it's puffing out of the walls in wisps. A beam of warm orange light shines from the cabin's only window, which is small and divided into four square panes. I move slowly along the cabin wall, feeling carefully with my feet in case I step on something sharp, balancing myself by pressing my hands against the wall-boulders. I edge up to the window and stand on tiptoe, which allows me to see in through the corner of a low windowpane. It's dusty and criss-crossed with old cobwebs stuck to the pane, so I have to peer through a penny-sized clearing in the glass. I see a big fire in an open grate, licking the chimney stones, and some of the smoke is spilling into the room in blue-grey swirls, small backward waves. On my right I see a large head – a movement catches my eye and I strain to see what's happening. The head shakes and there's a jingling noise;

then I see a steaming flank and a saddle – it's a horse! Creamy with a light mane and mud caked in its fur – I think they're called palominos. This creature is in the cabin and horse-napping, rattling its bridle when it wakes briefly. I can hear its shoes clunk on the floor as it moves its weight from one side to the other. After resting for a bit I stretch myself again and look some more through the peephole. It's all a bit dim, because of the wood smoke and lack of lighting, but to my left I think I see a narrow bed covered in a jumble of blankets. Directly opposite me there's a framed photo on the wall, I can make out something like a ship with an angel hovering above it. Below it, in the room, I see two shapes, one of them curled up on the bed. It's a child and it has its back to me. I think that shape is me, or it could be my dad, because this cabin was in his past, not mine. It's the same angel, sitting there with his wings furled and his arms stretched out on either side, his hands planted squarely on the edge of the bed, as if he were a bit drunk and concentrating on keeping upright. I look at this scene for some time, until the angel looks up at the window. I duck quickly, trying to stay unseen. Then I start peeking again, but the angel's still looking in my direction; this time he's got a smile on his face, and he winks. In that moment it's as if his feathers shimmer all over, like a blue butterfly caught in sunshine, and I think I hear him speak, but I'm not sure. It's a lovely sound, a cross between soft music and running water. Then the experience ends, suddenly, and I'm back in my bed at home, my feet still cold from the snow on the ground. After that I go into a very deep sleep and I wake up in the morning feeling good, completely refreshed. So meeting my angel in the night can be a good experience.

And there's a third meeting with the angel, different from the others. Again, I'm lying between my pink sheets and it's three in the morning, when – pow! – I'm flying again, rushing through the night air, but this time I'm high above the sea, and the *shhh* noise I hear is the wind in my nightclothes, chilling my body. The moon is shining on a vast expanse of water, and the waves are a pattern of shadows, motionless and silent. After a while – not long – I fly along an estuary, into a wide canal, and I see a ship moored to the right bank. It's a coaster with huge black lids over its hold and a machine squatting on its deck – a big metal crab with a long claw-arm. Instead of pincers it's got a massive bucket, to remove stuff from the ship's belly. The first thing I see is the ship's name, painted white on its black stern – *Clydenes*. I land on the deck and immediately I smell coal; it's a bulk carrier holding tons of smelly, dirty coal. There's no sign of life anywhere, though there are red and green lights on the masts.

Slipping through a heavy metal door, which I only just manage to open, I walk along a corridor, looking through portholes as I go. There's nothing much to see: the corridor is well lit, but the cabins are in darkness. Passing one room I smell queasy kitchen smells, then I clamber down a metal ladder and pass along another corridor. Engine smells now, and snores from a darkened cabin. At the end of the corridor I see a beam of hot light pulsing from a porthole, and I edge towards it. Without looking, I know what I'm likely to see. When I look through the thick glass I see a made-up bed, not slept in yet, and there he is – my angel, sitting with his back to the hull, hunched up with his hands clasped around his knees. There's another sepia photograph on the wall – this time it shows something like an old shed, I think, with an angel standing on the roof, in the process of taking off (one foot's already up in the air, climbing an invisible stairway). I peek again at my angel through the porthole, but as soon as I look at him he glances sideways at me, gives me a nice warm smile, as if he's been waiting for me. But there's a difference. In this scene, there's no-one on the bed with him. No-one at all – I am not there, and nor is anyone else. The angel is alone and waiting for me.

This time I feel my heart quicken; a kick of adrenalin enters my system. My senses are heightened; I hear the slap of the water on the ship's side, a strange bird-scream in the scrubland on the bank. There's a loud snort from a sleeper, and a few mumbled words in a foreign language, Russian or Polish perhaps. The ship rolls and creaks. I feel slightly nauseous from the coal and engine oil. I begin to panic, so I edge away from the cabin door. Soon I am running along the deck and then flying through space, into the moon. Almost immediately I'm back in my bed, the smell of coal still heavy in the air around me. Then I sleep, but it's bad sleep, fitful and jerky and sweaty. I cry out in my sleep and mum comes to my bed; she holds my hand and feels my brow. This is the angel dream I don't like. It leaves me tired and exhausted for days afterwards. My angel can make me happy, but alone in the ship at night he is sad, he worries me. I feel the need to help him somehow. But how?

And then it all changes, in a single night. I don't go to the angel – the angel comes to me. For months nothing happens, and I think maybe the angel thing is all over with. He begins to fade, and I have trouble remembering the exact shade of the blue of his skin, lighter than the shade of his wings. Then he comes to me. In my bedroom. I'm fast asleep, but when three o'clock arrives I wake up suddenly from the black emptiness of sleep, and he's there besides me on the bed, looking at me. The way he sits on the duvet and the way he looks at me reminds me of a doctor who came to see me when I was small, when I was really ill. I remember it well, even the smell of the doctor's hands. Now, on my bed, the angel's wings pulse and glow like my fibre-optic lamp. But I don't feel scared. I lie on the bed, still curled up and sleepy, looking at him. When he speaks to me I understand him but I can't really remember the sound of his voice. He doesn't touch me at any time, but he indicates somehow that I'm safe with him. This is what we say to each other, more or less:

I'm an angel.
What's your name?
My name is jupin-3.
Where have you come from?
A special world inside your head.
You mean you're not real?

Yes and no – I am real to you, but not to anybody else.
Why are you here?
Because you haven't been to visit me for a while.
Are you going to hurt me?
No, never.
Are you going to stay with me for ever now?
Only if you make me.
Why would I do that?
Because there's nowhere else for me to go.
Haven't you got a home?
You haven't made one for me yet.
But I thought angels lived in heaven?
Maybe they do, but you haven't made a heaven inside your
head yet.
Yes I have.
You've made a space ready for a heaven maybe, but you
haven't filled it – nobody finishes the heaven inside their heads.
How do you mean?
The heaven inside your head is a place with nothing really in it
– no houses, or animals, or cars, or seas. Do people eat, cry and
go to the toilet? Do they have pets in heaven? Do they get to
see the people they loved when they were living? Do they play
games, do they laugh at silly jokes?
*I don't know, I haven't thought about it. Anyway, I don't really
believe in heaven, or hell for that matter.*
You don't have to. But if you could imagine another place I
could live in, I'd be grateful. A place where an angel could be
happy. The cabin on the moors and the coal ship are OK for a
bit, but I need to spread my wings.

I laugh at his joke, but he doesn't know why. Maybe angels don't
have a sense of humour, or maybe he's preoccupied. He doesn't
seem to be a happy angel, so I have to do something about it. But
when I think of his future I get a feeling inside my chest which
makes me cry. How do I make a heaven for my angel, a place

where he can feel at home? Only jupin-3 himself can do that. What can I do?

I'm lucky, my angel is patient. Thank God, I've made a kind, forgiving angel. He's not going to bring me strange or worrying news, like the angels in stories, I'm not going to get pregnant or anything like that. All he wants is a place where he can relax and feel OK with life.

He's been coming to see me every day before dawn and I've woken up with him sitting on my bed, looking at me, waiting for some news. In the end, we agreed on a plan. We had a good chat about it, and I'm feeling a bit more relaxed about things. He's going to live in my dad's garden shed for a while, until all this is sorted. There's room for him in there, and a bed where my dad goes to sleep when he comes home drunk or when he's had a row with mum. I'm going to tell dad a bit of a fib, a little white lie. I'll tell him I want to paint a big picture of an angel in heaven. He'll go overboard, he'll try his best to help, I know that. He'll buy me a big canvas or a piece of board from the DIY, and he'll prop it up ready for me in his shed. I'll say I want to do it all alone, I'll make him promise never to go inside the shed until it's finished. Every day after school I'll go in there and help jupin-3 to plan a perfect place to live in. It's going to take some time, working out the sort of country he wants to live in. He's strange; his expectations are different from a human's. He doesn't want many people but he wants lots of animals. He wants total harmony and a place to meet jupin-1 and jupin-2 whenever he needs to. Poor old jupin-3 wants to be off as soon as he can. Who can blame him. He's painting a picture of heaven in my Dad's shed. He's painting it in sepia – because nothing in life is completely black and white, he says, and the only colours he wants to see are the ones in heaven.

I never thought you could imprison angels. But you can. That's the curse of humanity, he says. We can dream angels into existence – but we all forget to create a place for them to live happily in peace.

Maybe I can be the first. I hope so, jupin-3.

blue

I BOUGHT her on the internet one Monday night round about midnight, got in a right tangle about spending money I didn't have, and then worried myself silly about internet fraud – what if some bugger got hold of my bank number? Couldn't sleep a wink all night, tossing and turning. Worst days of my life, everything out of kilter. Big space in the bed too after Wendy went. Couldn't cope with it, needed someone to cwtch up to. No mucky business mind, don't go in for that sort of thing. Never had the chance to do anything exciting anyway, not with Wendy – we had it once a month, on payday, lights out at ten sharp.

Pull my nightie down when you've finished, that's what she said before we started and I always did, never forgot. But we hadn't touched for years, no wonder I was lonely. Bugger off she did, just like that, no note or nothing. The Plod never believed me, round every week saying they were going to dig up the patio, but I says please don't do that, it was the first patio in Glynneath, people came from miles around to see it and I paid a fortune for the fancy bricks with holes in them. Can't think why they cost more than real bricks if there's half of them missing.

On Saturday morning a white van arrived with a box and I took her out careful like in the back bedroom. Blew her up and I thought she looked lovely, bit small but nice in bed by my side and I talked to her for hours. Caerphilly outfit made her, same lot who make Dolly the Inflatable Sheep. I was worried in case someone in the factory knew me, or somebody told Doris Doom down the road, everyone would know before daybreak, before the bloody milkman came round.

Perfect for any stag night or novelty event, it said on the box, *an inflatable wife, the only woman a man needs. True, our product doesn't cook, can't read a map and won't satisfy you in bed, so what will you be missing? Comes complete with user manual which covers Romance, Dining, Biology, Exercise and Finance.*

As I told you, no dirty business – I put a pair of Wendy's elasticated knickers on her, I never looked down there. Strictly for company. Spilled my heart out to her I did, her plastic breasts got quite sticky with all the sobbing I did on them, had to clean them with a J-cloth. When one of the boys in blue found her he laughed, said she'd be easier to get rid of than Wendy.

One problem though, she didn't have a name I could use when we was snuggling up. Couldn't call her Wendy, could I? Then I saw the white light of divine intervention again, that's what they call it down the evangelical church. Me and Wendy had started going to pray for a kiddie, I went with her because she said I'd never touch her again if I didn't. But no matter how much we prayed, no kiddie came along.

This white light of divine intervention happened again when I was standing in Oxfam's, looking for some trousers – I came across a book called *The Penguin Book of Chinese Verse* and it said *With all my love, Sigrid xxx* on the flyleaf and that was it, I took it home and read it to my new plastic wife every night in bed. I called her Sigrid from that day on. Lovely name, Sigrid. Romantic, makes me think of snow and fir trees and rally cars and saunas. Them Scandinavians treat sex different from us, don't they? No big deal, they just gets on with it or they go on a suicidal bender and watch depressing films – if you're lucky you get an eyeful of tit now and then. Life was pretty good with just Sigrid and me, I used to call out to her when I got home from work every night, I'd shout *Hia Siggy love, I'm home!* at the bottom of the stairs and I'd run up and have a few words with her before tea, tell her about my day and all that, what me and the boys had got up to.

Then, messing around on the computer one night, trying to stay off the porn sites, I came across an old story about this Sigrid from way back in the past. She was tall and blonde and beautiful and she used to live in a cave by a fjord – every night she'd prowl along the edge of the water in the moonlight, waiting for her bloke to come home, some hero who'd gone off to war and never come back, same old stuff in every country isn't it? This Sigrid had a long red mantle and a crow on her shoulder, and then another crow when that one died, she taught them all to say her lover's name, Haraldsson or something like that. One day when she was in her cave her boyfriend comes back from the wars covered in scars, and he finds her by following the crow saying his name. You can imagine, they had a bit of catching up to do that night inside the cave and they got so fired up and emotional the mountain shook, there was a landslide, and all three of them got trapped inside for ever. You can still hear them laughing and talking to each other behind the rocks, that's what it said on the computer. Or sometimes they sing like they're in a Wagner opera. Bullshit, usual tourist guff. Got me thinking though, that crow did. Used to keep pigeons, runs in the family, but I got bored and gave them away. One of them kept coming back for years, I got so pissed off with it I caught it and pulled its head off. But if the Sigrid in the story had a crow, it only made sense for my Sigrid to have a bird as well. Budgie, I thought straight away, that's what she needs for company, I could teach it to say my name instead of Haraldsson. Went round to the pet shop and bought one, last one there, bog standard blue and green, put it in the bedroom with Sigrid so we could listen to it. Taught it to say my name, Iestyn, over and over again, all day long. Lovely like, much nicer than a crow. Every night me and Siggy would have a chat, I'd read some poetry and we'd have a laugh listening to the budgie, then we'd go to sleep after a bit of a cwtch. By now Siggy was wearing one of Wendy's winceyette nighties, the one with pink flowers all over it. She looked lovely my Siggy, with her blonde hair spread all over the pillow, much nicer than Wendy's hair, like a Brillo pad it was, permed so tight it nearly took my eye out when I tried to kiss her. I was much happier with Siggy, we held hands under the duvet. Sweet it was. Tidy. But one thing was missing, I needn't tell you what. Just now and again the urge got too strong – but I wasn't going to touch Siggy, no way Jose. Siggy was pure, she was untouchable. I went down to the evangelicals one Sunday to ask for divine interven-tion because I was shaking every time I went on the computer, tempted by the Devil. The pastor seemed to know all about the porn sites. He said he'd pray for the white light of divine inter-vention – and sure enough I was alright within a week. It was thanks to Wendy, in a way, because she hadn't come home and the police were still nosing around. Every Wednesday night they sent a lady copper round when I got home from work to hold my hand and coo-chi-coo with me, just in case they'd got it all wrong. They'd had a look under the floorboards and found nothing. Bloody fools, as if I'd put her there anyway. This copper who came to visit me was a real peach, about five years younger than me and smallish with blonde hair in a bun and nice blue eyes, bit like Sigrid's, sort of innocent and pure. After a few weeks of talking about Wendy she was really sorry for me and she'd cry, she'd let me put my head on her shoulder and she'd stroke it like my mam used to, all gentle, and she smelt nice too, warm and womanly with some perfume on her skin, all soft and white. She told me to get rid of Sigrid, it was unnatural and anyway I was still a young man and decent looking, plenty of fish in the sea. I got very upset at the thought of Sigrid going the same way as Wendy so I had a good weep. Tell you what, says the lady copper, put her in the wardrobe for a bit, then the spare room, then take her downstairs and after a bit she can go in the garden shed – put a bit of distance between you gradual like, till you can do without her. Seemed sensible to me. Could I keep the winceyette nightie in the bed with me? I asked, just to ease the pain, even though there was nobody in it. To cut a long story short I put Siggy in the wardrobe and the policewoman put the nightie on for a while to ease my pain. It was outside the line of duty but she lay in bed with me every time she came, until I was ready for the big break. One thing led to another and soon we were living as man and wife, me and the policewoman, and the budgie of course, with Siggy in the shed by now. What with moaning Sigrid in the policewoman's ear more than once when we were having sex (what would Wendy say!) the name sort of stuck and soon I was calling her Sigrid, even when we were in public, or when she was in uniform and I had to pretend we hardly knew each other. This went on for some time, me and Siggy Copper stopped pretending I was still being counselled and she moved in, lock stock and barrel. I took Wendy's clothes down to Oxfam after checking there was nothing in the pockets, though why I bothered I don't know because they'd already been to forensic. The budgie got to be a bit of a nuisance saying Iestyn all the time when we were making love so I moved him to the garden shed with the plastic Sigrid. I could still hear him though, even with the windows shut. Once or twice he came close to going the same way as the pigeon. Siggy also called out my name when we were in the throes of passion and sometimes I could hear a strange echo as my lovely new girl and the budgie called out at the same time. This state of affairs might have gone on for ever if Sigrid's brother hadn't turned up in a right old state one Saturday night after a big rugby international. Pissed as a fart he was and swaying all over the place, sick in the garden too. Turned out he was a copper like his sister, he'd been turfed out by his missus because he'd gone home drunk, massive lovebite on his neck. He was innocent as it happens, or so he said, he'd got it doing a scrum-down with his mates in the pub at half-time. He slept in the spare room that night and the night after that too, his missus wouldn't have him back and I couldn't put him out on the street in case Siggy my lovely copper got upset, so he stayed. It was like having Wendy back again, we couldn't have sex in case her brother heard us through the wall. We lay there in bed every night and I could hear the budgie chirping away in the shed and Siggy's brother snoring in the spare room – it was back to square one, hell on earth again. Bugger me if Sigrid didn't play a prank on her brother one day and put the plastic Sigrid in his bed stark naked, they laughed themselves silly but plastic Sigrid never made it back to the shed, I noticed that when I went to feed the budgie.

Enough's enough I said to myself one day. Something's got to give, so I goes down the road and has a word with Doris Doom. Seems to know what to do in an emergency, she fought for Franco's Fascists in the Spanish Civil War just to prove she was more of a rebel than her six brothers on the other side. She was standing by the gate smoking her pipe as usual when I got to her house, and I loitered for a while until she said:

– *What yew want then Iestyn*

and spat a big yellow gob on the path, big as a hubcap.

– I'm needing some sound advice but my mammy died so I come to you I answered truthfully.

– *You did right there see, Iestyn*

she replied, and we enjoyed pleasant small talk for another hour or two, until eventually I told her the exact nature of my plight, except the bit about going on porn sites.

– *Iestyn, yew got to wrest the plot from society and make the story your own*

she said to me, leaning on the gate and puffing vigorously on her briar, as she always does when she's making a dialectical point.

– *Iestyn, it seems to me you've three basic choices*

she continued, her dark eyes either fixed meditatively on the slopes of the Black Mountain or scanning my face for a response.

– *Yew can take the typical Welsh route, give up without a fight, sign your house away, go and live in the shed with the budgie and drink yourself to death,*

she mulled fatalistically,

– *Or perhaps yew want to take the American route, put everyone under the patio, including the blow-up doll and the budgie, but that's not really you either, is it?*

she continued, her white-hot pipe sending a shower of sparks into the encroaching gloom.

– *My preferred option is this Iestyn. Go down to the Miners' Arms tonight with a pocketful of money, get Psycho and his mates hanging drunk and then take them home to sort it out for you, send Sigrid packing and her sponging brother too. By the way, he's not her brother really – look at his eyes, they're just like the milkman's.*

Soon as she spoke I knew she'd uttered words of pure wisdom. By closing time I had Psycho and his mates, plus a carry-out and a good quarter of skunk, staggering up the garden path behind me and in no time at all Sigrid, her brother and all their possessions were out in the garden. There was a nasty and unforeseen twist which had me and Doris worried for a while. Psycho and his mates proved hard to dislodge – they stayed for ten days in all and left the place wrecked. The only reason they went was because one of them wanted to buy a horse at Llanybydder Fair.

When I popped up to tell Doris, I took her a kilo of Kosovan Shag for her pipe – she was overjoyed, hadn't smoked anything that strong since the Civil War, looted it from a body she had. We was buddies by now.

– *Get rid of the budgie too, take it back to the shop*

she advised, bathing me in a warm smile.

– *Show your compassionate side, spare the bird or they'll think you killed your wife*

she said and I did as she asked. He's been bought by Mrs Prytherch at Number 37 now, I can hear him calling my name from her living room when I go to work in the morning. Iestyn! he says through the window, and I feel a wave of *hiraeth* sweeping through me as I think about Sigrid, and being in bed with her by my side in Wendy's winceyette nightie, reading Chinese poetry. What was I to do with my beloved Sigrid the plastic doll, I asked Doris. I couldn't put her in the bin, the binmen always rifled it for valuables. She said

   – Iestyn my lover, there are some things a man has to decide for himself, and Sigrid you'll have to sort out on your own, then peel some potatoes for tea will yew…

Was it the little green-eyed monster I saw in her eyes that day? After a lot of thought I decided to bury Sigrid under the patio – if anyone asked me where the missus was I'd say

   – Under the patio!

And I wouldn't be telling a lie. But I made sure her eyes were directly under a crack so she could see me if I ever had a barbecue – never had one despite all the cost, I used it to park my sidecar after the suspension went. I sold the house to the Chief Inspector – he said he'd fallen in love with it when he came to interview me. And that was that. I took lodgings with Doris and it worked out fine, we went on holiday to Spain. She got to visit her old battle haunts and I had a lovely tan coming home. I never saw Wendy again. Nobody did. But I wake in the night and my mind is troubled. Worry has furrowed my brow – the doctor says I've an ulcer and Doris says I scream in the night, it reminds her of the wounded in their death throes at Guernica.

I think about her lying there under the patio, so cold and lifeless. The only woman who gave me real pleasure, even if she couldn't cook, or read a map, or satisfy me in bed.

So pure and innocent, Sigrid with the lovely blue eyes…

indigo

YOU were the cause of it all, Daddy, with your tall stories and your strange ideas.

All the other girls managed to find normal fathers – men who worked for the council or delivered mail; blokes who drank too much, ran the football team, grew dope in hot silver tents or sold pirate DVDs. Men with debts and ulcers, sometimes worried and watchful, other times funny and tired.

The kids in my class were all caught smoking or found drunk as a skunk outside the Spar, but no not me. I was the one who ended up with nice manners and twelve stars shining brightly on my GCSE results, thanks to the alien who lived in the same house as mum and me. A six-foot-seven weirdo with a million-volt shock of wiry grey hair – a stooping, preoccupied shadow who wore sandals, even in winter. Not that I didn't love you, I loved you sure enough. But why did you have to be so different? Why did you make me blush every time I saw you at the school gates?

When I was six I used to practise saying it in my bedroom mirror, having no idea what it meant: *Pro-fess-or*. I said it over and over again to myself, twisting it out of shape, my hot little breath misting the glass. It took a long time to say it right.

It doesn't matter sweetie pie, you'd say as you passed my bedroom door, smiling at me. But it did, it mattered then and it's mattered all my life.

Sometimes – whenever you could – you went to a distant land, a place of mystery, spices, silks and otherworldly music. You were my own living Ali Baba, flying into the distance on a magic carpet, and the paradise you went to was a romantic vision for a child, but too strange and vast to be understood, so I made do with dolls and dreams until I was old enough to comprehend that other half of you which lived for months on end on another continent, where you existed without me – a place where you disappeared to, coming back animated and thin, gusting new and puzzling smells. You brought back things I was seldom allowed to touch: an exotic sari for my mother, who wore it on Christmas Day, or a painting – a new miniature showing a Moghul garden perhaps, with richly brocaded men and half-naked women doing strange crooked things.

If you're in Heaven, Daddy, as you surely must be, or with Shiva, listen to me now. It started with you, yes, it started with you and the indigo bedroom, because I wanted purple, the same as the other little girls in my class. Why do little girls like purple, why do they want purple bedrooms with purple desks and purple doors? There must be a reason, and I had the same reason as everyone else for wanting a purple room. I wanted to be clever like you and mum but first I wanted a purple room like Emily Davies who pulled my hair in the playground and whispered *Professor Pissface* in my burning ear. Purple is the colour of little girls' dreams. I asked for a purple bedroom and I got an indigo bedroom, it said so on the paint pot.

I said: Daddy this is indigo, look at the label.

But it made no difference, you didn't listen.

It's purple really, sweetie pie, you replied, and I was lost, perplexed, didn't know what to do. The seed of uncertainty was planted then, that very day – soon I was living in a hayfever cloud of doubt: suspicion scabbed my skin and clogged my lungs. When you unwrapped my first inhaler, took it out of its box and read the instructions while I rotated it carefully, looking for its mysteries, I think we both noticed that its plastic sleeve was more indigo than purple. Did I comprehend the subtle irony, even then?

I itched and I scratched; the fray became a rip – within a month the tin which said indigo had torn me into two little sweetie pies.

Purple you promised, but it said indigo on the can. It didn't matter that the colour was right, because the name had to be too – that's the way it is in little girls' minds.

We're talking about important things here, Daddy. The same thing happened with mum: you didn't listen to her either when she tried to tell you about something which was important to her, something close to her heart. It wasn't a big thing, but women can't live in big houses for days on end waiting for something to happen, because it never does. Perhaps she never understood the quiet affection you showed her: if your love had been strange, unruly, outsized and pungent, like your body, then the marriage might have lasted. Your trips grew longer, and when you came back it was her turn to vanish, it was she who went away to a far-off land, a place inside her head which even I was never allowed to visit – and the only presents she brought back were the dirty plates piled up in the kitchen, the silences, the unwashed clothes of depression. Her pain, like yours, was never unpacked or laundered, never aired.

No-one's fault, nobody to blame: that's the mantra, isn't it? Your generation was taught to think it and to say it to each other, then to all the world: when two grown people can't keep it together it's fifty-fifty, six of one and half a dozen of the other. But while you went south to Asia and mum went north to iceland, our family went west. Kaput. One flew east, one flew west, one flew over the cuckoo's nest.

I was living in two homes soon enough, you and mum sharing me down the middle. Did you haggle? I can't imagine it, somehow.

You can have the TV and the three piece suite, I can have the…

So the rip continued, and I was torn in half. Not exactly, Daddy. You can't cut love just so, faithfully in half; you and mum, with all your brains, should have known better – someone will surely get too much pastry and someone will get too much jam if you cut a little sweetie pie in half.

If mum was purple and you were indigo, all those many years ago, and that's the way it seemed to me at the time, I lived in the shade between you, trying to love you both the same, measuring my raw and childish love in two little heaps on my plastic kitchen scales. And so I learnt to divide and apportion, count up days and allocate the hours with precision and exactitude – so that you both got your full share of me, your sub-divided sweetie pie.

Mum was for talking and shopping, painting our nails together, minor rows over nothing much, and decorating my new bedroom, purple of course... and providentially, miraculously, I can't forget our slow journey together, a return to her homeland from the Arctic Circle, hand-in-hand. She became happy again, and it suited her, painting my nails pink in the purple aura of my attic bedroom, and laughing. I found male things once or twice – a tie unravelling from below her bed, a note on the kitchen noticeboard which she hadn't noticed, with a phone number. But I never mentioned them to either party. Mum's the word, and frankly, I didn't want to know. Like all little girls, I wanted – expected – you both to do the decent thing and get back together again. Still do, inside my skull, in the place where nothing bad has ever happened, never will.

Daddy, you stayed in the old house and my room stayed indigo. You never touched it again, never looked inside the door, so it became a mess in there, a jumble of clothes on the floor and cobwebs above the wardrobe. I liked it that way; anarchy seemed to suit our new relationship. Staying at your place was good for other things too – for cadging money, smoking in the greenhouse, dreaming, planning which university I'd go to, and camping trips in the mountains with fresh bread and sausages and tins of beans. We went up there often, crawling and panting up their flanks, sharing water bottles; as you got older you slowed down, your eyes weakened, but I was still your sun, your little sweetie pie.

We'd go your favourite route, me walking behind the gorse ring of your hair, burnt out in the middle by baldness; up we went, onto bald Drum, along the fence to Foel Fras, onwards to Carnedd Llewelyn, dipping down to Yr Elen because you always wanted to look down the valley to Bethesda. Then onwards to Carnedd Dafydd; we'd sit on the summit, me leaning against you, and we'd look towards the heart of Wales, to the south east. I'd put an arm around you (only one, the other was for mum) and you'd go through the roll call of mountains as they faded away from us in blue and purple silhouettes. Moel Siabod was nearest: a loner, idiosyncratic – unchained from the rest. I think you felt an affinity with Moel Siabod, ostracised by all the other ranges.

Your melancholia dwelt there on Carnedd Dafydd: each time you'd recall the hero-prince who gave the peak its name; hanged, drawn and quartered in Shrewsbury, his body dragged through the streets and dismembered. York and Winchester fought like dogs over who got his right shoulder. And I wondered, as you spoke, about my own body, about being cut up and divided among you two, my parents. Which parts would go to whom? Some bits were obviously my mother's, but my hands and feet were yours. They were out of proportion, out of step with the world. And my hair – who would want my hair, with its crazy mix of copper red from mum and frantic frizzle from you, Daddy?

Up there in the hills was the only place where you and I were completely happy together.

One by one, in layers, the mountains receded from our view, from the Christmas pudding blob of Arenig Fach, flicker-flamed in burning vapours, to ghostly Arenig Fawr, dowsed in methylated spirits and haunted by eight American servicemen.

Living with mum during the week and with you over the week-ends, in the old house, was never schizophrenic but it changed my body-and-soul clock; a mirrored duality was spawned in me, a taste for two separate identities. I became two different people: I dressed differently at mum's, talked differently when I was at your place, Daddy.

I smoked in one house but not the other, slept longer at mum's but better in the old place with you…

Later in life, not content with one home or one husband, I wanted two: eventually my deeply cloven nature, my duality got the better of me and soon I was living a double life, married to two men in quick succession: one of them a dark, squat Welshman and the other a lanky, fair-haired Englishman. I forgot to tell either I was married to another and spent years, willingly, being shared – I felt as if I were a coin, being tossed into the air repeatedly, seeing the sequence of my life unfold. The first house was tidy, the next unruly. In one I smoked, left the washing up, and cadged money; in the other I painted my nails, scoured e-bay for bargains, and cleaned the cupboards wearing purple Marigolds.

I moved between them as the mood took me and opportunity allowed. The only way I could express love at all was in two equal parts, as you, my parents, had configured: I became a fruit tree with its branches trained along espaliers to the left and right of me, strung up on wires, unable to grow normally, towards the sun. In one home my bedroom was purple and in the other it was indigo – in both I pleased my husbands in equal measure, in exactly the same ratio, without an extra kiss for one or the other, nor one single disproportionate moan or stroke of affection. I was strictly fair, counting each and every sexual encounter so that both my husbands achieved exactly the same amount of pleasure in exactly the same positions in many of the same locations, though making love in a toilet near the top of the Eiffel Tower was slightly more enjoyable with the Welshman because the novelty had worn off somewhat by the time I went there with the Englishman; however, I balanced this by taking the Englishman to the Ritz and making love to him there first. I'm glad that I never wanted to make love to both men at the same time, though it could have been arranged. You know what men are like.

To each husband I gave a boy and a girl, and all four I loved equally. At last the curse of my manifold divisions was lifted: no half-loves or semi-hemispheres of affection partitioned my maternal instincts, since the wholeness of my devotion covered all my children without isolation or segregation. We carried on like that for many years before I was discovered. Now it's the children who feel the need to measure their love for me, but they dispense it in uneven and unpredictable portions. A little from one, too much from the other. My formula for eternal fairness has gone astray, for ever I presume, unless it's found in a dusty cupboard many years from now, or resurfaces mysteriously, as if it were a great-grandmother's prized recipe for chutney or raspberry jam.

Sweetie pie, you said one day, on the summit of Carnedd Dafydd, promise me one thing...

And I did, as I promised mum to be careful with men and never go to India, because that's where it all started she said, all the bad luck and the separation. Was she using a mother's intuition, or merely being unreasonable? Parents, after all, are testing grounds for irrationality and unpredictability – with Large Hadron Colliders below the shallow surface of their outward calm, where the atoms of childhood innocence are smashed together to reveal their true constituents. Even Barbie dolls have a god particle, seemingly.

Daddy, you wanted one last favour from your sweetie pie. So I promised to take you to the top of Carnedd Dafydd, when it was all over, and scatter you to the four winds.

Go to the top and look round Wales for me, sweetie pie, take me to the place I love the best, you'd say.

As for mum, she's made no request at all. It's up to me what I do with her afterwards. I have to guess, and that's what I've done. Sitting in my cell I've had plenty of time to think about such things, and one day I decided (wrongly, probably) that she'd want to spend the rest of her ever-diminishing existence under the ground, out of sight if not entirely out of mind.

Daddy died a couple of months back. They let me out for the day, supervised, so that I could go to the funeral – it was just a small do, no fuss despite his international reputation. He didn't have many friends left by then, not many still alive anyway, as his Guardian obituary pointed out (it made no mention of me, thank God). I suppose it's a wonder he lived so long, considering what I did to him. They wouldn't let me go up Carnedd Dafydd to scatter his ashes. They sent them to me by courier, here in Scotland (one of those progressive open prisons for women). I've got them in my boring little room in a plastic jar. It's matt grey, which is quite appropriate really, because black would be over the top, don't you think? His ashes make a shushing sound when I shake the container, like the noise of maracas. They call it an urn, but it's just a plastic jar really, a bit like one of those old sweet jars. My favourites were rhubarb and custard, just like daddy. I can taste them now…

I haven't opened the lid yet, I couldn't bear to look inside. Mum wanted nothing to do with his remains. She said I'd killed him off anyway. She never came to see me, but she sent me letters on cheap, lined notepaper. He'd died of a broken heart, she said. She can be mean, my mum. She said he'd died because he couldn't tell his stories to me any longer, and he'd faded away because there was no-one to listen to him after I'd gone. She wrote to me in her prim and proper writing: *If you hadn't been so selfish and got yourself two husbands none of this would have happened. He didn't know what to do with his life. And the shame of it all.*

She said that to me, and other things too. Why so cruel?

So, every night I watch the light fade on your ashes, Daddy, thinking about the day when I can leave prison and go up Carnedd Dafydd. If I'm lucky the mountains will fade into the distance in shades of purple and indigo, looking like a huge rack of triangular toast, uneaten, left on an abandoned tableland, going blue with mould. I'll scatter you into the wind and I will think of you, the way you were when we were together, making a roll call of the mountains as they faded away towards the heart of Wales. But I've an admission, Daddy – I'm going to cheat a bit. Because one day you explained to me, on that mountain, why you'd chosen indigo for my bedroom. The name comes from the River Indus, you said, in India, your second favourite place on Earth. Or it could have been your favourite, since you didn't like to choose between two loves, in the way I refused to choose between you and mum.

So when I get out of here I'm going to sneak off to India, where my mum said I was never to go, not ever, no. And I will take half of you with me, to the banks of the Indus. That way, Daddy, you will get – in death – what you never got in life: India at your feet, for evermore.

And for one whole day at least you'll receive something you never got before. My complete and undivided love. Every little bit of it, not just half. Jam, pastry and all – for you and you alone, a whole sweetie pie.

opaque

IT happened on a bright spring morning not so long ago that I observed an elderly man leaving a house in the mercantile quarter of this city. I was on business and I had lost my way, since I am not well acquainted with that area – it was out of bounds to us when we were children, though I am uncertain why. I do remember, however, my mother admonishing me tearfully one afternoon when she caught me prowling among those well-proportioned Georgian houses, with their uniform black doors, brass door-knockers, polished nameplates, and sharp palings, which always remind me of crocodiles closing in for the kill. I am told the houses have long cool gardens at the rear, very private, having many different types of trees which begin their yearly cavalcade with the magnolias and flowering cherries, troupes of ballerinas twirling in pink.

I watched the man as he made his way, gingerly, down a set of newly washed slate steps, onto the street, clutching the railings with one hand and a walking stick with the other. Although it was warm he wore a heavy black astrakhan coat and a homburg hat. Our paths met and I had time to study his face, which was sallow and rather melancholy. It occurred to me that he might have been ill recently, for he seemed frail and preoccupied with his foot-work. I surmised that he might have been handsome when young, since he still had a striking face, with a strong nose and clear dark eyes, perhaps those of an Armenian or an Eastern European Jew. I did not know his name, but I did possess a titbit of information about him, which was intriguing: my elder brother had remarked to me once, as we walked towards him on the esplanade, in his astrakhan coat, that this man might have been our mother's lover many years previously; furthermore, that I myself had been planned and conceived as an antidote to the near-dissolution of our parents' marriage consequent to the affair, which had been brief but intense. Or so my brother informed me. Looking at him now, with his crooked legs and his deflated body, I thought of the act of love; I imagined my mother's mounting excitement, an episode of passionate but guilty pleasure, and then the pain and heartbreak caused by this little man, now a remnant of his sex. He paused to look at me as I passed, and I had time to register a determined mouth, slightly downturned, and two half-moons of darkness beneath his eyes. There was no escaping an aura of sadness around him, of physical defeat and inner fatigue. I passed by, nodding courteously and mouthing a rather old-fashioned *Good day to you sir* as if I had strayed into an Austen novel.

By one of those strange quirks I came across him yet again later that afternoon. Having not seen him once since my early twenties, probably, I was to encounter him twice in a single day. Following our initial meeting I left him to totter down his slate steps, reminding me of an injured crab crawling from below a rock to meet the tide. I walked briskly – and as elegantly as I could – along the whole length of the Promenade des Anglaise, as was my custom, saluting everyone I knew, and taking in the sea air. Our main entertainment was the passage of a yacht from the horizon, slowly along the flat calm sea, into the harbour, where it disgorged an affluent Greek and his entourage. Either covertly or directly, all eyes were fixed on his party as they gathered in a circle of dazzling white around the magnate, conversing fluidly in their incomprehensible language; everyone watched as his harem – for so I took them to be – swept regally up the quay, some ten yards to his rear, having waved aside the gig waiting to ferry them to the resort's premiere hotel.

I rested on one of the long green seats stationed along the promenade, watching the crew unloading their craft before anchoring it out in the bay. It was a lively and noisy scene, with matelots shouting raucously to unseen crewmen below deck, underneath a makeshift halo of screeching, wheeling gulls. So engrossed was I in the scene that I failed entirely to notice a stooped figure passing through the melee of boys in front of me: the first I saw of his astrakhan coat was a black shimmer which appeared in the corner of my left eye. I looked round and caught him staring at me; again, I raised my hat and bid him good day. After a peremptory nod in my direction he sat down at the opposite end of the bench. We both contemplated the scene in silence, he immersed in his thoughts and I in mine. I composed a vignette in which, through a keyhole, I saw him dancing with my mother clasped to his chest, in a Victorian drawing room, the Blue Danube waltz wavering on a wind-up gramophone; all I could see in the gathering dusk of my daydream was a silvery gleam in my mother's eyes, a moist sheen on her parted lips, and the silhouette of her dark hair cascading onto her bared shoulders, or so I imagined her, since I had never seen her with her hair down.

I was awakened abruptly from my reverie by a loud cry. It seemed to come from a woman, close by, who was staring in our direction. Almost immediately her male companion, much taller than her, with remarkably long white hair falling onto his shoulders, exclaimed loudly and pointed towards our seat. As they hurried towards us, with the tall stranger almost dragging his companion along, tugging her arm, I searched my memory with increasing desperation, since I could not for the life of me remember either of them. I stuttered to my feet and prepared to make small talk, in the hope that their names would come to me eventually.

But it was not I whom they greeted now, with great warmth. It was the old man whom they fell upon, she grasping his shoulders from behind and kissing his cheek, her companion falling on one knee before him and clutching his hands, all the while saying *Eugene!* over and over again. The woman was the more excited, saying phrases such as:

– It's you again my old friend, at last!
– How marvellous to see you again!

But the old man was just as confused as I; he remained seated, and hardly acknowledged their salutations, since he too failed to recognise them.

I watched the yacht riding at anchor in the bay, appearing to move in the water but chained to the sea-bed; and I smelt the air around me, the stirring scents of spring, which awakened in me a strong desire to move on to another place, to see new sights. In the meantime, as this desire for change overwhelmed my senses, I listened to the conversation between the old man and his new-found friends.

– Surely you remember us?
– No, I'm afraid not.
– But you are Eugene?
– Yes, my name is indeed Eugene.
– And you were a gardener once?
– Yes, I have been a gardener all my life.
– But you have retired now, surely?
– No, I still tend my plants every day!

And so on, until the old man became irritated by all the attention he was receiving. He stopped answering the fusillade of questions fired at him, and sat resolutely with his hands resting on his stick in front of him, as if he were about to pull a lever which would open the ground beneath these silly people buzzing around him. Realising the effect they were having on him, the woman put a finger to her lips, urging her companion to be quiet, and then sat by his side with one hand curled around the collar of his coat and the other folded over his hands, which were shaking by now and making his walking stick tremble. She steadied his hands and soothed him. After a while he appeared to relax in her embrace, and his eyes closed. Then she told him a story, and I listened to her voice which was clear and melodious, the voice perhaps of a singer or an actress. She soothed me also, I believe, for I too closed my eyes and listened to her, while registering the sounds and scents around me – childish merriment, dogs yelping, gulls calling, and the smell of women passing: eau de cologne and the newer French perfumes; occasional jasmine wafts, and the bitter smells of the awakening earth, all mingling on the cool, sharp breezes of spring.

It appeared that Eugene had visited this couple many years ago, when they were first married. He had been recommended to them, and he had turned up on their wedding day; everyone had laughed at him as he stood on the lawn, cap in hand, unshaven and unkempt, incongruous in his black peasant's boots. A ripple of mirth had sounded among the guests, seated in white pavilions under yellow swags and bunting; the string quartet had stopped playing while he was ushered from the scene, into the servants' quarters. This was the story she told him, but he had no recollection of it.

The woman's companion sat down also, and relaxed by my side, pushing his legs out in front of him and resting his head on the bench, his hat balanced over his eyes to shade them from the sun. It appeared that Eugene had returned to their garden later that month, after the honeymoon. He had been hired to design and plant a beautiful and extraordinary garden to celebrate the marriage and to harbour the couple in their retirement; in the same way as their wedding ring avowed the eternity of their love, the garden would signal the eternal nature of their intentions. And so Eugene had designed a garden for them, and planted it with lovely and unusual plants which appeared in rotation to match the seasons and provided forever a soothing and inspiring haven in which they could walk together, talk together, and rest together.

Eugene was some sort of rustic Capability Brown, evidently.

Now, as he sat in a huddle, held gently by this ravishing

example of womanhood, he asked for a detailed description of the garden. She outlined its main characteristics, and as he listened he unfurled slowly, drawing himself upright.

This garden, it was in the English quarter?

Indeed it was.

At such-and-such a house, with a Cedar of Lebanon in the far corner?

Yes, that was the place.

Did this happen in the year of the president's inauguration?

Yes, he was perfectly correct, because they had delayed the wedding so that it did not clash with the civic event.

Eugene became animated, almost excited, his gnarled fingers pointing at imaginary borders and flower beds in front of him as he described the trees and plants he had installed. He wanted to know which had survived. At this juncture the lady sprang to her feet and said: But you have no idea how glad we are to have found you. We have been searching for you, both of us, and our servants, all over the town. We had given you up for lost, almost! We are having a celebration! As a mark of our own daughter's impending wedding we have commissioned a statue and a plaque to be erected in our garden and we want you to be there! Will you come? Please say yes, it would be so wonderful if you could come, you would make us both so very happy!

I listened to all this while pretending not to hear any of the conversation, but as I looked round now at the group my eyes met those of the woman's companion, who had removed the hat from his face and was now regarding me with... I'm not entirely sure... distaste perhaps, or cynicism. Was it suspicion I saw in his eyes? Meanwhile, his wife, or so I took her to be, continued: Do please come Eugene, do please say yes. We have such a wonderful surprise for you. My dear Eugene, the statue is of you! I have made it myself, with my own hands!

I was startled by her speech, and must have expressed myself in some way, because they all looked round at me now, even Eugene. I was immediately struck by the looks in their eyes.

There was little doubt that the man sitting next to me, with his mane of white hair, looked distinctly discomfited. The woman appeared excited, and her eyes gleamed with emotion; they were lustrous and moist. Eugene's eyes, I couldn't help noticing, were fixed expressively on the woman, and he too appeared to be moved by the proceedings. I apologised for eavesdropping, while also expressing wonderment concerning everything my ears had just heard. I had been deeply moved by their conversation, I admitted. I was touched that they had found Eugene after so many years, and I hoped he would visit the garden he had created all that time ago. Appeased by my apology, and pleased that their story had been so entertaining, they invited me also to the unveiling of the statue. I accepted readily, since I had my own motive for seeing Eugene in stone or bronze, or whatever her medium – since he had forgotten the garden until this pair had so unexpectedly thrust themselves back in his life, I wanted to see his reaction when he saw his creation again. I might also be granted an opportunity to broach a subject close to my heart, vis-à-vis my own mother, and Eugene's 'friendship' with her all those years ago.

A date and time was appointed for our meeting in the garden.

I was standing in front of the house, hesitantly, on a warm but showery morning, when a phaeton came into view at the end of the street. In no time at all it had stopped by my side, and since it was Eugene who sat in it – as I somehow expected – I opened the door and helped him onto the pavement. In a trice the door of the house had opened to us and we were whisked as quickly as Eugene's legs would allow into a large waiting room where we were welcomed by the lady and offered refreshments etc, which we both declined, listening instead to the animated introduction delivered by our hostess. It was clear from the contents of the house that we had entered the residence of one of the old patrician families of the city, possibly an equestrian dynasty, since there were portraits of fine stallions and mares everywhere on the walls. We were not the sole guests, evidently, for soon the house and garden were full of prosperous traders and merchants accompanied by their wives. After a discreet interval we were ushered into the garden and encouraged to group around a perpendicular object of about six feet in height, on a plinth and covered by a plum-coloured cloth held in place by a golden cord with tassels at both ends. Our hostess led Eugene to a solitary chair below the plinth and pressed him onto a plum-coloured cushion. By now she was magnificently attired in a light blue gown offset by a single-strand pearl necklace, though I am no expert in these matters, merely informing you that the stones had a milky opacity.

I noticed that Eugene was wearing white gloves, and I surmised from his newly brushed hair that he had been spruced up by the servants. But he was ill at ease throughout, fidgeting with his hat, which he held in his hands between his legs, and casting nervous glances at the people around him.

Mercifully, the lady of the house made but a short speech in which she alluded to her wedding day, the arrival of Eugene on their lawn during the celebrations (laughter), the construction of the garden, its formal opening, and the awards which had followed (applause), its development and maturation, and its role now in the hearts and minds of those who knew it, walked in it, and loved in it. They had sought out the garden's creator and he was the guest of honour that day (more applause), for he had returned again after many years to witness a day of celebration and joy, marked by the unveiling of a suitable statue. Without further ado, our hostess untied the golden cord and a servant whisked away the wrapper, revealing a bronze statue of a young man under an apple tree, about to pluck a fruit from a lower bough. In all respects it was most realistic, partly because the tree was a real apple tree, contained in a large terracotta pot. The likeness to Eugene was apparent only in the characteristics of the face, since we had here a young Adonis in his pomp, well muscled and strongly built. His hair was wreathed in laurels and his left hand held a cornucopia, full of fruit, into which he was about to place an apple from the tree; he had the aspect of a god of fertility greeting the spring. The head, and in particular the nose, was perfectly recognisable, however, and drew admiring glances and exclamations from the throng. Eugene was pressed to say a few words, but declined clumsily. Instead, he asked our hostess if he could be taken on a tour of the garden, to the Cedar of Lebanon and around all the delightful attractions he had constructed all those years ago. He tottered off, and I followed, admiring the lady's bearing from behind, though knowing little about the flowers and bushes which grew in profusion – yet with great subtlety and delicacy – in their allotted places. As we approached the huge tree which dominated the far end of the garden he stopped by a small artificial waterfall, near a weeping willow. He looked at his guide, who seemed to understand his wishes. She looked at me, then at him; he looked around at me, shrugged his shoulders and mumbled something, then she parted the descending willow fronds and led him into the tree's ambit. I followed them, at a slight distance, until I too was underneath the willow's umbrella of foliage.

After a while, when my eyes had grown accustomed to the gloom, I saw them approach an irregular doorway, which turned out to be the boulder-strewn entrance to a picaresque grotto, glinting with reflective stones, and revealing gargoyles, daemons and hamadryads moving in and out of the rough-hewn walls. At the far end, in a pool of light created by a cunning aperture in the grotto roof, I could see a comfortable divan covered over with a deep crimson wrap and bathed in the soft green leaf-colour of the weeping willow outside. On it was a young woman, very pale and distracted, with her shoulders hunched and her hands clenched between her knees. She was introduced to me as the lady's daughter, about to be married. I congratulated her and tried to make small talk, as one does with a stranger. And yet she had familiar looks. Surely I knew her from somewhere else? I searched my memory. There was something about her face – the nose, the bone structure; her expression when she looked at her mother, at Eugene, and then at me. As we all sat in silence, with the pale young woman and her mother on the divan, and Eugene and I on cast iron garden chairs painted white, on either side of her, it became clear to me suddenly that I was about to learn a very shocking secret.

green

DURING that chimeless hour before midnight, between the last glass of wine and bedtime, I go to sleep for a while. The girls have gone, taking all the oxygen with them, and in the dry heat my eyes droop; my brain shimmers into a faraway camel moving slowly in a desert heatwave, and I drift pleasantly into a little nap among the crumbs. As I crumple slowly into a punctured balloon I nod off to the sound of a bluebottle flying lone sorties around the room. It speeds up and down the valleys between the mugs and the jugs, strafing the leaning towers of crockery and, in the eerie silence between its full-throttle dives, I know a Dream is about to come my way.

It's so strange, the world inside my Dream. I'm alone in the house and I'm pensive. I call out to you, as I always do in my Dream. But you're not there. You've gone again. I try to say some words but my mouth won't work. I'm trying to say: *Please come home to me – let that door open now, let it be you. I won't care if you leave oil stains on the handle or cement dust on the carpet...*

But nothing at all comes out, not a word.

When a Dream comes I go to another country, but you never seem to be there. I'm always looking for you. I go out in the shimmering silence of first light, as the songbirds start to sing, looking for you under a shiny new rainbow. I'm in my flowery plastic mac and favourite red Wellingtons. I skip out of the house and storm down the road, full of wonderment and puzzlement, walking in any direction, looking for you. The Dream's in colour, it's nice and bright in here. Pausing for breath by the school I encounter a small table, draped with a red damask cloth, on which someone has built a makeshift shrine with a crucifix and a picture of Jesus, bearded, smiling in his flowing blue robes. A candle burns in a glass lantern and there are prayer beads, a holy book, and messages of hope scribbled in childish writing. Among them an upturned fly, dead, and a note, in your hand: *Please pray for my wife Rachel, about to be troubled by a Dream.*

A small boy dressed in the crimson and white of a choirboy kneels by the shrine and I ask him: What is the meaning of this?

A small girl, he says warily, noticing my wild air, *is in a state of exultancy: waves of great emotion pass over her in the classroom – one minute she swoons in a paroxysm of sorrow, the next she cries out in ecstasies of happiness.*

I also scribble a message and leave it on the table: *Come back to me Benito, I love you more than all the flowers of spring.*

Homewards I wend, already exhausted. I crawl fitfully under a marigold sun and the garden wilts without you, Benito: a robin in a scarlet cope celebrates mass in the shrubbery, singing a canticle for your safe deliverance. Sitting on the stairs I weep in a white cloud belching from the great swinging incense-burner you've constructed on a whim in the hallway. Now my brain crumbles: through the window I see you walking intently towards the woods… yes, it's you, stepping into your willow cathedral. A troupe of mistle thrushes, finials on every treetop, sing you in with madrigals and tropes.

What a Dream I'm having, Benito.

Filled with trepidation now, I don my red Wellingtons again and follow you into the trees… but what's this? The Dream's going bad! You're nowhere to be seen, Benito. I'm in a sylvan snare, trapped by the Green Man. I can sense him, my body's going hot and I'm making whimpering sounds like a sleeping dog.

The Green Man has found me out. Lurking near a massive oak

he scents me and yowls pitifully. His massive lugs swivel towards me – two fleshy, algae-mottled satellite dishes, furred with age; his eyebrows unfurl and move towards me on the wind in dense filaments, sensing my humid core. Sequinned with seeds, he dazzles. He sibilates in his ancient language, a primeval earth-moan, words dribbling from his mouth in a thick, green chlorophyll slime. His feet have disappeared: he sways plant-like, up to his shins in loam; his loins are wrapped in pantaloons of rotting humus. His eyes scan me for blight and mould; he beckons with his branchlet arms, urging me upwards through tangled leaves which darken the sky. Into him and through him I climb, panting, raking my shins on his spiny bark. Up among the cumuli, in a cloud-halo, I find a flower-strewn platform, a pixie place bathed in lantern lights – a fairy citadel glowing in soft, diffused colours. On the wind comes a haunting melody, a shepherd's lament wafting from ancient reed-pipes. In the distance I see you Benito, my paramour, I see you writhing and weeping in the long grass. *Benito*, I cry. *Benito my own true love.*

Opening my lichen-tinted hand, I drop a dead fly into the awaiting moss bowl. A shudder goes through the Green Man: my token has been accepted. Enfolding me tenderly in swathes of fine tendrils, he scans me for the knowledge he needs; then he downloads noisily, sucking my brain through a straw. My head whirrs; he rewards me with sensations far beyond human emotions: sensual tremors sweep through my body in waves lasting hours, maybe days. Now I must fly from him. He gurgles with pleasure as I rend my clothes in a frantic helter-skelter descent. Lunging at me, his fronds try to pod me, to rip away my fragile anthers. Running now, I laugh and sing on the dusty road as I flee. The people I meet on the way are Tylwyth Teg, elfin and animated, returning from their revels, a night of moonlit dancing on the green. Greeting me boisterously, they drive their miniature cattle before them, lowing and heavy with milk; in their arms they hide stolen babies, mewling and wan. I will away to the savannahs, to find Benito. I climb upwards through a ravine, among colossal boulders, to the tableland where three rivers meet, then I hit the Roman road: a white weal in the moorland, a dribble of history along the mountain's bilberry tablecloth. Far below me on the yellow strand, where I first laid eyes on you Benito, a mermaid sings among the wandering sailors, blind and bumbling men with broken nets and broken dreams. Her tender young body indents the summer sand, warm and golden. At last I reach the Druids' Circle, ashen with exhaustion.

Ah, my lovely Dream. My sad, mad Dream.

Benito, he's so brazen. Just as I expected, he's drunk again, or drugged with happiness – stretched out languorously at full length on the short-cropped grass, propped up on his left elbow. His flowing locks and moustaches glow in a ray of preternatural light; his blue overalls, spattered with paint, have been cast aside. He's as naked as the day he was born. Tears well up and spurt onto my cheeks. *Benito, you break my heart,* I whisper.

In his left hand, I think, he holds the Pipes of Pan; in his right hand a crystal glass, which swirls loops of effervescent wine into the refulgent air as he sways to the rhythm of his dark music. Flushed, his face glows with pleasure. His luminous, intoxicated eyes stay on her throughout, lovingly, as she poses and pirouettes, executes perfect arabesques in the soft green grass. His crazy, adoring inamorata. A woman in her eighties. The shame of it!

She is dressed – undressed? – in a harebell costume, barefoot, dancing around the standing stones, tinkling a song of enchantment and sleep. Yes, dammit, in a lawn green pixie dress, torn (by him?) in provocative places. And the *giggle* on the girl.

On top of a monolith her cat purrs a mighty purr, her back arched with pleasure.

Behind them twelve white rabbits, in top hats and tails, throw themselves into a Moulin Rouge can-can. He ignores me. *The bastard.*

I flee homewards, plastic Wellingtons chaffing my legs. The

cock crows thrice at Cammarnaint Farm and I am forsaken. At eight bells I weep in the heather. Now my lover is Caliban, dancing with fell Sycorax the witch; I am Ariel, imprisoned in the cloven pine. My teeth ache with longing – for his hot breath in my hair, for his arms around me. Oh! – to hear the hiss of his spit sizzle in the fireplace on a stormy winter's night.

As I descend, pathetically, into the town a fine rain arrives in ribs of white which drift slowly across the valley, dreamlike towers of foam disintegrating in slow motion onto the land... handfuls of chalk thrown to the wind. On the shimmering roads I walk on water, and my steps hiss in the trees. I am an insect drifting on a melting ice-mirror. I am nothing without him.

The bells on the fuchsias toll for me.

Drunk as a lord and pawed wantonly by matelots singing rude hornpipes in the Victoria Hotel, I shed all my inhibitions and dance naked on a sticky table. My toes are crimson with bilberry juice or blood. *Retribution, Benito.* I have a jamjar of gin in my hand and jack tars aplenty to keep me amused. Cuckolded by an eighty-year-old pixie? Not me, not gracefully. Landlord! – pour some more gin in my jar! Slop my future into a bucket and throw it to the pigs!

Twilight and evening bell,
And after that the dark!
And may there be no sadness of farewell,
When I embark …

My dream, Benito, it's my Dream again.

Furiously, I tell them everything, those fuddled fools dribbling into their black porter. One of them raises his shipwrecked eyes from the flotsam beer mats and eyes me as steadily as he can. His voice I don't recognise, but there's something about the twitch in his right hand which reminds me of… yes, it's Cadfan, the town scrivener, missing presumed drowned for fifty years or more. On his eye-patch the Old Testament writ complete in a lovely monastic script. Medieval Welsh – a speciality in these parts. I greet him warmly, fondle his stump. He has been on a voyage to fetch green tiger beetles to make his ink, iridescent and everlasting: he is ready for his first commission. A scroll of calf-skin vellum on the table already bears a massive decorated capital in the shape of my naked body caught deliciously in flagrante. The likeness is remarkable, down to the goosebumps.

Take a note, Cadfan, I boom magisterially through my plentiful tears.

> Dear Pixie,
>
> I will have my husband back without further ado. Whatever your magic, ancient and horrid hag, unfetter him now and send him home to his beloved (me). Shipwrecked he came ashore and shipwrecked he will soon be again, on the rocks of your lust. It was I who saved him with love and broth, who made his thighs the girth of a small bull and his manly item as big as a fencing post. It was I who bought him his first plas-tering trowel down the market; it was I who carried his first sack of lime from the kilns on my bent back; it was I who cooked him supper every night, the hod still stuck – with sweat – to my exhausted body, you witch. It was I who tended his manly wounds with waterproof plasters and it was I who bore him twelve children (all of them done well, three of them doctors and one a prophet).
>
> May the fleas of a thousand camels infest your ****.
>
> Yours, Rachel (daughter of Jones the Postman).

Homewards I wend my weary way, in my red Wellingtons, naked in the streets and humbled. Toothless grandmothers, sitting on their doorsteps in black, laugh at me, saying they will be next to woo him. Outside the school Christ is weeping tomato ketchup from his stigmata, and the school kids smirk at me.

Pixie, Pixie, Benito loves a Pixie they chant in unison. My own little Megan among them, there's no pity to be had. Crouching again under the great incense-burner in the hallway I blub and flay my skin with a torn picture of him, my poor Benito. What I'd give now to hear the clatter of his hobnailed boots in the yard, the roar of his voice in the pigshed. Instead I see a note being pushed through the letterbox, and I recognise the inky green fingers of Cadfan, no less. He beats a hasty retreat whilst I read the scrawl, which glows beetle-green.

Dear Rachel (daughter of Jones the Postman),

I have been to see for myself what they're up to, your husband and the pixie, still on the mountain they are and dare I say it, fallen into sin with night fast approaching and danger at every turn on the lonely moor. The music I don't mind but I draw the line at wine, men should stick to beer. I agree that lawn green suits her exceedingly, and the distressed hemline, slanting from her left thigh to her right knee, was a subtle and provocative masterstroke. Her dancing, like Isadora's at its best, was simply divine. The rabbits were superb and fulfilled their obligations to the letter. Rachel my love, you are radiant, you are sunsparkle on the shimmering ponds of heaven. I include herewith a solution to your problems and a relevant recipe.

All my love, Cadfan ap Iago the Younger.

PS. I am only sixty-seven and carry with me always a diploma in calligraphy from the Benevolent School for Retired and Maimed Sailors.

Naked under my see-through plastic mac, iconic in my red Wellingtons, I skip out of the house joyfully and storm the shops, grabbing goods off the shelves willy-nilly. I career up and down the Co-op, scouring every aisle for delicacies and scattering shoppers with my overloaded trolley. I pay for it all with promises and daisy chains. Soon I am ready to execute the coup de grace. Oh, my beautiful Dream.

Benito, I am writing in my beautiful Dream!

Dear Cadfan ap Iago,

As you suggested, I put the dish before him in his love bower at the height of the revelry; if I might say so, your recommendation – wild mushroom, chestnut and sage penne was a brilliant choice. After selecting the finest ingredients: penne pasta, Umbrian olive oil, Sicilian butter, fresh porcini mushrooms, garlic, sage, parmesan and freshly roasted chestnuts, accompanied by a poignant Chianti, I cooked the feast alfresco on the summit of Dinas, on a fire fragranced with wild mountain herbs. Needless to say, the first mouthful dispelled his fantasy and within seconds he was back to normal. He returned penitent to the lowlands, holding my hand like a naughty schoolboy. After a satisfying and complete repast, three bottles of wine and a nap in front of the telly, he's back to his old self again. I would be grateful if you would send me a bill to cover your costs. Please advise the octogenarian pixie that her cat has fleas. More important, please inform her that my lover has reclaimed his sanity, and that her wiles will work no more. Tell the old witch she's no match for my love – and fresh porcini mushrooms.

Tell her also that the fly she put in my ointment has been disposed of.

Yours appreciatively, Rachel.

Sometime before the chimes of midnight I wake suddenly after a little nap, my head resting on the table, nestling in the crook of my right arm. I'm still holding a knife and my hair's sprinkled with breadcrumbs. It's almost dark in the soft glow of the telly: there are shadows among the crocks and the cruets. The furry taste in my mouth, tinged with garlic and wine, reminds me that we've just enjoyed a large and pleasant meal. My eyes focus, slowly, on a fly. It's dead, I think, lying upside-down on the table-cloth, a small black blob. I flick it away and it disappears among the cups and the plates – a miniature china city, deserted.

My wonderful Dream is over. How long have I slumbered?

My cheek is rosy and numb, indented with the outline of my watch. My hand is wet and warm with the dribble of sleep. I've been dreaming about him again. It's the Dream... about another woman. The pixie.

Is he being unfaithful to me again? Why such dark doubts? It must have been the cheese...

He's asleep, wine glass in hand as usual. Snoring gently. The slob. A Fellini film drones in the background; the one with a dwarf nun climbing a ladder lodged in a tree; in the top branches a haggard madman shouts *I want a woman, I want a woman...*

Ample, saucy evidence of my love lies spattered all over his overalls (such a messy eater, but my own true love). Wild mush-room, chestnut and sage penne – his favourite meal. And a lot of wine. Frascati, Chianti. Valpolicella in a red rim around his mouth. Gradually I come to, though my head is still muzzy. Sitting by the fireside, poking the fire, I drift in a calm sea of fuzzy thoughts. How funny he is when he snores in Italian, when the moon hits his eye like a big pizza pie...

The pixie in my Dream is asleep and all is well. Surely he's not at it again. Who else would want him at his age? Such a belly on him too. Bald as a coot and sagging everywhere, even down there.

So foolish to have suspicions again. Love is so wobbly. A wobbly tooth to worry me all day. The tingle. My love is a tingle in a wobbly tooth.

Time for bed. I'll take the glass out of his hand, leave him where he is to sleep.

He can wash up in the morning. My voodoo lover, who dances naked with his pixie on the moors. In my mad, sad, wonderful Dream.

gold

GOOD on the island now, plenty of food again and no killing. Every Season the men come in fast boats to make sure we work, no guns. Since No World we grow food and sleep in the big house. Goog tell us what to do every day. Better since No Hope and I work with my Spade all day without wanting the Old Time again. My Spade is My Friend.

Goog has told me who to Love. I go with the men in the fast boat and they leave me on another island, not so far. They say the woman I will Love sleeps on her own in a tent away from their big house. She has Food Land and a Spade but no Love.

I beat my Spade with a stone and leave Spuds by her tent and Seeds, custom.

Goog says she is my only Love in the world that is left, in all the islands. Nobody else can be my Love, destiny.

In the morning Spuds and Seeds gone, custom. On the tent blue dog picture, I shout Dog and beat my Spade with a stone. She does not come out but smoke and crying.

I am hungry so I root in the woods, sleep in the grass till noon. I go back to the tent and she is in the Food Land, digging and crying. She is ten or twenty years more than me with hair like a rope on her head. She has good tits but legs like a hen, too thin. Her face fatty white with blue paint on her cheeks, pictures. Long green dress, no boots. She digs the Earth, still strong. I beat my

Spade with a stone by the edge of her Food Land, custom. She shouts at me, no words I know. She waves her arm, throws stones at me. Custom on this island maybe.

I sit by the edge of the woods, hungry, looking at her tent and her Food Land. I am hungry, but not angry, I am No Hope now. Why is Dog my only Love in the world. Why not Beth in the big house? Goog says so.

Three days I wait eating rabbits and roots, then the boat men come find me. They take me to the tent and talk to Dog, no words I know. Dog's tent is big, made of skins, warm in there. Skins on her bed too, fire in the middle of the floor. Pot for cooking and a loom for clothes, pretty stones from the beach and flowers hanging from the poles, good smell. Child toys and child clothes by a little bed but no child. Dog has many pictures made on slates taken from the Old Homes under the water I think. The boat men shout at her and point to me, they are angry, but no killing. She cries, they go. After, she makes me a bed by a Child Picture, away from her. In the night when I am in bed she goes out and comes back wet, more slates in her arms. She swims for them in the sea, looks like she gets them from the Old Town in the water and dries them by the fire. Quiet now, no crying.

I am No Hope, no matter she does not want Love, custom. Morning she gives me cold food and takes me to the edge of her Food Land. With stones she makes a Square on the Earth, big, and points to my Spade.

I beat my Spade with a stone and shout My Spade is My Friend. She throws a stone at me and hurts. She takes me to the Square and starts to dig with my Spade, then gives it to me and points. I am No Hope, I dig all day in the sun, she brings me Water and sits on a rock to watch me. Smoke from the tent by night, she makes hot food and we eat on a rock, looking at my Square. I make a hole in the edge of the Square for my Shithole, then I shit. She points to the stream and I wash, then bed, custom. No light in Dog's tent so she sits in the tentdoor, under the Moon, with a slate. She makes Words with a nail. She has made Words all day with her finger in the Earth by her tent. Some days she stamps on the Words in the Earth and starts again. In the night when I pretend sleep she goes to the Words in the Earth with her slate, writes them down. Finish, she sleeps.

Days this goes on, I dig all the Square and fence about, spend time in the woods thinking. She has not told me to Love her yet, she pushes me away to my bed. Goog says she is my only Love in all the islands, but she does not Love me yet. New Season and our island is hot, the men come in boats with guns. They ask if she has Loved me but I say no. There is more anger, they hit Dog and I watch them. I am No Hope. I ask what is wrong. They say she is Mad. But she is not, I have seen Mad Dan and Dog is not Mad like him after the World drowned. In the beginning many went Mad from the Silence, Dan went Mad too. Noise all over the place before the World Drowned, but new Silence on the island too much, hurt their heads.

The boat men go away and Dog cries, I put my arms around her but she shouts and runs to the woods. I try to read her Words but only a few I know, Spade and Man and Child.

Dog stays in the woods for three days, comes back Mad, breaks many slates and rips her tent pictures. For a day she sits on the child bed, playing with toys. No Spade work, no planting in the Food Land. No hot food, no Words on the slates, only crying. Next day Dog makes me sit on the rock and she paints me, blue on my face and red on my chest and back, patterns. She rips her dress and paints her body red in patterns, custom. She sings a baby song, then we Love each other. This is my Love, Goog told me. Every day we Love and Dig, she writes Words on her slates and I plant the Spuds in her Food Land, Harrow the Square and fetch firewood from dead trees. One night she goes from the bed and sits in the tentdoor, moon shadow. When I wake she has gone. Maybe she has gone to the big house or the woods again to think. I look at her slates and they are full of Words, there are Words in the Earth and painted on the tent, all over it. They go round and round the tent, red Words painted with her finger. For days I wait for her to come back and then I go to the big house, but she is not there. I look in the woods but it is empty. I shout Dog and there is an eko but she does not come, the world is empty. I am No Hope but I feel again, hot pain in my chest. More days go by and the men from the big house come to the tent, angry. They push me and beat me, I don't know why. I speak to them but they do not understand. They take me to the edge of the water where she went for slates, and she is there, on her face in the water. Dog is Dead, I run in the water to pull her out, but she is blue and the paint has run on her face. Her eyes are not there, her face nearly gone, but it is her, blue and Dead. Her hair like a rope is loose on her back, green with weed. Her mouth a bit open and there is a gold tooth, it shines in the sun, and a green crab in her mouth too. They leave us, I make a hole in the woods and I put her in the Earth, custom. A hot burn in my chest and I am feeling again. Years without crying, now my face wet again. For many days I do nothing, leave my Spade and eat the Spuds I put in the Earth. I try to know the Words but no good, I give up. At the end of the Season the boat men come for me. They ask me for Dog and I point to the Earth in the woods. They go to the big house and come back angry. They tie me up and take me in their boat. I try to tell them but they do not listen. On the way to my Home they leave me in another place, a small island with no people, no trees, no animals, no birds. They are going when I cry for my Spade, I shout My Spade is My Friend. They throw it in the water, I go in and get it. Only me and my Spade on this island, No Hope again and no animals, no birds. I am No Hope. There is no water, for days I suck the leaves at dawn, no food but roots, I sleep in the sand and I feel again, my chest is hot and I cry. I write in the sand with my finger, Dog and Spade and Love. I write My Spade is My Friend with stones, and much bigger, HELP in stones on the sand. For days I sleep, hardly move, a pain in my belly and my Spade is rusty, I look at the brown on its Blade every morning, getting bigger. When I am No Hope again a boat comes, it is Beth and a man from the big house. I cry, I have Hope again, it is an old feeling and it makes me ill. I hold her dress and I cry, there is sand in my mouth which is dry and my lips are big, they will not move. I say to Beth Goog was wrong. Dog not the only Love for me in the world, in all the islands. I say to Beth the truth, Dog is Dead and Love is Dead. She asks what happened and I tell her. There is no Dog for me to Love, she is Dead in the water, drowned looking for slates in the Old Town under the water I think. I tell Beth about the Words and the Pictures.

They take me in the boat to my Home and we go to the big house, they make me better. Did you kill her they ask, I say no but I put her in the Earth, custom. Every night when she comes home from the Food Land she sits by me, Beth, and asks me the same thing. Did I kill her. No I say. I promise her. She makes me tell her many times, over and over again. I tell her about the slates, and the paint on her face, the Words in the Earth. I tell her about Love.

At last they let me go, with my Spade but it is brown now, rust on it. My Spade is My Friend, but I am No Hope again, I do not dig in the Food Land with the rest. All day I walk in the woods with the animals and the birds, I go thin and weak.

Beth comes to find me and sits with me under the trees, we talk about Goog and my only Love in all the world, Dog who is Dead. I am without need for my Spade, I do not want to Labour in the Food Land, but Beth brings me a bit of food and a skin to keep me warm in the wood when it is dark. I am No Hope, I walk about in the green wood, I call to the birds and the animals, making their noises and whistles.

When the Season ends the men from the boats look for me with guns but I hide. In the rain and the mud I make a place to hide, cover it with branches and leaves. When it rains I sit there and listen to the rain on the green leaves, and the sound of the wind in the green trees, I listen to it for ever. My Spade is with me, it is brown now. I look at it and ask if I will use it in the Food Land again, with the others. No is the answer in my head, never again.

I am thin and my hair is long, my beard on my chest. I paint my cheeks blue, a picture like Dog made, and I make my hair in a rope. I look for slates in the ruins and I make Words I know, Spade and Dog and Tent. In the days of sun I collect stones from the ruins and I make a House of Stone with a roof of branches and mud. I beat the earth to make a floor, I cover it with sand from the beach. On my slates I draw pictures with my Knife, pictures of me and Dog and our Days of Love. It was the best Love in all the islands, in all the world. I will tell my story on the slates. On the biggest slate I make a picture of Dog. In the Big Slate Picture she has a green dress made from moss stain I rub in with my finger. Her hair is real, made from Beth hair. I do not know how to fill her smile, I have no gold for her tooth. I have asked Beth for gold, she has seen the picture. I have been in the mines and there is yellow in the rock, I will make a tooth for the Big Slate Picture and She will be perfect. Beth says for me to go to the big house now, they want me to Dig again with my Spade but I will stay here. If I go with her the boat men will find me and take me away, custom.

I have been to the mines but I can't make Gold. Beth brings me no food now and I am thin, weak from roots and berries, no hot food. In the nights I think how to get Gold and I see a way. When the boat men are here to tell us what to do I will steal a boat and go back to Dog, take her gold tooth out and bring it here to the Big Slate Picture, put it in the stone. Make candles all round it, go to it every morning and talk to her, my only Love in the islands.

Today they come from the big house for my Spade and I am angry, My Spade is My Friend. I kill two of them fighting, there is rust on their faces, a strange light in their eyes. I beat my Spade with a stone and shout My Spade is My Friend. Black crows all around me, they will feed well tonight. Many I fought, strong was my arm, two will sleep forever tonight. As the crows fatten there will be many tears in the big house, no fire on the hearth, my brothers and sisters will cry in the dark. In the morning they came boastful, shaking Spades, shouting Come Out No Hope, fight with us or we will take your Spade. And I answered them: no pup will take my Spade, I will fight with you. And they came from all around me through the green trees shouting and waving their Spades, but I met them fast and strong, I killed two where the crows walk in their cold black blood. Crying tonight in the house of their sisters and wives, their rooms will be cold and their children hungry. I talk to Dog in the small light before dawn, she tells me to have Hope. She will look after me. She says I must kill Beth to get Gold, she has a ring on her finger.

I have killed Beth in the afternoon. She brought me food and I killed her outside the House of Stones. She was not looking, I did it quick but not with my spade. My Spade is My Friend. Then I looked at her and cried, no Love now for me or her. Her gold ring I beat flat with a stone, it is in the picture of Dog. My Love is pleased with me, my work is good. I take the dead people to the mine and cover them with stones. After many days I take my Spade to the Food Land and start to dig. The others stay away from me, they leave me alone. I beat my Spade with a stone and shout My Spade is My Friend, custom. They gather round. I tell them what to do now. Goog is no good now. When the men in boats come we will kill them. I am the Goog of the big house now, Goog of the Spade Men and I Love all the women, destiny. All the women have blue paint on their cheeks, pattern like Dog, every woman has her hair like a rope on her head, custom. Every day I talk to Dog and she is Happy with what I have done, I have Hope.

Written in the House of Stones, in the First Year of Dog.
Custom.

pink

AN old man sits in a room, alone. He lives in the country, in a house set apart, grey and silent. Autumn's infringing sadness billows the turquoise curtains with earth-cooled air and invades the house with spores, invisible moulds and nostalgia; another tired year is turning over in bed. Time has tipped to over-ripeness.

The old man feels sad. After dinner, in an infant gale which doesn't know its own strength, he watches the Sunday afternoon film without moving once – without taking a sip of water or nibbling a biscuit. Of all the films in all the world, it's Casablanca. He considers the great romantic films. He can't remember many.

After tea on his own, sardines on toast and a tin of rice pudding straight from the can, cold, because he can't be bothered any more, he sits down in his deep armchair and imagines his own Love Story. A strong evening sun, beating through the window behind him, projects a yellow screen onto the wall in front of him and he sets his own film in motion – his own *Cinema Paradiso*, or maybe *The Last Picture Show*.

Then, in his imagination, he stops the film and makes a few telephone calls. Still sitting there, he looks at the yellow screen on the wall and invites some friends round to watch his film. He needs a Love Committee: a handful of people who've been around him for a long time, to sit in the room with him and mediate.

He mumbles to himself as he picks his Love Committee. He chooses them in the way playground captains pick their football teams at school, instinctively and cunningly.

Big burly Tom the policeman, red with effort and drink but still functioning in the upstairs department – Tom will be able to jog his memory and remind him of his first days of love. Primavera. They're the same age; he rewinds the tape some fifty years, to the time when Tom was a rookie copper on the night shift. Every night for a summer, when the town clock struck twelve, Tom would rap his friend's bedroom window with his truncheon to wake him up so that he could run barefoot across the dewy fields to Morfudd in her father's barn.

He will need Frances there – the librarian: proud, punctilious, much too frank with the drink inside her, tragically dismayed at her own marriage. Impeccably dressed in plum or serge, her perfume armorial, not an invitation... her miniature affairs dotted on her skin, freckles of ardour. Three decades of calm punctuated by a handful of brief volcanic eruptions; frantic couplings separated by years of formality and politeness, her inner heat invigilated by the lifeless books in her library. Her passion was governed by the laws of diminishing returns, since every Heathcliff or Darcy in the town had aged or gone grey with doubt. But real love was all in the mind; real love was different. She mourned it and put a spade in the ground every night, wanting to find it like a crock of gold.

And who else should be there in his Love Committee? Jonty, undoubtedly. A haggard man, thin and secretive – retired from the sea but still in love with the waves. He seemed to live in a crow's nest near the top of the cliff, a niche on the path which dropped to the shore, his berth a double seat carved into the rockface. He sat there every day with his binoculars, on a water-proof cushion which he stuffed into his coat when he left the place, if he ever did. He knew about the creatures of the deep, and their watery romances. Whales tended to be promiscuous. Dolphins copulated belly to belly after lengthy foreplay. Like humans they had sex just for fun occasionally, and got fruity with other animals, even humans. Dolphins could be gay, too. Jonty divulged all this in a sad monotone, never looking at the listener, his eyes forever scanning the sea for fins and spumes.

Why was Jonty invited to the screening? Because maybe he had a woman in every port once. No, that was unlikely. Because he watched and waited so patiently? The old man has no idea why he wants Jonty there, but he does.

The old man sits in his crimson chair, watching the square of yellow moving slowly along the wall. He clears his throat politely and addresses the phantom Love Committee in a level, dispassionate voice. He no longer smokes, but feels the event would be more atmospheric if Frances – perhaps – smoked moodily in the corner, looking like Anais Nin, fresh from another wanton sexual encounter. He would watch the curls of smoke wafting across the screen – yes, that was appealing. They would need plenty of drinks on his long low table, in glinting decanters; a bucketful of ice and some tumblers.

Everyone settles into a chair. Frances lets the ice clunk and swish in her glass then she sucks neat vodka from a hole in her cube – a little trick of hers; a trademark drinking habit. She looks round at the old man and her eyes gleam in the murk. They're ready. He starts talking…

My friends – the fragrance of new-mown hay is the nation's favourite smell, I'm told. But did you know that only one type of grass leaves that distinctive tang in the air?

He hears Frances whisper its name.

Yes Frances, sweet vernal grass. When it dies it leaves a wonderful fragrance. Once the old people made bonnets from it, and whenever the bonnets got wet they gave off the same sweet smell, months or years after the plant's death. And that's what I want to show you first, on my screen – an evening in a garden, many years ago. It has stayed in my mind, vividly. As soon as I think of it the smell of a freshly mown lawn seems to fill my nostrils, and I'm taken back to that time. My memories of one particular aspect of the evening are as powerful as they were then.

Jonty sits in his chair unmoving, staring at the screen with an intensity he usually reserves for the boundless sea. He considers an unlikely fact: ambergris, expelled from the intestines of the sperm whale, is a powerful source of perfume. Jonty knows he'll get drunk and quite probably aggressive... will he make a fool of himself in this place too? Will he have to move on again, to another solitary cliff in a strange place, full of people who won't know him? His secret crouches inside him – a ship in a bottle, broken and irreparable. Wife beater. Child bruiser. He blocks it out again, sinks another finger of Scotch and listens to the old man, his ridiculous testimony. How could anyone his age be so naive, so romantically stillborn?

It was summer. A warm evening in June, in the Marches, where Wales meets Shropshire, by a river. I'd walked along a water meadow by the Severn, picking my way through marsh marigolds and thistle clumps. At some point I was surrounded by a herd of young heifers: I was enveloped in a cloud of milky cowbreath, with insects buzzing and chirring, the smells of warm mud and cowpats on the riverbank...

Frances closes her eyes and joins him on the screen, walking by the river. She sketches in a kingfisher darting from the bank and a trout rippling the water, then she adds some sound effects – the swish of the heifers' tails, the suck and gurgle of the river, a woodpecker cackling in a spinney above...

The old man continues...

I was on my way to a party thrown by the editor of a local newspaper, who lived in a large Victorian manse – crumbling a bit, with a portico and balustrades, plinths and statues. Catholic family, used to be posh but struggling to keep it all together – I think perhaps the party was a big family effort, their once-a-year attempt to stamp some order on a place beyond their energies or bank balance. The terraced garden fell in folds to the riverbank. I remember a row of weeping willows, and yellow roses in full bloom. Old English, probably. We were coming to the end of a long hot summer, and when I arrived the event was in full swing. Butterflies and silky insects shone in the air around us. This was about thirty years ago, so most of the people were formally dressed – the men in white shirts and grey slacks, many with ties... most of the women in print dresses, with pastel patterns or flower designs. Diaphanous in that light – quite exciting for a young man. People were in motion everywhere – moving between groups, forming into clusters then disbanding, veering erratically from one centre of attraction to the next.

Tom grips his glass and contemplates the party on the lawn. He thinks of water coming to the boil, atoms becoming more and more volatile under the influence of heat. The people on the lawn are over-excited atoms, coming to the boil under the influence of alcohol. Tom hates parties and leaves them as soon as he can. People became unpredictable, ungovernable. He seemed to bore them. Standing with his back to a pillar or a wall, he'd await a darting visit, try hard to be interesting, then watch crestfallen as the visitor darted away again without probing him for his meagre nectar. What did they feed off? They perplexed him. He eavesdropped on conversations, hoping to pick up some know-how, but the conversations seemed trivial and vapid. Perhaps it was the delivery and presentation that counted. He should giggle and wiggle his eyes around, perhaps. He couldn't be bothered any more, didn't even try.

He looks at the screen on the wall and mulls gloomily on the old man's magical party. What will happen next? Will a female guest tear off her clothes and dive into the river? Will there be a hush as everyone else turns to watch her surface in a ring of foam? Will the rest of them join in? He imagines a wild bacchanalia, a writhing mass of pale flesh tuna-threshing the water, laughing and squealing... orgiastic sounds from a couple on the bank, their entwined limbs mermaid-green in a willow's watery shadow...

The old man continues...

And then it happened. I saw her out of the corner of my eye, moving coolly from the nearest group, towards me. Dressed differently from the rest, in a white muslin dress which ended a few inches above the knee. No hat, so I noticed a difference immediately – her hair, normally kept up in a bun or a chignon, curled and flowed around her shoulders in a blonde cascade. I hardly recognised her.

Frances thinks: God, he's almost gaga. Lost in the shrubbery of dementia. He's obsessed with the film he's directing, the scene on the lawn. He's dredging his pond for a lost and idealised love. She places another figure on the screen, under a weeping willow: Dante Gabriel Rossetti, about to dig up his wife's grave to retrieve the love poems he wrote long ago, before she overdosed on laudanum; their child stillborn, like the emotions being exhumed today. Frances contrives a title for the film: *Onsra.* In a certain language it meant *to love for the last time.* That's what he's doing, she thinks – trying to invoke love for the last time. A young grub of love struggling inside an ancient, decaying chrysalis.

The old man continues, running his last picture on the grainy screen...

I was leaning against a statue. Later I found streaks of old, creamy paint dust on my suit. I was disengaged from the party around me, resting in the sunshine, enjoying the coolness of the stone, the match of its contours to my own body. Feeling nice and relaxed, languorous, drowsy in the summer heat. Cigarette in one hand, glass of wine in the other. She came towards me and slowly I recognised her shape; she was a family friend. An aunt but not an aunt, if you know what I mean. One of those women on the periphery of the family, not a blood relative but still called Aunty by the kids. About forty. Forty-five? Hard to say... she was quite a bit older than me, certainly. Old enough to be my mother, as they say...

Tom closes his eyes and brings up a picture of his mother. He'd never seen her demonstrate a single sexual trait. How many times had she had sex? Just the once? Had she been a human variant which had hermaphroditic sex on a preordained day in her life, hanging upside-down in the attic, merely to reproduce? His father had died in a POW camp. After that, nobody. Perhaps his parents did it once with their eyes closed, and his father in uniform. Full battle dress, trench coat too. Maybe he put it through a buttonhole and sang hymns very loudly to drown out any embarrassing noises. Sex was the ultimate taboo. Even when he was older the TV was off in an instant if as much as a bra strap appeared...

She came up close to me and put her hand on my chest, as if to balance herself. One of her nails, painted pink, played with the top button of my shirt. She leaned on me slightly and looked into my eyes with a warm fuzzy look, slightly myopic. Indulgent. Green pupils with flecks of hazel, and laughter lines, slightly whiter than the skin around her eyes. She'd been laughing a lot... I remember her laugh. She was slightly drunk by now, but still in control. She teased me about some-thing and did up a button – a sort of mock modesty, tutting and fussing about my appearance. I was suddenly aware that this woman was quite different from the one I knew as Aunty Marian. A woman with pink nails, with her hair let down, enjoying herself, confident and talking to me invisibly with her fingers, pressed softly – meaningfully – onto my chest.

Jonty creaks to his feet and shuffles to the drinks table, sloshes himself a large dose of whisky. He must leave after this one, make his excuses. The anger has caught fire inside him, the flames will incinerate him soon. He can feel the roar in the chimney, but he doesn't know why he gets so damned hot when he drinks. And angry. Prometheus on the rocks. An eagle eating his liver, the past eating his brain. No love for him now, not even his children's. Didn't know where they were even. Back in his chair, he takes two big gulps of whisky and tries to focus on the screen. All he can see is a huge bottle with a ship inside it, ablaze…

Then she turned away from me and studied the party for a few seconds, taking in the scene. She obviously thought it was funny, because she gave a gurgle of amusement. I was dreamy, looking at the fine hairs on her neck, funnelling into a V of silver before disappearing into her clothes. I looked at the zip on her dress – pink like her nails, and so inviting. I touched it, lightly. The smell of her was the smell of a woman, it made me feel drunk. It wasn't perfume, it wasn't soap – it was the smell of a clean healthy woman in the sun, a warm brown smell… I can't think how to describe it. Hot skin rubbed with aromatic leaves, stroked with sandalwood. No, that's not right. It was the smell of her whole being – it came off her body as if the fine hair on her skin had been mown, and was sending out a signal like the sweet vernal grass around us on the lawn…

Frances feels a toothache coming on: the ice has begun to hurt her right molar, the usual place. Tender is the right. Abscess makes the… she gets more vodka to dull the pain. The film is coming to an end, she can feel it is ending. Incest in the sun. But it wasn't incest. A young man waking up to… no, it was something else. Something special had happened that afternoon on the lawn. First love? But hadn't he described his former wife as the love of his life, the only one? The screen on the wall freezes – she puts the film on hold. The kingfisher hangs in mid air; the whole party becomes a silent frieze of statues. She's intrigued. Her own past is in grainy black and white. But the old man is showing the first film he ever shot in full colour. Yes, that's it.

His voice drones on in the corner…

Now she moves back slowly and rests her whole body against mine, but not centrally. She's a lynx on a branch, using the left hand side of my body as a resting place. I think she closes her eyes for a while. The noise on the lawn is a soft drone in the background. Human sounds are so ridiculous when you remove yourself, listen dispassionately. She relaxes her hip into the waiting groove between my legs. Her head is on my shoulder and her hair drifts against my cheek. Our bodies are almost conjoined physically. There is no sexual tension. She is merely being her: a woman. I am merely being me: a young man.

The old man halts his story to top up his glass. He looks around at the Love Committee, but they've disappeared: all he sees is three empty chairs, all askew, as if his witnesses left hurriedly. He tops up his glass with soda: he doesn't want to get drunk yet. That'll come later. He wants to finish the film, even if he's the last one left in the cinema.

She stays like that for five, maybe ten minutes. She becomes part of me, almost. I am rooted to the spot, I hardly move. I flick away my cigarette and hold her bare shoulder with my hand. I feel the almost imperceptible crater of an old smallpox jab. Her skin is so nice to feel. Is there anything nicer? Finally, she rights herself, moves away slightly and smoothes her dress. She turns round and smiles at me gently, slightly woozily. Her hair is disturbed so she flicks it back with her hand, pats it down. She kisses her right forefinger and dabs my cheek with it. Then she says Ciao! *and heads for the melee again. The interlude is over. I relax and light another cigarette, but I stay where I am.*

The old man gets up, moves to the window. He stands there, looking out at the meadows. He can smell smoke, searches for the source, and finds it drifting from the woods in the middle distance. Autumn is here again, sporing away.

He closes the window and turns to the screen on his wall, but it's gone. The sun has dipped below the horizon, night is coming on. He sits in his chair, with a full glass, and gets drunk in the gathering gloom. His eyes close and he drifts towards unconsciousness, the glass tilting awry in his hand. Before he goes, he talks to his phantom Love Committee one last time...

When she left me my body felt as if I'd been standing too near a fire, I was burning. It was as if she'd left an imprint on me, branded me with her own flesh. And it seems to me now that she shared something with me that afternoon, without intending to. The woman I thought of as an aunty revealed to me a part of herself that she'd shared with other men over the years – her immense sensuality, the sort which so many women have but which only a few are able to share consistently. It flowed out of her and it left its heat on me for the rest of my life. I can still feel it there now. I was unable to find it with another woman, not even my wife. Strange, that. Perhaps it was all in the mind. But it was powerful, unforgettable. So powerful that I described it to my wife once, and that was the biggest mistake I ever made.

The old man goes to sleep. His glass tilts further and weeps whisky onto his pullover, then slumps onto its side. A dark stain spreads over his clothes, onto his skin, but he feels nothing. The old man sleeps on...

silver

ALL my life he's been with me. For as long as I can remember – from our first day at school until now. He's almost part of me. Brother, friend, drinking buddy. We've shared wet days, dry days, a lot of happiness, some misery and at least three girl-friends. He's my mate. We've talked the talk and walked the walk. We've travelled in many lands together. Never equal but always compatible. He was the clever one. Miles ahead of me. Miles and miles in front.

His brain was a mystery to me and to nearly everyone else from the start, from our very first day together at infants' school. He saw things I never saw and he felt things I never felt. I wasn't the only one who realised he was special – for a while he was quite famous. Among his many talents was an amazing ability with maps and charts. He could look at a map, no matter what scale it was, and interpret it so brilliantly he could actually describe the landscape almost exactly as it was. I suppose he was a mystic, really, because he saw more than any map could possibly describe. He looked at that square yard of paper, which had taken cartographers years to compile, and he could form a picture of it immediately.

The Ordnance Survey made him into a bit of a celebrity on a TV show, and the army tried to use him too but he wasn't that type. The poor bloke had enough wars of his own to fight. But that knack of his was quite brilliant. Recently I came across a word which describes him perfectly – he was a *hierophant*: a man who could explain mysteries. He could decipher and enlighten. But as with all great minds, this wasn't enough. He wanted to take it a step further – into the unknown, into a realm of the brain which no-one had entered before. And that's when he went beyond my reach. After that I lost him, in a way. We weren't close again for a long time.

His descent started a few years ago, and I can tell you where – precisely. If we could find his battered old maps, which he used to keep in a locked cabinet by his bedside, I could find that house for you today. God knows where the maps are now, but he still has the key on a silver chain around his neck. He seemed always afraid of losing those maps, as if he'd die or get ill if they were taken away from him.

One day when we were sitting in his kitchen and he was recreating a map in his mind's eye – he used the word *imagining* – his forefinger fell on a solitary house in a certain part of the country which is far away from all the primary routes.

'You know something,' he said meditatively, 'I can see that house right now. It's something to do with its position in the landscape. It will always attract a certain sort of person. Location and all that. The way it faces towards the river, in a bit of a hollow. It feels lonely, patient, resilient. It's the sort of place which attracts compassionate people. Retired teachers. *Guardian* readers. People with empathy. They try to cheer it up. I can see bright colours. Turquoise curtains and outbuildings which are really bright red I think.'

He described the place in detail.

To cut a long story short, we got in my car and we went looking for that house. We didn't need a map, of course, because he took us there as truly as if we were guided by satnav. And when we found it, on a rather dangerous bend in the country, it became quickly apparent that he was absolutely right. We had to park in a lay-by for a while because someone had driven into a ditch and

I'd had to call the emergency services; but we stayed long enough to confirm his 'intuition'. I knew from the outset that he wasn't playing games; he was never a prankster and he disliked anything that smacked of dishonesty.

I left him at his door, expecting to see him the next day, but I didn't see him for a month. And when he reappeared he was a different person. He rang the doorbell at one in the morning, when I'd just dropped off to sleep, and I answered the door to a man who was almost dead on his feet, as if he'd just ran a mile with a pack of rottweilers behind him. When he recovered I gave him a bottle of brandy and a duvet because he was too far gone to make any sense that night. In the morning he'd disappeared, leaving a note which left out more than it said. I've still got it:

> Sorry about last night, thanks for putting me up. Owe you a bottle of booze. Can't tell you much at the moment but I broke into that house we went to and took it all a stage further. Very exciting. Old geezer asleep upstairs. As I thought – *Guardian* reader, film fan etc. Searched the place and eventually found what I wanted, some maps. Bullseye! Superb quality, among them an early Bartholomew chart of a region in Scotland. Beautiful. Took it with me and 'imagined' the place as well as I could in a night, then caught a train up north. Picked up a girl on the way, going to the same parts. Just been ill, on her way back home. Want you to meet her. She can do the same thing as me but with paintings, found she could do it when she was a kid, something to do with angels. Hah! The Scottish map took us to a wild part of the world. The place I 'imagined' turned out to be a croft with a rusty roof and little more than a woman inside it and an urn full of ashes – I'd predicted the woman but not the ashes. This time I didn't break in, telling the truth seemed easier so she invited us in and we stayed a couple of nights. Bit of a weirdo. Clairvoyant, read my hand. Not very good news at first but she says things will turn out OK in the end. We got some good lifts all the way back to Wales... then something strange happened – we got a ride

which took us past that house on the bend, the one with the red barn. The woman in Scotland had mentioned it. That house keeps on cropping up. Spooky or what! It's up for sale now. Anyway, must dash – will let you know what's happening ASAP.

Again, I heard nothing for several weeks. Then he arrived at my door again in a terrible state, shaking all over and covered in scratches. For a day he said virtually nothing, sitting in an old deckchair at the bottom of my garden, wrapped up warm in a rug. I managed to get some soup down him but he seemed stunned, and he was a lot thinner than before. I got just a few facts from him; he'd lost the girl during an escapade which had nearly cost him his life. Wishing to go one step further again, to push the boundaries of his world, he'd visited the council archives and studied – for days, it transpired – an antique map of the nearest city, and then he'd imagined it as it was in the early 1900s. Unable to speak by now, he wrote a note to me laboriously on a notepad I gave him, and I was shocked to see that his handwriting was in copperplate:

On May the first, shortly after four in the afternoon, I successfully 'imagined' the northern suburbs, including a section of the promenade, sometime in the past. It was the first time I'd tried this technique and I didn't get it quite right – there was a time warp and I became confused over which age I was in. I entered the area during Victorian or Edwardian times; the very first man I saw was wearing a homburg hat and an astrakhan coat. The street names seemed to be in French, which I cannot account for; perhaps the map I studied had been lying next to a map of France. I followed the man – who looked remarkably like my father – and watched him enter a house. Finding my way to the back of this house, via a back alley which I had stored in my memory, I climbed over the garden wall and hid in the shrubbery, from where I witnessed a statue being unveiled in front of a large group of people. While I was watching them my experiment began to fail, due to a lack of concentration I think. The scene in front of me faded and I found myself in the present. At this point I noticed a wonderful aroma wafting from the same house – delicious chocolatey smells, which were so intoxicating I made my way to the back door and knocked, overcome with a desire to taste the cake being made inside that house. I was so absorbed in my own thoughts that I failed to foresee what the reaction might be to a stranger appearing out of thin air, so when I came face to face with a rather frail old woman she screamed and started to lunge at me with a chocolate-covered knife. I ran away as fast as my legs would carry me, through the next garden along, which is why I'm covered in scratches.

With this he burst into tears and struggled past me, pushing me out of the way. That glimpse of his tearstained face was the last I saw of him for six months or more.

In early December I responded to a stern rat-a-tat on my door and opened it to a distressing scene. Two policemen, looking as if they meant business, stood on either side of him; he was handcuffed to one of them. I invited them in but they declined, wanting only confirmation of my friend's identity. After I told them his name and last known address they took him away to the police station, and I was allowed to see him only briefly after all the interviews were over.

It seems that he'd led a wandering existence based on crude maps he'd picked up at tourist information offices. He'd been to the Loire Valley, picking fruit, and many other places in Europe. In a bizarre twist, he'd felt so homesick while in Spain he'd stolen a map of Britain from a library in Madrid so that he could gain enough impetus to return home. He 'imagined' a place in Snowdonia so well that he soon found himself living in a hut somewhere in the mountains, where he'd been found by a man inspecting a new wind farm up on the moors. He'd nearly starved to death, and was hallucinating by now, imagining that he was living with angels.

After his visit to the police station my friend disappeared from sight for a long time, almost a year. The seasons came and went, and I'd almost forgotten about him when I received a letter from a hospital to the south of the country. This is what it said:

Dear C,

I beg of you one last favour. My journeys have got me into trouble again, and I'm in a hospital somewhere but I cannot find my way back home. After promising the magistrate never to look at a map again I did keep my vow, but one day I started looking at some of my old school text books and came across a map I'd drawn in pencil when I was in primary school, showing all the rivers of Wales. Unfortunately I found it impossible to resist temptation so off I went again. I was doing fine until I was taken in for questioning after being caught on private land. Eventually they brought me here in a van with no windows so I've lost the thread of my journey and no amount of imagining will get me home again. So I'm trapped without a map to get myself out again. PLEASE help me. They won't even let me out in the garden. Can you find me? I want to come home now.

Your old friend, A.

It took no great feat of intelligence to trace him, and I found him in a psychiatric unit in Carmarthenshire – the silly sod had been following the River Teifi from the mountains to the sea. He was overwhelmed with emotion when he saw me and cried with gratitude, holding on to my arm as if he feared I would go without him. Passing myself off as his brother again, I eventually secured his release and took him home with me. He seemed to get better and by the end of the year I'd found him somewhere to live in a block of council flats at the other end of town. I went to see him now and again, and was saddened by the slow change in him. By then he was hitting the bottle quite heavily and I'm not sure if he was fully sane. He was telling me a great deal about his fellow residents, not that he'd met them. Having vowed never to touch any form of map ever again he'd turned to the postal service, in the way an alcoholic moves from whisky to meths. It transpired he was 'imagining' his neighbours from their mail, their newspapers, and any other documents he came across, such as delivery notes. He was particularly interested in a sleepwalking builder on the top floor.

When I arrived at his flat one day the place had been boarded up. But it didn't take too much 'imagining' to know where he was. I found him at the local hospital, in a sorry state again, having succumbed to the booze and general despair. Again I had to lie, telling them I was his brother so they would let me in to visit him. He was in a six-bed unit with a motley crew around him, people he seemed to know quite well already – there's a camaraderie among the sick if they're well enough to care. They all looked at me as if it was my fault, so he introduced them with a certain dignity, something he'd always done well; it was the child in him. They were a bunch of freaks, worse than him.

Next to him was a woman being visited by a strange-looking man in a pork pie hat and white trainers clutching a posy of sweet peas. Over the aisle there was a bloke who looked surprisingly like a Mexican, having a blood transfusion, then an old man who was really ill, surrounded by monitors.

Look, I said to him, after a bit of a chat, this lot are in a worse state than you. But there's hope yet. I've got an idea.

It meant taking him home to my place, cleaning him up, and getting him off the booze. He was pretty desperate by now and he wanted to live, so he agreed.

I gave him a clean batch of clothes and he moved into my spare room. I also gave him a map, a camera, an artist's set and plenty of paper. And then I drove him around Wales for a month until he'd got the hang of what I wanted.

What I'd bought him was the Ordnance Survey's historical map of Ancient Britain, showing all the Mesolithic, Neolithic, Bronze Age, Iron Age, Roman and Medieval sites in the whole island. All he had to do when we got to those places was to imagine them in the past.

He took to it like a duck to water and produced an outstanding body of work which has been used by almost every publisher in the land. He's a contented man these days, gone a bit thick round the middle and prone to afternoon naps.

But he's back among the sane again, and he's in the land of the living. Sitting with my back to a standing stone on Anglesey one day I told him the worst secret I'd ever kept to myself – that I'd slept with his ex-wife one night in the distant past.

I know, he said calmly as he sketched a vibrant mass of people eating frog and fish stew at a spot not so far from us. I've known for a long, long time.

It transpired that his wife and I had gone for a walk soon after our misdemeanour, using one of his maps, and he'd been able to imagine what had happened from the way we'd folded it.

He even made a sketch of the scene, with the two of us talking about what we'd done and deciding that we'd never ever tell him.

His gift is stronger than ever now, but he's learnt how to use it in a way which gives pleasure to himself and other people too. Life has a funny way of surprising us. After he was released from hospital he continued to call on the ward for a while to visit the people he'd met. He came home glum one afternoon because the old man had died and most of the others had gone home. I was worried in case he started to drink again. But in the following weeks he returned a happier man every time. The sole remaining person – the woman in the next bed to him – was making a steady recovery and was expected to live, against all odds. My friend seemed very happy about this, and he's been cheerful ever since. I think maybe there's a love interest by now. Initially he'd been touched by her devastating story – she'd had to close her post office business, and her husband had run off with someone else at the same time as she'd become ill. She'd almost given up. But she was on the mend, and in their mutual catastrophe they'd found friendship... maybe more. She was going to buy a house in the country, and he was thinking of moving in with her.

Life goes on, he said to me yesterday, with a pastel crayon in one hand and a beautiful drawing in the other. He folded the map away carefully and sat in the sun for a while, looking at me. And then he smiled that old smile of his again, and went indoors to make us both a cup of tea.

Essays

north ~ south ~ east ~ west

north

I WENT north into Liverpool Bay on board a great little ship which pulls in the water as a ratting terrier strains at the leash. I spent a day on the sea, and it was good.

A few years ago I walked completely around Wales, a journey of a thousand miles, and then I walked across the land seven times. The next journey to take my fancy was a trip around my homeland on the water, by sea and canal. I'm not sure why; in an age of great uncertainty maybe it's a way of seeing with my own eyes what's going on. I'm a journalist, and the original reporters, or *intelligencers*, were little more than spies.

With me as I started this jaunt was the actor Steve Huison – the tall ginger one in *The Full Monty*. As we surged through the Menai Straits, graveyard of so many ships, I saw him swallow a tablet. Yes, the man who can face any audience without qualms gets sick in a boat. Conversely, I can bob up and down on the water without a care in the world – but put me in front of an audience and I'll sicken and quake. Thank god we're all different.

We were on a day trip from Caernarfon to Liverpool on the Balmoral, a pleasure boat which plies her trade around the coast of Britain. Built just after the second world war, she was pensioned off as a floating restaurant in Dundee for a while – and having tasted captivity she's enjoying her freedom again, waltzing through the water in a *when I am an old woman I shall wear purple* sort of mood. Amazingly, this svelte little ship can take up to 750 passengers, but the cargo that day was smallish, a motley crew of people, mainly middle aged and Welsh; we might have been a handful of west-coast families heading for Liverpool and the New World two centuries ago, escaping poverty and the perennial religious divides which plague mankind. I spent a day on the water with those disparate people, most of them whiling away the hours of retirement, some of them reinforcing a long friendship with the sea. There is a nakedness about people's faces when they're on ships: performance is abandoned and everyone reverts to type for a while. Eyes glaze over, faces slacken; we all become versions of the ancient mariner, scanning the sky for an albatross. The vessel's heartbeat throbs through our feet and travels up our legs towards our own little engine rooms. Slightly tipsy and flushed after her leaving party, our ship blew bubbles coarsely in her bath and emitted a big wet fart when she departed. To emphasise our exodus from little old Wales, the crewmen crackled in Russian, Polish and Lithuanian as the Balmoral detached herself from a spiderish web of ropes glued to the harbour wall.

After picking up passengers at Menai Bridge and escaping through the jaws of the Straits we saw our pilot, Richard Jones, hop onto a charter boat which zoomed alongside; Richard is the seventh generation of his family to do this romantic but dangerous job. After threading our way through a flotilla of canoes, a burst necklace of colour on the polished surface of the sea, we dashed between Puffin and Penmon, towards the open sea. Almost immediately a smoky pall descended on us, isolating us from the landmass, which soon seemed no more than a bulky presence – a sleeping Hitchcock behind a stage curtain. Divorced from the land, I leant on a rail and dwelt on the future. I'd been restless of late, unable to find a comfortable bed, rotating on the spot as a dog tends to do, twirling around in its basket before settling down for the night. As the ship disappeared into a sea-gloom I mulled on the meaning of the word *north* – a word which actually came from the east, spilling from the mouths of prehistoric Indo-Europeans whose root word *ner* probably meant *to the left of the rising sun.*

North is one of the four cardinal points but let's not forget *here* as a place; neither should we forget the navel or *omphalos*, also an important spot on the map. Both Wales and Britain have a traditional north-south divide. England's halfway mark, famously, is Watford. There's a tradition that Wales' belly button is Pumlumon, which I see as a rather boggy centre circle on a football pitch, with the goals at Cardiff and Bangor. Aberystwyth is the spot where the ref blows his whistle to start the game. Historically, in Western culture, north is regarded as *the* fundamental direction and it defines all other directions.

But I tend to think of north as a place, not a direction. If you look at a political map of Britain it's clear that the north and west are more 'liberal' and left-leaning than the rest of the island. There are almost no Conservative MPs in Scotland, Wales or South-West England, and socialism as a concept is stronger in those regions. No doubt the main factor is the historic poverty of the outlying areas; but I have a notion that the matriarchal Celts nurtured a healthy concept of fairness when it came to land ownership, since they practised gavelkind – the division of land between a dead man's sons, including those who were illegitimate. It was the nauseating Normans who brought the curse of primogeniture to Britain – the inheritance of all property by the eldest son. This led to great power and wealth being concentrated in a few hands, and set the scene for modern imperialistic Britain with its male-dominated, pyramidical power structures, ranging from companies with their managing directors to most families and societies. But I'm not talking about historical accuracy here; I'm describing my perceptions of the north. I was born in the north and I live in the north; I am in thrall to *the pale, unripened beauties of the North* as Addison put it. Besides, could David Lloyd George have been forged in Kent? I think not. Nonconformism also played a part in generating a breed of regional rabble-rousers, republicans, radicals and anarchists. Jac Glan-y-Gors is my personal favourite, a satirical poet and pamphleteer who spent much of his life running the Canterbury Arms at Southwark. Jac was a bar-room fundamentalist who led a spiritual and political pilgrimage to his own pre-communist version of the promised land. He was a six-pint socialist, as the South Walians say.

A ship's rail is a great place to enjoy a five-star reverie and I remember leaning and mulling, looking at the faint trace of the shoreline around my home in Llanfairfechan. I'd recently enjoyed a cuppa with the violin maker and restorer Dewi Roberts, who lives with his musical family on the foreshore at Aber. At some stage he handed me a violin and invited me to play it. It was such a sweet instrument I almost managed to sound competent. I asked where he'd acquired it.

It belonged to a Mr Melville Cooper, who died recently, said Dewi.

And my mind flew back, over forty years, to an upstairs room at Llanrwst Grammar School, where a peripatetic music teacher known to me as Mr Cooper, patient and kind, had instructed me in the basics of violin-playing – and instilled in me a lifelong love for a few bits of wood which, glued together, can make such a beautiful sound. I learnt the violin merely to dodge treble physics. As I played Mr Cooper's violin in Dewi's house I became aware that I'd been a young boy when I'd last held this instrument in my hands – deeply unhappy, and willing to spend many hours in my own company, with a fiddle, merely to escape from the world. A lot had happened in forty years, and Mr Cooper's violin was a link between two very different people, both of them me: a troubled teenager, on the verge of running away from his father, and a middle-aged man sawing away at wood and words, finding happiness in small things after a circuitous life-journey.

Out on the sea that day, aboard the Balmoral, our trip became a journey into smoke, a nether world of Hadean gloom. Even out there, on the wide watermass, man is encroaching. Wind farms and oil rigs clutter the water meadows of the wine-dark sea. Our last clear horizon is becoming obscured by man's relentless colonisation.

And then we came to land again, and the dream was over. We docked at the Pier Head after a calm and uneventful passage into the Mersey estuary, with an elderly and very lame Liverpudlian excitedly pointing out all the landmarks.

After that journey into Liverpool Bay I was to embark on a series of mini adventures, in search of something which was intangible. First of all, I was determined to conquer my fear of flying so I flew out to Italy with my teenage daughter. It's never going to be my number one hobby, but now I can take to the air without going to pieces. Bravery was never my strong point.

Rome is a gigantic ruin, a huge heap of stones, a coliseum within a coliseum within a coliseum. And a parable too: the Vatican City is encrusted with precious stones, a citadel of wealth, while outside its massive walls the city is awash with beggars, alcoholics and thieves. While the Pope fiddles, Rome burns; twice we were robbed. After four days of stumbling around this great ruptured mausoleum we found Florence and Pisa besieged by humans, vast termite mounds of tourists being hassled into culture. We escaped to the west coast and found a place to relax, a nice little clifftop town called Castiglioncello, on the rim of Tuscany; just about everyone hit the beach during the day to swim, sleep, or to parade their physical wares; then the whole town came to life at night in a warm, dreamlike sanctuary of bar babble, book stalls and fairy lights. It was nice to be with normal Italian people. Close by are the 'mountains of marble' from which Michelangelo ordered his raw materials. I know it's a beautiful country, but I couldn't live in Italy for long. All that heat. So little damp greenery. So few sheep. So many excessively right-wing people…

Whilst flying over the Dolomites I became aware how childish my geography is. Looking at a map or a globe, I still think of the north as 'higher up' than the south, and I think of Cardiff as being lower down, geographically, than Bangor – as if I were observing the south from an eyrie in Snowdonia. Of course I know this is nonsense but I can't dislodge the notion without making a conscious effort. These are the misconceptions of childhood, echoing down the years.

After our trip to Italy the wandering continued. I jumped on a plane with Edwin and Ella, the youngsters in my life, and headed for Prague. We meandered around this beautiful baroque city, lost in another world. I realised during those five days why I've been such a poor traveller all my life. I'm not good at moving between worlds. Maybe this has something to do with my upbringing, on a remote hill farm; maybe not, since I've seen TV footage of Amazonian tribesmen wandering around New York, completely unfazed. Prague reminded me a little of Britain thirty years ago; the Czech people are mostly conservatively dressed, friendly but dignified. The great god Mammon hasn't quite got the place by the throat yet. Another thing that's really noticeable: there are hardly any black people. We 'did' Prague – the famous clock, the churches, the puppet shows, the jazz bands; we sauntered along Charles Bridge at dusk and watched hot air balloon flights over the river; we listened to musicians, we made way for a Hare Krishna sect snaking its way through the crowd, chanting and beating drums. It was nice to get my first sight of onion domes with the kids, since it made me feel young and still capable of wonder. Then I stood in St Vitus Cathedral, within the castle complex, and I was overwhelmed by the sheer mass of the place. It's vast by any standards. Huge. Standing inside its hush, I became aware of the importance of stone in man's journey through the world. All around me lay millions of tons of dressed stone, piled into patterns which have different meanings for each succeeding age. I was overwhelmed by stone – its bulk, its martial presence, its dictatorship over the senses. I became aware of the enormous reservoirs of human energy tapped to make all the stone buildings of man. Standing in this gothic edifice, which took almost 600 years to complete, I was numbed by stone. On a lesser scale, perhaps this was how my ancestors felt when they first engineered the masterpieces of Neolithic Wales – the 150 or so cromlechi in the country.

We stepped out of the cathedral and wandered around the rest of the castle buildings.

Inside the White Tower we learnt about Katerina Bechynova, a cruel woman who murdered fourteen people, mainly young girls (she was said to cut their skin with a knife and put salt in the wounds). Katerina was lowered to the bowels of this tower to die of starvation, thirst, and cold. One of its more famous prisoners, according to legend, was the bogus necromancer Edward Kelly, nemesis of the Welsh-blooded alchemist John Dee, who has a chapter all to himself in history.

But I was more interested in the tale of the Dalibor Tower, named after a man who was sentenced to death and imprisoned there for giving shelter to rebel peasants. It's a sad but lovely story. Every day, as he waited to be executed, Dalibor played his violin, and the people of the city were moved deeply by the beautiful music which poured from his lonesome tower. He became famous and the authorities repeatedly delayed the execution, fearing civil disorder. But then, one day, Dalibor's fiddle fell silent and the people of Prague had a little less light in their lives. By his silence, they knew he was dead.

My wanderings were nearly over: the year was coming to an end. Our last trip was to Robin Hood's Bay on the eastern seaboard of England, for a reunion and birthday – nine of us, ranging from fogies like me to young Tom, aged four, staying in the youth hostel at nearby Boggle Hole. We wandered around the quaint streets and narrow ginnels of this old fishing town, which suffers from exactly the same second homes problem as most of Wales.

Smuggling was a way of life here once and the womenfolk

apparently poured boiling water from their bedroom windows to fend off the excise men; contraband could pass from one end of the town to the other without leaving the houses.

We admired their homes, charmingly quaint and huddled close together as if forever awaiting the last tempest; we ate fish and chips and we borrowed a bucket and spade from the street-side repositories provided by thoughtful locals; we built sandcastles, caught crabs, joked and bantered, took photographs. At some stage my daughter and I peeled off to comb the crumbling cliff-edge for fossils, an east coast speciality.

As we stumbled around in the scree, heads bowed, scanning the stones, our hands met and curled around each other: we hadn't done that for a while and the sudden convergence of fingers felt natural and good, surprising us both with its power and warmth. We became father and child again, rather than two people orbiting each other. We looked at each other and smiled, acknowledging this moment. At the same time I noticed many other things held in an age-old clasp around us: sea meeting shore, shells closing and knitting, the people around us darning friendships, using new words to bind old feelings. During the ensuing night my daughter and I both had nightmares about each other, dreams of danger. Was there a significance in that? Every time we experience a perfect conjunction, hand meeting hand unexpectedly, does the inner mind always freeze the final frame and imagine the worst possible scenario that might follow? Do we pause to think, unconsciously, about that final moment when each of us, from mammoth to trilobite, from human to mouse, is grasped by mud and stitched into place, a knot of bone in the rock-hard Bayeux of the untouchable past?

The journey has ended for now; I still haven't finished the voyage around Wales by water. Perhaps I never will. Winter came and we all went back to our homes. I rather like the eleventh century Irish story about Athairne going on a journey in the autumn to the home of his foster-father Amhairgen. As Athairne prepares to leave, Amhairgen finds a reason to detain him because he doesn't want to lose his company; so Athairne stays for the whole season, and when he prepares to leave, Amhairgen finds another ruse to keep him there for the winter, and yet another for the spring too. But when Athairne prepares to leave in the early summer Amhairgen lets him go, saying: *A good season is summer for long journeys; quiet is the tall fine wood, which the whistle of the wind will not stir; green is the plumage of the sheltering wood; eddies swirl in the stream; good is the warmth of the turf.*

The year's restlessness has been quenched, the door has been locked and the fire lit. There will be no more a-roving before the spring. So I've started playing the violin again. It's not the first violin I ever owned, though I still have that too – I bought it when I was a young boy, from a man living in Llanfairfechan, little thinking that years later, when I was twenty-six, I would come to this town again for a day visit and stay for the next thirty years. I often pass that house where I bought my first violin and see a little boy in an upstairs window, with a fiddle tucked under his chin. Our eyes meet. I wish I could ring the doorbell and meet that little boy, tell him that everything will work out all right, that life will be worth living. I want to tell him that he will surge through later life in a *when I am old I shall wear purple* sort of mood.

Yes, that little boy is me. Never wanting to be far from each other, we both still live in the north.

south

I WENT south to the Black Mountains in May, when the whole country lay as still as moss on a tombstone, and the greens were countless. Tawny owls sounded all night in the cloisters of Capel y Ffin and a green woodpecker cackled by day. I knew from the first morning that a special time was upon me: I felt a calm clemency below the wide blue sky. For the first time in many years I met a woman I desired, an old-yet-new feeling which arrived, embarrassed and flustered, like a latecomer to a concert.

I was staying in the country's oldest youth hostel, due to close that autumn. Standing on Gospel Pass I surveyed the wooded cleft of the Vale of Ewyas, scraped out by meltwater and bearing almost as many Christian symbols as a saint's festival in Spain. But I felt nothing of its holy past, not up there. Great change was afoot. I met a farrier-publican who told me that the old families were disappearing rapidly and centuries of border Welsh tradition were coming to an end; as if to illustrate his words, I noticed a large farm being renovated meticulously near Cwmyoy Church, at huge expense. A millionaire, I was told. New money was flooding into Ewyas, as it was pouring into the rest of Wales; it was a time of plenty for builders and a time of lean for the old and tetchy as they witnessed a disappearing world.

On the first day I walked down to Hay with the Bluff on my right and Lord Hereford's Knob on my left, on a morning as sharp and bright as fresh linen drying in a sunny garden. Bullfinches and goldfinches flitted upwards into the hawthorn bushes as I walked on, and there were warblers everywhere. I snacked on wild strawberries shaded by the roadside flowers – including yellow archangel – and my spirits roared. Down below the pass I met a tall man with a white moustache standing by his camper van; he willingly took my camera and snapped me with Hay Bluff rearing up behind my back. Five years previously I'd spent one of the happiest hours of my life sitting up there with the patchwork fields of Wales at my feet and a miniature farmer on a Lilliputian horse whistling to his dogs in the amphitheatre below. I'd travelled without a camera then, and this was an effort to recapture the past, but it didn't work, because the image was sterile – in fact I felt rather like a revisionist, distorting history for my own ends.

Having your older body photographed as you stand awkwardly in revisited places is the closest you'll ever get, probably, to experiencing multiple lives, as a new image – a palimpsest – overlays an older one in the memory. On the way into Hay I encountered two attractive women taking a small dog for a walk, and felt smitten. Maybe the sunshine was infiltrating my hormones; maybe the change of scenery was sharpening my senses. Maybe I was in the mood for love – or maybe I was just an old fool, I thought to myself as I surveyed a broad reddish weal slashing the countryside from left to right – the new gas pipeline. Traversing South Wales, from Milford Haven to Gloucestershire, this 197-mile tube was due to cost about £700 million when completed. A few men would make a lot of money and the plebs would pay, as usual. Trying not to get upset over the rape of Wales (a full-time occupation these days) I reminded myself that the Amlwch-Stanlow pipeline which went through North Wales in much the same fashion thirty years ago is almost completely anonymous now, in fact few remember it's still there. Back to the here and now: Italian welders working on the new pipeline were getting £500 a shift, I was told by locals. Rumours abounded of fabulous wages, and the natives were agog as they passed the news from ear to ear.

Down in Hay I popped into a store and chatted to the woman at the till; she was a Welsh-speaker from my own region and I asked her what she was doing among the southren folk. She'd traced her father after more than thirty years' separation, she said, so she'd settled here. Wondrous news; a new life superimposed on an older one; a picture within a picture. I wanted to hear her story, but she was busy dealing with an infestation of bookworms attending the annual Hay Festival.

On the second day the youth hostel was full of people from the Central London Outdoor Group, who were trying to recreate the capital's rush hour traffic conditions in the kitchen, as if they were an urban re-enactment society. It was Sunday and the heavens had opened in the night – we had the wettest day of the month loitering outside the windows of our hostel, a squat old farmhouse lodged on a sharp incline. There are otters in the area, apparently, and I considered joining them for a good soak in the nature reserve close by. Instead I onioned myself in a double skin of coats and walked down to Llanthony Priory. Conditions were dramatically different from the previous day: I bobbed through a waterfest extreme enough to suit Noah himself, and my ears were caroused by the splish and splash of a trillion raindrops. The road-tunnel through the dripping trees gleamed with sheets of shape-shifting floodwater, and hawthorn blossom, dashed from the trees, lay all around me like confetti at a mermaid's wedding. Because this is a region of red sandstone (in the deep past it lay at the delta of a vast river) the water was terracotta red where it stood in puddles. The valley is also a busy equine centre and hoof-prints decorated the ground here and there in red crescents. The ever-present cow parsley plants, weighed down with water, bowed their umbelliferous heads penitently on either side of me. Wet? You know it's utterly wet when there's no point sheltering under trees. First stop was the entrancing church at Capel-y-Ffin, a pocket venus with teddy bears on the organ and lovely posies in the windows. Two small headstones in the churchyard were carved by the typographer, artist and pervert Eric Gill.

At Llanthony I joined an American party who ignored me studiously in the ribcage of the ecclesiastic skeleton, then I padded around the drab little church alongside, built on the site of St David's early cell. What did they live on, those holy men – handouts from the local serfs? No Tesco, no weekly Giro. Still, they didn't have to hang around waiting for planning permission, or a delivery from Jewsons. There's a hotel glued incongruously to the side of the priory complex, and the whole place is a sort of Blue Peter cut-and-paste model gone wrong. If you want to learn how the arrival of someone with loads of dosh and big ideas can seriously piss off the locals, read about the Victorian writer Walter Savage Landor's involvement with this site. Famously temperamental, he is caricatured in Dickens' Bleak House.

Onwards and downwards I stumped to the fantastical little church at Cwmyoy, bent out of shape by convulsions in the bedrock below – the tower leans drunkenly and 'no part of it is square or at right angles with any other part'. A seventeenth-century monument to a local man, waiting to be called up to heaven, bears this verse:

Thomas Price he takes his nap in our common mother's lap waiting to heare the bridegroome say awake my dear and come away.

Charmingly, the words mo/ther, bri/degroome and a/wake are all broken, signifying an age which was less obsessive-compulsive about straight lines, superficial appearances and passing fads.

Just like my own photomontage near Hay Bluff, histories have been superimposed onto each other within this building. I quote a church pamphlet:

The medieval cross in the centre of the church was discovered in 1871 at the nearby farm. It is thought to be one of the crosses on the Pilgrim Way to St David's. It was transferred to the Vicarage garden, and eventually in 1935, placed in the Tower inside the church. In 1967 the cross disappeared, but not before a photograph of it was taken. This photograph was shown to the Keeper of the Sculptuary at the British Museum, and the Keeper not only dated it as being 13th century, but also said he had seen the cross in an antique dealer's shop in London. From there it was recovered. The original thieves were never traced.

From Cwmyoy I laboured over the ridge to the Grwyne Valley to visit the famous church at Partrishow, in a field by a farm. It was too wet to visit St Issui's famous well because the rain had become passionate; besides, I remembered that Issui was murdered by an ungrateful traveller who had received hospitality in his humble cell, and such stony fables as these can gather much moss on wet green Sundays in Wales.

The church, which has a magnificently carved screen, also has a starkly medieval representation of Time painted on the west wall of the nave – a skeletal figure with a scythe, hourglass and spade, meant to be a macabre reminder to the illiterate peasants that the wages of sin are death. Again, I quote the church pamphlet:

The artists were itinerant painters. Their range of colours was limited. We find a lot of red and ochre. These were earth colours, easily dug up. Black was provided by soot from lamps. James I ordered that all such 'Popish Devices' should be white-washed over, and suitable texts painted there instead. At Patricio today, we have a number of such texts, but if you look carefully you can still see traces of these pre-Reformation paintings pushing their way through the white-wash around the texts.

Tired by now and half soaked, I realised that I'd bitten off more than I could chew, and getting back was likely to be an ordeal. The ridge loomed above me Everest-high and the rain intensified, seething in drainpipes and overpowering the pathways. But fortune smiled on me, as if I had offered prayers and been rewarded (though I am a rank atheist, oddly invested with a great love of churches). I was joined in the chamber by two marriage-related families and we all poked around politely, trying to make room for one another, tinkling money into wall safes and studying ancient artefacts in the gloom. I must have looked forlorn, for mercifully one of them, a Maesteg physiotherapist, offered me a lift back to Cwmyoy, his family cramming into the back of their steamy car so that I could be accommodated. Their children looked at me as if I were a strange antediluvian monster or a coelacanth netted during a storm at sea. But boy was I grateful. I stuck my thumb out at Cwmyoy and the first car which came along took me all the way up the valley to the youth hostel. I outdid the sky in outpourings, in my case a deluge of gratitude.

After I'd peeled off everything soggy I put wedges of cheese in some bread donated by departing people and chewed contentedly, greeting the London lot as they dribbled back to the glimmering kitchen. A sheep and her lamb stared cynically at us through the window, unimpressed by this moving tableau in their upland Tate. Soon I was in a scene from Good Companions, or sheltering in a smoky inn of old as travellers found sanctuary, a safe house secreted in a gauze of wet white mist. One of them had a fresh round face which reminded me of the gilded angels down there in the churches, painted in vegetable dyes by local artisans; the bright naive colours are still optimistic and fresh, but the painters' formula was lost over 150 years ago. A woman among our company, Jewish and musical, made the magnet in my compass lurch around and the bread was dense in my mouth. Too late, I thought. Too late on a wet day in Wales. If there's such as thing as regret without melancholy, but with a touch of hiraeth perhaps, I felt it then. Like the walk I had planned along the tops of the Black Mountains that day, it was best left to that part of the brain which deals with what might have been; the mind's draughtsman, sketching glorious plans for an idle master who never goes beyond the dreaming stage. The older version of me sitting at that table thought of the young man who had been able to contemplate such things. I was a coat of whitewash daubed over him. My desire was merely an old fresco on a church wall, seeping though to the surface many years later.

On the third day I walked down to Hay Festival, in sunshine again. This time I knelt by flowers in a field by the Craswall turn-off and took photographs of spotted orchids with slender green beetles nosing around their nectar cups. My sojourn was drawing to an end and my name was being called out in the classroom again. Society needed to check my credentials: it was time to sign on for my small dole of public recognition. My attempts at self-expression had engendered a strange baby – a book which had little resonance among the people around me (and was therefore a failure, presumably) while winning the approval of competition judges (and was therefore a success, presumably). I did the interviews and played the game, but I was unconvinced by my own patter. I watched the literati come and go, talking of Michelangelo, many in long gabardines and bushwhacker hats; I felt inadequate and micro in this macro setting, this town-sized Petri dish gathering clumps of etymological growths. I watched throngs of people in bookshops and on pavements, within pubs and in large white literary tents, patterns of iron filings grouped around hidden magnets. Words were important, yes I knew that. Probably our last stab at democracy. But their piling up in this place was an artifice and a conjuration; the festival tents were a glossy dental enamel painted on the yellow teeth of literary endeavour: a snowstorm of words come to earth without wonder. There was a sense of over-feasting, of the castle hiding its caried teeth with a genteel hand and sighing; when the belch came it would be described fulsomely, in the chatter of the cover blurbs, *extraordinary* or *vivid*, or even worse, the dreaded *remarkable achievement*.

So I took my smallness away homewards. I hitched a lift to Abergavenny and it was good to walk around the busy streets. Alexander Cordell listened to these people and was inspired. Among them I saw relics of the past, walking as if they were ghosts: rustics with check caps aslant and sticks in their gnarled hands – the farmers of old, a hobbitry of endangered beings, each taking with him, to be burnt, a book of discreet knowledge, the lore of planting and reaping, hedging and husbandry.

In the train, almost alone, travelling in heavy sunshine, I saw the south recede, hedgerow by hedgerow, stream by stream, sheep by sheep. On my map of the Black Mountains I had smoothed down a new transfer tracing my spoor – fresh signs and markings, a gloss on the earlier chart. I would keep that new picture of myself by Hay Bluff to mark the lesson it had taught me in emotional triangulation, and for no other reason. But again and again I would seek to recreate the experience of sitting on the bluff on a summer morning in 2002, with a year of living dangerously spread out to dry below me.

The woman in the Spar, who went south to find her father, will stay with me – as will the Jewish viola player. Their footprints are on my map, moving away from me at the crossroads. But the people I will remember best are nameless, faceless.

One of them is the unknown carver, perhaps Welsh, perhaps Flemish, perhaps Italian according to some sources, who carved his soul on the Irish oak screen at Patricio Church for considerably less than £500 a shift; a craftsman who worked a pattern of wooden flowers of great delicacy, and imprinted on his bresummer beam a dragon, signifying evil, consuming a vine, the emblem of good. And when I consider the figure of Time on the wall, faded but still clearly discernible, I think of the unknown painter in that greatly underrated film, *A Month in the Country*. Those travelling artisans will forever be unknown, but their anonymity carries a certain power, a voltage which still illuminates a rare and singular lamp, unwired to any mains.

There is another figure I will remember, with golden hair and golden wings, a girdle of gold around her plump waist too. Hovering in mid-air, she blows a golden trumpet but still she manages a lop-sided smile from a rubicund face; her dress billows around her, and her cheeks are flushed with girlish effort.

She is a country girl going to heaven; she is a medieval angel painted on a memorial at Cwmyoy Church.

A few days after I wrote these words – a fresh inscription on the walls of my own life – I became aware that the anonymous, long-dead artisans of the Black Mountains were already seeping though my handiwork, just as their murals had re-emerged through the pious scripts in the Church of Merthyr Issui at Patricio. It is their work which will survive, not mine – and that's just fine with me.

So I will make myself busy again, and move on.

east

I WENT east to the border country, where I saw the biggest box of cornflakes in Wales, possibly the universe.

They could have filmed *Aliens* in it. An immense hangar full of flaked-out people working for a corny old American corporation – the Kellogg's factory.

Other industrial units lie all around: as I passed by I couldn't help wondering how many people actually enjoy working in them. Not many, I suspect. Instead of tricking people into a life-time's servitude with baubles and mirrors (the old slavery) the trick nowadays is to get people to labour all day making baubles and mirrors which they then buy back for ten times their value (the new slavery). What do the words freedom and democracy mean in such a context?

As I entered north-east Wales along the Expressway I felt the arteries tighten and clog with dirty lorries (*also available in white* scrawled on one of them) and stressed-out company men bumper-surfing, scuttling between the mass-produced tin shacks they work in nowadays, their cars badging their status: you're no-one unless you drive a BMW. All of them trying to look busy in one of capitalism's eddy pools. And if I sound like William Cobbett repeating his rural rides in t-shirt and trainers, so be it. In my nice bauble-filled flat I'm a beneficiary like everyone else, and I'll acknowledge the hypocrisy. But deep down I know the price is too high, and so do most of us. What happens when people take a wrong turning? They end up on the industrial estate. That's an urban joke, by the way.

I'm in Wrexham Maelor to meet a man who was born way out west, on Bardsey Island, a place with no factories or pollution, and almost no people either. A place of dreams and flowers, saints and birds of passage – mystical and part mythical.

His name is Bob Williams, and his journey from a mini-paradise on the western seaboard to a landlocked industrial city is a paradigm for the age we live in.

Now, for the first time in man's complicated history, more people live in urban areas than in the countryside. And look at the consequences.

Bob was the last boy-child to be born on Bardsey, and I'm visiting him at his home in Maes Brenin, Pentre Maelor, on the outskirts of the industrial estate, near Wrexham. We're only a couple of miles from the confluence of the Clywedog and the meandering Dee, which doodles a slow squiggle – the border with England.

Bob lives on a large and well-designed estate, airy and confident, built for key workers who went there to work in the new factories after the last war.

The name, Maes Brenin, means king's meadow. And I'm reminded that Bob's old home, Bardsey, had its own elected kings – complete with ornate crown – from about 1800 onwards. The last, and most famous of them, was Love Pritchard, who died in 1926. Apparently he volunteered himself and all the men of Bardsey for military service in the first world war, but was rejected – at seventy-one he was considered too old. According to legend he was so incensed he declared Bardsey a neutral power and may even have sworn allegiance to the German Kaiser.

But I've rushed into the story, and that's a mistake. I've careered along the Expressway and charged willy-nilly into a half-baked critique of modern life. So let me start again, only slowly. That's the trick: to take a stroll around the garden, sniff the early morning air, wash the dishes, tidy up a bit, have a little read. Let's slow it all down.

This is how my day starts: with a summer dawn gathering strength on the other side of the multi-coloured curtains in my bedroom. The hues in the fabric embolden slowly, giving a soft stained-glass effect. Then I go back to sleep, until seven or there-abouts. As I get older I'm slowing down, and the waking process is less dynamic. I'm turning into a sloth, after years of springing out of bed, getting the kids ready, making their lunch boxes, getting them ready for life in the rat race. But now I drift into the world on my own stately bashed-about barge. As the world comes into focus I sense an oxygenated freshness and a new sky, after days of summer rain – there's a cool fresh smack to the airflow gushing in through the windows. The sky hasn't cleared completely: it's a milky blue, and what catches my eye immedi-ately is a towering cathedral of cumulus clouds in the west, a fantasy backdrop for trumpeting angels or retributive gods winging earthwards. The cloudbank is a vast candyfloss tumult and it's awesome. Then I turn my head to look the other way, and amazingly, there's another one – a twin – out to the east over Rhyl, big and brash, a bouffant hairdo snatched up by the winds and hung over a peg in the sky. I get ready for the day slowly with a bath and a shave, clean shirt, lots of tea, and a bowl of cereal (not Kellogg's).

I've borrowed my ex-partner's car for the journey, since I'm trying to be eco-friendly and she's trying to be reasonable.

There's no point dawdling on the Expressway so I put my foot down and get there quickly, though I get lost for a while in the Borras Hall area; I'm surprised by the leafiness of this lacuna between town and country.

I was welcomed at the door by Bob's wife Doris – Dot to family and friends.

Bob is nearly blind, and I could sense him checking me out

with his other senses as I sat down in their front room and made small talk.

The couple were looking forward to their fiftieth wedding anniversary, and Doris provided a helpful commentary as I began to question Bob about his boyhood on Bardsey. In a conversation embroidered with the shy humour of the old western folk, he revealed that he was brought into the world on a tempestuous night – with his father as midwife. Bardsey wives were normally taken to Aberdaron on the mainland before the birth, but heavy storms kept his mother Jane on the island. A neighbour from Carreg Farm was enlisted to serve as midwife, but the occasion proved too much for her – so Bob's father, William Hugh, came to the rescue as the storm raged around them and he delivered the child himself. Although he lives on the other side of Wales by now, Bob still feels half-rooted in his old *cynefin*. To accentuate this duality, he's known as Gwyndon on the Llŷn peninsula while in Wrexham he's called Bob.

He was born in 1929 at Nant Farm, one of five children. He remembers playing happily for hours with his siblings. They'd play in the fields or along the shore, collecting firewood or helping their parents with the churning.

One of his chores was to run along to Mrs Murray Williams the schoolteacher, where he'd collect the weather forecast scrawled on a piece of paper after she'd listened to it on the radio – the only one on the island.

We were very happy – it was an ideal place for children because we didn't know any other sort of life, though it must have been terrible for teenagers, says Bob.

He has few memories of those times. He recalls a pianola at the school, and the skin of a huge snake on the classroom wall. 'It must have been an anaconda or something because there were no snakes on the island,' he says. There were no rats either – but there were mice, and they were extra large, he seems to remember.

He recalls saying Bible verses in chapel with the grown-ups towering above him and the minister looming like a giant in the pulpit. There was no established home for the minister – he went from hearth to hearth, sleeping where there was a bed for him.

There were three lighthousemen, says Bob, and they gave all the children a gift at Christmas.

But life on the island was very harsh and took a heavy toll on its occupants, who eked out a living by farming and fishing.

A year or two before the second world war, when Bob was about eight, his family left the island for good, taking all their animals with them on the boat. The shadow of the first world war had continued to loom over them, and with the threat of another war the Bardsey people decided that enough was enough. They nearly all left at that time.

The Williams family rented a farm on the Llŷn peninsula but tragedy struck almost immediately – Bob's father died in 1938 at the age of forty-two. He'd worked himself to death, says Bob. We were extremely poor after that.

Almost destitute, the family moved around, battling to survive. Two of the boys went off to war, while Bob's sister Mary was forced to leave school at fourteen to look after her ailing mother.

Bob did his National Service and then moved to Wrexham, where he found work as a labourer. After marrying Doris he settled down in Pentre Maelor by the industrial estate and they have five children. Bob has returned to Bardsey three times: in the 70s with a television company, aboard a helicopter, to make a documentary, and twice since then with his wife, who also loves the place. They hoped to return again to mark their anniversary.

I talk about Bardsey all the time, but you can't go back into the past, can you, says Bob. There's something special about the place in January and February, when it's dark and lonely.

His face breaks into a smile whenever he mentions the island, and he's requested his ashes to be scattered there.

Migration from the country, mainly to the English cities, has been a dominant theme in recent Welsh history. And there has been a counterflow: in the last ten years a tide of refugees, fleeing

English urban conditions, has flooded rural Wales.

Before my time there were four main avenues of escape for those who didn't want to work the land, or couldn't: they became teachers, preachers or soldiers – or they emigrated. My own generation was the first to go en masse to the universities and then chase jobs all over the world. The decision to stay or to leave was a fundamental rite of passage in young people's lives, equivalent to circumcision in many early societies. I decided to go. Born on a hill farm in wildest Welsh Wales, I left the land for a medley of reasons. I'm glad I did. Farming has to be in the blood for it to be a happy occupation, and it's not in mine, not truly. It destroyed my father.

Recently I returned to spend five days on the farm, alone – the first time in forty years I'd been that close to my past, and for so long. I was standing in for my cousin Morus and his wife Gwenda, who were taking a very rare break from their endless workload, with a foreign holiday. For me there was no sense of going back to a biblical paradise – the Garden of Eden merely symbolised the home of early man, when he was nomadic. But his ideal state of existence was rendered impossible by population growths and mass migrations. Too many people on Planet Earth. Today, as Gordon Brown's government makes plans for another three million homes in Britain, hardly anyone considers other possibilities: proper use of the stock we have, containment of speculators, or an attempt to curb the population. It's quite simple: humans are bad for the environment. More people equals less nature.

But let's go back to the biblical past for another parable: Cain and Abel.

Abel was a shepherd who moved around on the landscape: his name signifies *breath* or *vapour* in Hebrew, meaning that he was a living, moving, transient being. His brother Cain got his name from *kanah*, meaning to acquire, own property, and ergo to rule or subjugate. Bruce Chatwin points out that Cain also means metal-smith, and there's a link in many languages between the discovery of metal and resulting violence or subjugation. The legend of Llyn-y-Fan Fach is our own equivalent.

Cain the city dweller killed his brother, a countryman, out of envy for his freedom and his life amid beauty.

But it's too simplistic to boil it all down to a country mouse/town mouse bedtime story. As I lugged a dead and smelly sheep into the back of my cousin's Land Rover in the pouring rain, I realised that my flight to town and desk had been an escape from all this shit and mud too. It's all too easy to file the past under Golden Age: as Raymond Williams demonstrated, humans have been rose-tinting their *temps perdu* since the father of history, Herodotus, started writing it all down in 450 BC.

As I stood in a pair of borrowed green Wellingtons, examining an ooze of cold blood from the sheep's behind, I remembered something else from my childhood: that disease and death stalk the farmer constantly. Nature wasn't created in the image of man's compassion, someone once said. Too bloody right. So I chose the other sort of Nature, the one I could visit on sunny days – a more agreeable sort of nature, dressed in pretty flowers, more appealing to aesthetic sensibilities.

Looking at the pitiless landscape of my youth, from the comfort of the Land Rover, I felt like a hermit crab who'd wandered back into a previously occupied shell. But another thing became apparent. For although I felt no rapport with these fields and hedges, which I knew so well, I also realised that all my internal maps were configured to match the patterns of this territory, its land and water: and if indeed I had sung the world into existence all those years ago I had taken my songlines with me into adult life – and they were better than any OS map in existence. Family pictures show a wild boy, dirty and unkempt, with his own shotguns at the age of ten, tilling the land as a boy-child, milking cows before school, going to lessons with sheep's afterbirth still on his boots. His internal chart plotted the many lives which came into existence around him and then disappeared just as quickly under the land's contours.

And finally I saw – with a lovely clarity – a truth which had evaded me because I hadn't looked in the right places. The roles of town and country dwellers have been reversed. My cousin and his wife were drifting down the Danube towards Beethoven's birthplace (he's a farmer with classical tastes), having snatched a few days' respite from the never-ending call of the land, 365 days a year, twenty-four hours a day, but even while they tried to relax, on this rarer-than-hen's-teeth holiday, they'd be worrying about events at home. I realised that the modern pastoralist is more tied and trussed than ever; I realised that today's bucolic lifestyle is more confined than the nomadic shepherd of yesteryear could ever have imagined. Every day is a workday. Almost every animal is a dependent child. A day a week is given over to documentation and form-filling; our grandparents would be shocked and enraged. At the same time, the city dweller is freer than ever; his life is an exercise in liberty and leisure, no matter how much he moans. He can throw a sickie; the farmer never can. Society has become so fluid that the urbanite is now the true nomad; almost all roots have been torn from the ground – townspeople roam the land, far and wide, looking for peace, or property bargains, or a better lifestyle. They fly abroad at the drop of a hat. Yes indeed, the tables have been turned. As a Caribou Eskimo told a European traveller: *What can we do? We were born with the Great Unrest. Our father taught us that life is one long journey on which only the unfit are left behind.*

I left the farm on a wet Saturday morning, and eventually boarded a bus in Llanddulas. It was full of dreary people talking urban pidgin and oozing *Big Brother* incontinence. Am I being snobbish? Fascist? Reactionary? Yes, perhaps you're right. But I'm also trying to be truthful… the fields of Llanddulas, where once I ploughed, have disappeared under ugly little estates filled with a generation which has no concept of the people or the wildlife they've supplanted. What I see is the end of a certain way of life and the end of the vernacular tradition, throughout Britain.

For what? For the nothingness of modern urban existence? I could be wrong, and what does it matter anyway, because the rural voice is weakening all the time. The Welsh hills have bred hordes of fierce little autodidacts like me – socialistic, anarchistic, opinionated, consumed with egalitarian principles, melancholic, too sure of their home-grown beliefs. The rural communal memory, from which I draw part of my world picture, will fade eventually. It was rich and multifarious – a hoard of expertise and craftsmanship, hedged around with fable and lore. But it's already a receding memory. My own memory console blew a fuse some time ago. In a poem called *Access*, written a long time in the past, I looked at a faded Kodak Brownie picture of myself on the farmyard of my youth and addressed myself thus:

Like a dungfly
You squat in sepia on a handful of shit
Slung on a mountain – your birthplace,
Your midden on vertical slurry,
Your winter palace,
Your cowpat farm in ossified dung.

Pot-bellied snotboy
Smeared with my history,
You cannot destroy all my records:
I know of snowswirls in your bed,
The dogs you beat and wild strawberries
In your filthy childhood Wellingtons.

I have memories
As thin as wool snagged on scrubland gorse;
A deep dell, the little Amazon
Where your father,
Sent mad by mud,
Hid his dead whisky bottles, their insides
Fermenting a new culture:

His life in miniature within the glass –
Emerald moss, delicate and fated
Floating on slime, the musky smell of adult failure.

You are too young to keep my files:
Forty years is too long to sequester
Those secrets in your eyes.
Why deny me access,
Does it matter to you
Which trees I climbed,
Which nests I robbed
In the vertiginous years
Between you and me?

Yes, the past is a different country. But what country is this?

west

I TRAVELLED to the west in search of a tiny country, a nation-state lying off the coast of Wales and I found it, though it bears no resemblance to the island so fabulously described by countless travellers. Like Venice of old it once had a king or *doge*. Like Venice it was a centre for holy crusaders, and like Venice it had an ambivalent liaison with ships. Forever reliant on them for essential goods, the islanders also feared what their holds might contain: sometimes rapid change, sometimes pirates too.

Many people have identified a timeless air of mystery on this island, which like the Venetian *repubblica marinara* was a repository for holy relics. And since the words *quarantine* and *ghetto* were coined in the Italian city state, I was struck immediately by a similarity between the two places: a lonely beauty, a seclusion from the rest of the world, and an *apartness*. They even share the same outline in the sea.

We entered the rocky harbour shortly after noon on a bright May morning. I was ready for magic and mystery, as promised in so many books and personal accounts, so when I heard eerie sounds as we landed I thought they were the cries of the water monster *mamba mutu* – a fish-tailed human which raids villages and dines on the blood and brains of everyone it catches. But the grunts and groans came from a colony of very fat seals, about two dozen of them, sunbathing on nearby rocks.

I can hear you say *Ahhh, there's lovely.*

But they looked like a bunch of football hooligans on a World Cup bender – and they quickly dispelled any fairytale notions I had in my head. They sounded drunk and boorish; I wouldn't have been surprised if all of them had been clutching a can of lager and generally swearing, belching, farting and scratching their huge beer bellies. Seals behaving badly. When I hear young male seals having a pop at each other while lounging around I tend to think of Millwall or Cardiff City supporters, rounded up after a match and waiting for the Black Maria. Sentenced to a bit of mild corrective therapy, they're sent on an outward bound course at Aberdyfi, where one fateful day they're handed wetsuits and taken down to the shore for a spot of snorkelling. Unaccountably, they take to the briny like ducks to water and head off to sea, finding homes along the Welsh shoreline. Under those wetsuits I know they have smelly beer-stained football shirts, and the weird grunts they make are football chants horribly slurred after twenty cans of Special Brew. They're shifty and vulgar and they treat everyone like a referee. Or they're overweight divas with throat infections, never letting anyone forget they're ill by emitting a constant recitative of operatic moans and groans. At other times they remind me of blown-out lorry tyres abandoned on motorway verges. When they float in the creeks they always look inland, as if they were spies.

I saw a party of people arriving by boat and they passed those seals without seeing them. You could tell the seals were miffed. I could hear them hurling insults. The visitors were supposed to throw flowers at them and clap ecstatically as if they were at Glyndebourne, but they went straight to a little beach and loafed around themselves, as if they were method actors learning how to imitate seals for a *Pingu* voiceover.

Anyway, after that encounter with the seals I saw the island as an island and not as a grandiose chunk of mythology rearing out of the sea. Next stop was the lighthouse, a large complex posing as a whitewashed hacienda somewhere in Spain with a tower stuck in the corner. Here's an interesting fact about the modern lighthouse: it can never be allowed to rest. So the generators throb away day and night, and that poor light inside the tower goes round and round 24/7. Why? Because if it stopped rotating it might come to rest on a house or a sleeping baby or even worse, a sleeping sheep – and scorch it to a frizzle. I quite like the notion. Much more interesting than roulette: you could bet on where the beam finally settled and land a small fortune if a cat went up in flames. Apparently the lighthousemen of old used to draw curtains around the reflectors by day to prevent such carnage. Of course, there aren't any men up there now so the generators chunter away all day long, wasting vast amounts of fuel. A parable for the age, I hear you say. Indeed. Apparently scientists are trying to develop solar-powered lighthouses but things aren't going smoothly. There's an air of despondency and abandonment about this complex because the non-essential buildings have been allowed to decline, and one of the houses I entered looked as if it had just been ransacked by Vikings. A page three girl pouted and thrust her dusty bosom at me from an old copy of the *Sun* in the corner. The whole place is a photographer's paradise. Built in 1821 – and still the tallest square lighthouse in Britain – its completion marked the first major exodus to the mainland.

Wherever there are humans you'll find politics, scrap metal and myths. The island has all three. The boatmen who ferry visitors to and fro are at odds with each other: there's an English camp and a Welsh camp. Historians tussle over the true facts; one says this, one says that. And the spats go on...

Ornithologists, who flock to the place in migratory swarms which quaintly reflect the movements of the birds themselves, generally look up to birds and down on other people. They've replaced the druidic cast of old, believing that a little esoteric knowledge gives them special powers. That's my general impression of twitchers the world over. The bird people who visit this island are as pleasant as you'll find anywhere, but I'm not sure about all that bird-netting gear lurking in corners everywhere.

Are a few statistics worth the trauma felt by a little bird which has flown halfway round the world and desperately needs a nap?

Yes, the island is a tiny political state: an offshore Vatican and a microcosm of the world, as William Golding might have warned me. They knew my business; they knew why I was there. They have passwords, such as *look out for the icterine warbler*. And throughout my visit Mr Seal the Spy kept a baleful eye on my every movement.

Two mysterious islands are marked on old maps of Britain: insula avium and insula arietum. One was an island of birds *which held a fayre tree, full of bowes, and on every bow sate a fayre birde, and they sate so thycke on the tree that unnethe only lefe of the tree myght be seen.* The second island *was the ilonde of shepe, where every shepe was as grete as an ox and where there was never colde either but ever sommer.*

The island I went to is a marriage of these two places: I am talking, of course, about Bardsey off the Llŷn peninsula. Or to use its much sweeter Welsh name, Enlli.

I went on the back of a giant pondhopper – a twin-hulled boat which scuttled across the famously dangerous sound with alacrity. Bright yellow, it carries the colours of the Evans family, who spend half their year on the island and half on the mainland.

Ernest, a fisherman and boat builder, can trace his Enlli roots to 1770 and was the last child to be taught at the one-room school; his wife, Yorkshire-born teacher Christine is a noted poet, and their son Colin has followed in his father's footsteps while also dabbling in a whole range of other activities; in the tradition of the Welsh farmer-fisherman he can turn his hand to just about anything.

Chatting with Christine in her wonderfully peaceful home on the island, and heading for seal-size fatness myself thanks to her delicious fruitcake, I revealed that I'd been compelled – most unusually for me – to compile a list after a few hours on the island. She laughed. It was quite common, she said. Many people felt the same urge. I suppose it's because the island is smallish – about 440 acres – and almost everything can be quantified. So here's my own little list...

Three dogs: I saw only one, and he was sleeping in the sun. Bardsey had three 'kings' between about 1800-1926, the most famous being Love Pritchard, and the crown is still kept at the Liverpool Maritime Museum. Here's how one of them perished, as related in the Caernarvon Herald of April 17, 1841:

Having some business to transact at Pwllheli, John Williams, 'Master of the Bardsey Light Tender' and 'King of Bardsey', instructed his servant that morning between five and six o'clock to get a small boat ready, with a sprit sail, for the purpose of crossing to Aberdaron. But after the two men had gone some distance John Williams landed the servant on the island, saying that he could manage the boat very well alone. The servant went home but he glanced back and saw that the boat had capsized, John Williams struggling in the water. The servant dashed to get help and another boat was launched immediately and manned. The ebb-tide had already drawn John Williams a long way out to sea, his only support being two small oars, which he had managed to get under his arms. When taken into the rescue boat he was said to have been much exhausted. He spoke but a few words and expired. He was about forty-two years of age and his wife had given birth to a child the Sunday evening prior to this accident which made her a widow.

Apparently every dog belonging to successive kings was called Nol. Nice name for a dog, don't you think?

Twenty thousand saints: Not a sign of them, but I saw a red tractor harrowing a field and sending a curtain of dust out to sea... I couldn't help but wonder if that drifting soil contained the remains of at least some of the saints. Their ashes were being scattered at sea, in a way: not quite the ending they expected.

Three Muscovy ducks: Which showed their arses to me whenever we met.

Countless rabbit holes: But no rabbits, which were wiped out by disease. Some of the holes are now used as second homes by the island's A-list celebrity bird, the peculiar Manx Shearwater, which does a decent David Blaine impression and goes underground for a period during parenthood. Like the seal it emits a spine-tingling sound, a ghastly strangulated cry – Enlli's a good place for that sort of thing.

Fourteen caves: Including one for visiting robbers (Ogof y Lladron). My favourite was Ogof Gwr, named after an unhappily married man who spent a lot of time in hiding. Did some of these caves serve as boltholes for the religious community in times of trouble? Where else would they hide?

Lots of houses: A throng of them, at least eleven, but only one of them an original Welsh croft – the rest were transformed into grandiose town houses by Lord Newborough's men. Absolutely hideous and completely out of place. Their completion marked another major exodus from the island: some say that the locals never got used to their swanky new palaces, others say that the promise of big money and bright lights lured many away to the mainland.

Three hundred and fifty types of lichen: The clean air fosters a plethora of wildlife. I saw a splendid colony of yellow flag iris, and ragged robin, and blue carpets of spring squill everywhere.

More litter than you'd expect: Quite a lot of it on the shore. But no shipwrecked vessels, though many have been sundered on the rocks. Tomos Jones, who lived on the island for many decades, recounted some of his memories in a book written by Jennie Jones. Tomos recalled one stormy night when a barrel of brandy was thrown up on the shore after a ship foundered. After rushing up to it and tapping it, the men realised they had no receptacle to drink its contents; they wore wooden footwear in those days, so one of them removed a clog and they drank from that. Nowadays, Bardsey's human waste is recycled in earth privies. I came across only one conventional toilet, in the light-house complex – and you're not supposed to put any loo paper down the pan. There's a bucket for it. A small amount of house-hold waste is burned and the rest is taken back to the mainland for recycling at Cwrt Farm. Am I being too prosaic for you? Should I be twittering on about Arthur's last resting place or Merlin's magical kingdom? Sorry...

A few generators: Don't expect eternal peace and quiet on the island. When night falls there's a good chance you'll hear a gener-ator churning the silence to shreds. The lights flicker when power is supplied in this way, giving the impression that the house you're sitting in is a ship at sea.

Not many lobsters in the pots: May is a bad month for lobster fishermen. There's a tradition that lobsters go into hiding when the young bracken is emerging from the ground in green swans' necks.

Many empty rooms in unlocked buildings: A thing to gladden the heart. Being able to sit in the old school, alone, was extremely pleasant, listening to the silence and watching the sun move across ancient floral curtains; browsing through the musty books, watching shadows move along the floor. The chapel was also open and inviting. I say chapel – in fact it's a hybrid, the best compromise I've ever seen between church and chapel. The whole island is a place of trust: I left money lying around knowing full well that no-one would touch it.

A few children: Who seemed bemused by the island, less chatty than mainland children, watchful and reserved. One young person wore rubber gloves whenever I saw him: an allergy, apparently. Another was scouting the fields with a pair of binoc-ulars at six in the morning. I would have liked to question these kids about their lives on the island but middle-aged men can't do that sort of thing any more.

No moles, no skulls, no bones: I didn't see a single molehill. Presumably the little gentlemen in velvet waistcoats never made it this far. Neither did I see any of the saints' bones reported by some travellers; in one account femurs were plentiful enough to be used as fencing posts throughout Enlli. Tomos Jones, mentioned earlier, testified that many skulls and bones were ploughed up in the fields. He also revealed something of the lifestyle of previous residents, and the measures they took to stay dry: their outer clothes were covered in a coating of coal tar to waterproof them. This may have given them stiff, slightly robotic movements when they walked about in the rain...

Plentiful evidence of human toil: One of the features of the island is the *oglawdd*: an earth-and-stone partition between fields. In some parts of Wales the outer skin of these earth walls is strengthened and decorated with layers of stones set on edge in a zigzag or chevron design; I'm no expert, but the older walls seem to have a tighter weave with smaller stones, providing a lovely herringbone pattern. There are miles of these earthworks on the island, testifying to centuries of toil. Is there something about the Celt and earthworks? Is the act of moulding soil the most Celtic thing you can do – is it an act of ultimate atonement as well as a primal act of defence and artistry? Am I beginning to ramble? The gardens on Enlli have high walls around them, built by Lord Newborough's men to protect them. They have uniform arches – a very practical touch.

One view of the outside world: It's necessary to climb the hill which thinks it's a mountain on Enlli to see the rest of the world. This hump-backed hill almost obscures any view of the mainland. I sat on its summit and smelt the drying gorse, a variant called western gorse, dense and spiny. I listened to the stonechats and the warblers. I looked over the sea, towards the body of Wales. It looked most beautiful; smoky blue shapes, jutting headlands, bays in deep shadow, and rolling fields in a patchwork of colours, with brown ploughland contrasting elegantly with many greens; a country of verdancy and plenitude. I felt rather like Ellis Wynne, who took his telescope to the top of a mountain some three hundred years ago and dreamt into being a mythical and wonderful land. I realised then that I was a creature of the main-land, needing the wide open spaces of rural Wales in which to wander without limit or fetter. To me, the mystery of Wales lies not in the constriction of islands but in the never-ending surprises of the open country, and the unfinished journey. I'd walked completely around Enlli in a morning, and again by tea, and across it countless times by the following noon. It began to choke me in a python's coil; it began to feel claustrophobic. The magic of Enlli failed to work on me. I felt like someone at a party who'd been taking huge drags on a joint being passed around but who remained untouched while everyone else was giggling and gobbling chocolate.

So the next day, clutching my rucksack and the remains of my bread and cheese, I headed back to freedom. Because islands are mainly inside the head. More than anything else they are a state of mind. I went to Bardsey as an observer, and found a small island in the sea. Had I gone with a spiritual mindset, or a romantic mindset, I might have been touched by its fabulous history. But I wasn't. Mystery for me is serendipitous, a happening in unexpected places at unexpected times. Within my poor little brain it can never be pre-ordered or prefigured. My own numina – spirits of place – cannot be conjured up with a prayer in a building on Sundays; they come to me by accident in fields, or on mountains, or on dusty roads to nowhere; some-times on paths less travelled, sometimes in crowded piazzas.

So be it. The end of this book marks the end of a journey. Well, almost.

Seven years ago I nearly died of alcoholism, but I was fortu-nate and I survived. A blessing on those who helped me, and a blessing on those who didn't. Life goes on.

In giving up alcohol – my sweetest lover, my darkest enemy – I decided to go on a curious journey, a journey of my own: I would attempt to write three books, walk completely around Wales, walk across Wales seven times, and circumnavigate Wales by water. All those things I have completed bar one. I have indeed written three books, rather odd little things which have taught me much about myself; that I am a strange specimen of humanity, rather ordinary in most ways, but extra-ordinary enough to be me. I have walked completely around Wales and across my homeland seven times. I have had a wonderful time doing so. Indeed, I have had a most fortunate life. But I haven't completed the last requirement: I haven't finished the journey on water – partly because of circumstances, partly because I fear that an ending might be just that... an ending to me and my little life. And the beginning of another bottle.

So I have devised another journey – and hopefully my life will go on for a while. Because I don't want to leave this beautiful land. This beautiful life.

Just a few people have been with me from the start of my quest until now, the end. To you I say: Hail and farewell. I hope to meet you again on the highways and byways of Wales; on clifftops and hilltops. By riverbanks and in water meadows full of buttercups and hope. I think perhaps I'm some sort of numen myself by now: a spirit of place. Finally, at the age of fifty-seven – my father's age when he died – I have become myself. Lloyd Jones. Father, journalist, former farm worker and nurse. Extremely minor author. Hobbit-shaped wanderer. Lover of words, nature, secularity and freedom.

At last I see a figure coming towards me through the trees. It is me.

About the Author

A former farm worker, nurse and journalist, Lloyd Jones lives on the North Wales coast. After nearly dying of alcoholism and undergoing spells in hospital and living rough, he quit drinking and walked completely around Wales – a journey of a thousand miles. In doing so he became the first Welshman to walk completely around his homeland, and his epic trek was the inspiration for his first novel, *Mr Vogel*. For his second novel, *Mr Cassini*, he changed tack, walking across Wales seven times in seven different directions.

Mr Vogel (Seren, 2004) won the McKitterick Prize in 2005 and was shortlisted for the Bollinger Everyman Wodehouse Prize for Comic Fiction.

Mr Cassini (Seren, 2006) won the Wales Book of the Year Award 2007.